Stone Wall Freedom
The Islander

Stone Wall Freedom

The Islander

Part II

A fictional story inspired by the beauty and history of Block Island, RI

Mark + Mary;
Keep on sailing — on land or sea.
Dave

DAVID LEE TUCKER

David Lee Tucker

Two Harbors Press

Two Harbors Press

212 3rd Avenue North, Suite 290

Minneapolis, MN 55401

612.455.2293

www.TwoHarborsPress.com

A fictional story inspired by the beauty and history of Block Island, RI

ISBN-13: 978-1-936401-88-8

LCCN: 2011930679

Distributed by Itasca Books

Cover art by Eleni Tucker

Cover Design by Wendy Baker

Typeset by Nate Meyers

Printed in the United States of America

Other Works by David Lee Tucker:

Stone Wall Freedom – The Pirate

Introduction

Throughout New England, during the colonial times, the rocky soil was cleared to plant crops, and the rocks were piled up as boundary markers in the form of stone walls. In *History of Block Island*, a book published in 1877, S. T. Livermore describes the soil found by the early islanders:

> When they landed on the island, it must have been difficult in some places to have missed stepping on a stone. A glance at the walls now standing is evidence enough that before they were built the surface of the ground was well-nigh paved with small bowlders. It is no exaggeration to say that more than three hundred miles of stone-wall now constitutes the fences of Block Island ... While they so frequently disturbed the plow and the hoe of the pioneers, few, perhaps, thought of their value in future ages to fence the fields after the primitive forests had disappeared.

It must have taken a huge effort to clear the land for plantation farming and the pasturage that was created at that time. The extraordinary number of walls still in existence is evidence to that. It is believed that many of these stone walls date as far back as the 1600s.

The owners—or even paid employees—would not have built the walls if slave labor were available. If slaves did inhabit Block Island, it's reasonable to think that their labor was used to clear the fields and build the walls—there are records from southern Rhode Island that substantiate that this job was typically relegated to slaves.

From the 1600s through 1774, Newport, Rhode Island, may have been one of the busiest ports to engage in slave trade in the North American British colonies. Also, during the same time period up to the Revolutionary War, a plantation system of farming existed in southern Rhode Island. According to the *World Book Encyclopedia*:

> It somewhat resembled the plantation system of the South. The islands in Narragansett Bay and the coastal regions, known as Narragansett Country, were fertile and well adapted for grazing. Many wealthy planters had farms of 1,000 acres or more, and owned slaves who tilled the land and cared for horses, sheep, and cattle. The plantations produced great quantities of cheese for export.

In fact, the preamble to the Rhode Island Constitution, adopted in 1842, refers to the people of the "State of Rhode Island and Providence Plantations." This can still be found on some state letterheads. The original records of the purchase and settlement of the island by investors and settlers indicated that it was for the purpose of establishing a "plantation." Apparently, property had always been bought and sold quite frequently, but in the early 1700s, the island had consolidated into three regions, each having unique owners, people, and plantation life.

John "Ed" Littlefield, a nineteenth-century island editorialist and reviewer of Livermore's book, wrote:

> According to Livermore the early proprietors of the Island, Simon Ray, on the West Side, James Sands, near the Center, and Thomas Terry on Indian Head Neck, all lived on a grand scale with slaves and servants to run their extensive farms and large houses. They entertained many notables, and were socially intimate with many mainland families of consequence and means.

The first US census of 1790 revealed that there were forty-seven slaves on Block Island. Although slave trade was first ruled illegal in 1774 by Rhode Island courts, and emancipation legislation was slowly being adopted, it was not until 1842, with the ratification of their constitution, that slavery was officially abolished altogether. It was another twenty years later that the ongoing agitation between the North and the South culminated in the outbreak of civil war in 1861.

There are few documented references to substantiate that slaves built the stone walls, let alone earned their freedom in this way. However, in her *Block Island Scrapbook*, published in 1957, Mary Elizabeth Hyde referenced the story by saying that many of the stone walls were built by slaves, and then stated that four slaves actually achieved the goal and were set free, though there are no historical records to verify that this actually happened. While knowledge of the story is mixed among the islanders, there are those who always assumed this story to be true. Fact or fiction, this story continues to be propagated—but only through oral history and tradition.

The questions of why and when are inextricably coupled. The period of the late 1700s or early 1800s would seem to have been ripe for such events. The increased awareness of personal freedom as a result of the war for independence—and the growing activity of Christian church leaders and abolitionists in the North—resulted in the adoption of various pieces of emancipation legislation.

The emancipation that gradually occurred, however, was not driven by the legislation but by growing social pressure. The pressures came not only from outside forces but, most likely, from the slaves themselves. Because of the struggle for freedom that was going on around them, the slaves may have become more assertive about their own personal freedom.

What greater motivation could there have been than to create an incentive that addressed both the islanders' need to clear the fields and the slaves' greatest desire: freedom? The strong work ethic of the islanders of the day might have combined with these influences to suggest that freedom could be achieved, but the slaves would have to earn it.

Why, then, is there no record of this ever occurring? The answer may be that while slaves had been building the stone walls for years, any such "ordinance" might have been in effect for a very short time. Or it could have been that this occurred in the form of a few individual "manumissions," or written documents, freeing a slave for good service to the master who had this particular stipulation. Regardless, it is likely that few, if any, were ever able to accomplish the task and earn their freedom in this way.

Without any evidence to support if or when this may have happened, we can speculate that this could have taken place during the gradual emancipation period from before the start of the Revolutionary War in 1776 and the adoption of the Rhode Island law abolishing slavery in 1842. Based on the changing social and moral values in the North during that period, records show that growing numbers of slave owners, either voluntarily or under social pressure, provided for manumissions to a status of indentured servants or to full emancipation.

In Arthur Kinoy's published paper "The Real Mystery of Block Island—The Origins of the Island Colony," he concludes that the first settlers came to Block Island to escape Puritan religious persecution. They came to settle a land where they could freely live out the convictions of their Christian faith. The resulting form of town government is thought to have been the first real democracy established in America. A wealth of evidence indicates that the island settlers and residents throughout the years have been good, decent, hard-working, patriotic, and God-fearing people.

Some town hall records on Block Island from the late 1700s admonish masters for mistreatment of slaves, giving some indication that systematic abusive treatment was unlikely at that time. The vision of bullwhips and the stereotypical brutality of the Southern plantations in the 1800s likely was not the reality for most slaves in southern Rhode Island and Block Island. Slaves in the North could hold property and had a legal right to life.

There are indications that during this period, slaves were treated with some level of Christian dignity, beyond the status of a mere "possession." There remains the possibility that they were treated more as servants or, in some cases, almost as a part of the family. In fact, many slaves were typically identified as "members" of the slave owner's family. Still, slavery in the Northeast was a harsh system, providing living conditions that were consistently substandard. It demeaned human beings as possessions that were not afforded the same freedoms as other human beings.

There may be no more mystical or magical place on this earth than an island, and perhaps even more so, a small island. What is it that draws men to her soil? The seventeenth-century English writer and preacher John Donne wrote the famous words "No man is an island, entire of itself." The spiritual truth in that statement is also an indication that there is no greater test to a man's adventurous spirit, indomitable character, and unwavering faith than to make his home upon one. Why would those first pioneers choose this small island, while so much rich, virgin territory lay west of them on the mainland?

As an island, it is set apart by water and weather, with limited resources and little hope for rescue or help in time of trouble. Its clearly defined boundaries, its communion with the sea, and its independence said to those most stout pioneers, "Make me home, and I will make you men among men!" Those first families who pushed their cattle off the barges to swim to shore in full sight of natives who had killed white visitors before them embodied the greatest of pioneer qualities.

It was very likely that slavery in the 1700s was an invaluable source of labor that freed the Founding Fathers to engage in the great revolutionary struggle. Is it possible that their God could have used those enslaved men and women against that very system that enslaved them? Did their contributions help to create a nation founded upon ideals that would cause her people to face the inevitable job of tearing down their own system of slavery? The finished product of true freedom from prejudice and bigotry has been a long work in progress that continues to be one of the measuring sticks that determines just how free a nation we really are.

The people of Block Island, as part of the great state of Rhode Island, should take pride in the fact that they were the first to abolish the business of trading in slaves, even before they were the first colony to declare war on England. Both were giant steps in long struggles ahead.

Stone Wall Freedom—The Islander is part two of a three-part fictional tale inspired by the beauty and history of Block Island. It uses S. T. Livermore's *The History of Block Island* as the primary historical resource. The entire story was written as a tribute to the microcosm of the struggle for freedom that the men and women, both free and slave, faced on this blessed little land.

Part Two

Chapter One

Block Island
Spring 1776

Sea captain Alexander Hawkins put his face to the sun and felt its warmth. He breathed in the familiar island fragrances as his long brown ponytail snapped in the wind. He was back on Block Island, and its familiar sights, sounds, and aromas made his body tingle with appreciation of his island home.

Captain Bertram Spats's middling-sized open sailboat ferried Alexander from the mainland to the old pier in the bay on the east side of the island. The trip was a short one, with a good breeze from the northwest. Scanning the pier at Harbor Bay, Alexander could see that not much had changed during the months he had been away. The old pier itself, built in 1742, was in a shambles, awaiting the Rhode Island Assembly's approval to construct a new one. The fish houses still smelled atrocious. Harry Littlefield's tavern, known as the "Spa," and Nathaniel Briggs's mercantile store both seemed a bit more weathered but were still welcome sights.

Upon Alexander's arrival, there were warm greetings welcoming him home and numerous offers for rides to the farm. He chose to walk. His companion, Nathan, took a wagon with their belongings and went on ahead to let the family know they had arrived.

As he headed west through town, the concerns and troubles on the mainland seemed to melt away. Block Island lay no more than a few leagues of sea from the coasts of Connecticut, Rhode Island, and the Providence Plantations, yet he always felt transported a whole world away.

Alexander stripped off his heavy wool captain's coat and unbuttoned his homespun white cotton shirt to the early spring warmth. He wore brown breeches that came to just below the knee, white stockings, and cowhide shoes with large buckles, all bought new in Newport. He headed up Center Road, a cart path that led past Pilot Hill and then cut across his neighbor's broad open fields, crossing lots through the stone-wall gateways, taking the most direct route possible home. The fields he crossed were ones he'd helped clear, with walls he'd helped build. The route home was not even two miles, and though he was anxious to arrive home, the walk itself was a welcome embrace that he wanted to enjoy for as long as possible.

He climbed up one more gentle slope, and just as he came over the rise he looked across the field, and his heart stirred. *Oh, what fortune!* There, across one of the Paine farm fields, stood his Rebekah. Her bonnet was down, letting her full light-brown hair wave in the breeze. She strolled in the tall grass amidst the Queen Anne's lace, holding a parasol to protect her from the rays of the bright afternoon sun. Her young bondswoman, Abigail, meandered behind Rebekah, holding the reins to Swan, Rebekah's long-neck stallion.

Alexander took a deep breath and summoned his courage. Their farewell prior to his departure for his most recent voyage had not gone well. While he was at sea, she failed to return any of his communications. Yet Alexander hoped and prayed he could mend their differences upon his return.

He called out with excitement, "Rebekah! I have just now returned," as he waved and jogged in her direction.

He slowed to a stop, though, as her immediate reaction was not one of a warm welcome. Upon seeing him, she stepped back several paces, as if retreating from an enemy. She backed up to a stone wall and sat against it, slowly transferring her parasol from her right hand to her left and laying her right hand on top of the wall. She then called over to Abigail, who responded by bringing Swan over to Rebekah.

This was not the reaction Alexander had hoped for. He anxiously called out again, "Rebekah?"

This time she coolly called back, "Captain Hawkins, do not come any closer."

Alexander dropped his head in disappointment but continued to walk toward her. He was determined to try to make amends for their very unsatisfying farewell.

As he lifted his head, he saw something out of the corner of his eye and immediately flinched. A stone zipped by, narrowly missing his head. Incredulously, he called out, "Rebekah!"

Looking over to her, he saw another stone in her hand, with her arm cocked. She let fly and this time, Alexander knocked it down with his hand. He cried out in pain and shook his hand. Now his incredulity was replaced by anger. He yelled, "Rebekah, stop dismantling that wall! I had a hand in its construction, and there are ordinances against this behavior!"

She seemed to become only more incensed, grabbing for more stones so he immediately backed off, waving his hands saying, "All right, all right. You have made your wishes quite clear."

Rebekah said nothing more but took the reins of the horse from Abigail and mounted. She coldly stared at him as he backed away. Alexander took a deep swallow and shook his head. Her cold stare said all he needed to know.

Dejectedly, he continued making his way home, heading southwest to the Hawkins farm. His hand hurt almost as badly as his disappointment, but he soon found himself involuntarily smiling. What would he have expected from Rebekah Beach? Growing up, she had been as competitive as any woman—or even any man—on the island. She could throw stones as hard and as accurately as any mariner. Perhaps this was the chance for her to vent her upset. He hoped that with her anger now vented, he might have an opportunity for a more civil exchange the next time.

Certainly, this was not the warm welcome he had hoped for, but he refused to let it cloud his return to the place he loved. He was excited to be back on his Block Island, and there was much to enjoy and to reacquaint himself with.

Hiking past Fresh Pond, he headed south until he crested another hill. Alexander spotted the hollow and the corner of the Hawkins farm. His spirits were lifted, as he couldn't believe his fortune: With his arrival, the shadblow was in bloom, covering the entire hollow in a soft white. With the farm in sight, his pace quickened. Approaching the gate, however, he noticed the deterioration. The fences needed mending, and the brush needed clearing. The twinge of sadness he felt for the entropy was soon overwhelmed by his confidence that he could attend to these needs and see that the farm was back in order in short time.

The merchant voyage from which he was returning had been longer than expected. Alexander had grown anxious to return to help after he'd received word that his father, Joseph, was struggling with the failing farm. In addition, Alexander was anticipating a letter regarding his own commission into service from the fledgling American Navy under Commodore Esek Hopkins's command.

It was now two years since the New Shoreham town meeting resolution against the British duties on tea and almost one year since the Battle of Bunker Hill. Alexander knew that the colonies were scrambling to put together the requisite army as they prepared for war. He wondered if the small island's population had sorted through the township's official position toward the war. There was no question that the sentiments of the leading men of the island were to move in any direction with the American colonies for the maintenance of their most cherished rights and privileges. Their only hesitation was for the isolated nature of the island and the dangers to their families.

While Alexander was eager to plunge into the affairs of the farm, he decided he would immediately seek out the First Warden John Sands to find what the islanders had decided on the matter. If no decision had been made, then he was willing to assume the duty of obtaining a consensus from the islanders as to their position toward the impending war and find out how they would ready themselves.

As Alexander walked the long, shadblow-lined approach to his home, the substantial white saltbox house with its wide porch lining the front came into view, and he could see his family congregating on the porch. Upon seeing him, his house mum, Molly, began to excitedly lumber toward him. Following close behind were the bondsmen Cujo and Bolico. Nathan sat on the porch, relaxing.

Alexander quickened his pace with the realization that he was really home. It felt better than he'd anticipated, but then again, it always did.

From a distance Molly called out, "Alizander, you home! Could you save your Molly Mum a few steps an' move a bit quicker?"

Alexander had to smile. His Molly Mum's familiar deep guttural Creole formed from the mixture of dialects of numerous West African people groups warmed his heart. Hers was the very first voice he could ever remember hearing and it tickled his hears and warmed his heart to hear it once more. He ran the final few yards and embraced the heavy black woman. "I missed you, Mum! I missed this farm and this rocky island."

Molly answered with tears in her eyes. "Now maybe you have de sense to stay an' not go ridin' all over de world lookin' for all dat's right here."

"Maybe one day I'll grow to be that wise, Mum." Alexander acknowledged the other two slaves as they arrived and embraced him.

After exchanging greetings he began catching up on the current affairs of the family and the farm as they walked the final distance to the house. Alexander asked, "Where might my father and Stepney be?"

"We didn't know you was comin', or dey'd be here," Cujo answered. "De two of dem took de oxcart to Mr. Beach's to discuss a town meetin' dat be comin' up."

The group arrived on the porch where Nathan sat resting with a mug of water. "A town meeting?" Alexander said, turning to Nathan. "How about we take a ride over to John Sands's? I have a few matters to discuss with him that I'd like raised at the next meeting. We can see what has become of our island and perhaps avoid my father, who's sure to put us right to work. What say you, sailor?"

Nathan immediately jumped up, saying, "Whatever is my captain's pleasure."

"Alizander," Molly disappointedly interjected, "you two just arrived. You can't be stealin' my boy away an' just go ridin' off like dis."

As the two ran off the porch, Alexander called back, "Molly, we'll return shortly. Your boys are back to stay for a while."

"Mum, what can I do?" Nathan hollered back, palms raised. "The master calls!"

Chapter Two

Alexander called to Nathan, "I'll saddle up the black stallion, Nimbau. Nathan, why don't you take the gelding, Pouckshaa."

Nathan had served as a common seaman under Alexander, so there had been precious little time to share their friendship while Alexander was captain. Now, Alexander was looking forward to spending time with his friend outside the encumbrances of the formal chain of command.

When Nathan was younger, he was every bit Alexander's physical equal. The two had grown up together and both considered each other as friend and brother. As the "older brother," Alexander was always there for Nathan and protected him from scoundrels and bullies. Alexander remembered even interceding on occasions when his own father, Joseph Hawkins, felt it necessary to dispense punishment for Nathan's errors.

Alexander and Nathan immediately put their mounts to their paces and savored the sport they had missed while at sea. Their old competitive friendship took over, and the two raced past the onion farm and through a meadow of panic grass, asters, black-eyed Susans, milkweed, pasture rose, and Queen Anne's lace.

Alexander pulled Nimbau to a stop and listened for the nasal caw of the fish crow. He was pleased that the small crop of trees in the meadow still hosted one of the island's nests.

The two continued riding northeast, taking every opportunity to jump some of the shorter stone walls until they arrived at Fresh Pond, where they settled into a trot heading north on Center Road and past the Indian burial grounds. Arriving at Town Road they turned east passing through the small crop of buildings. As they rode up to the Sands's large stone house Alexander recalled how significant this house had been to the island population over the years. The builder had been John Sands's relative, Captain James Sands, an original settler and one of Alexander's three personal island heroes. He had grown up inspired by the stories of the settler leaders: James Sands, as the great statesman; Thomas Terry, the hard but courageous hero; and Simon Ray, the great moralist and spiritual leader.

For over eighty years the Sands's stone house had served as a garrison in the time of the fear of the Indians, as a hospital and place of refuge for the poor, and even as a house of worship. The Sands family had a plentiful estate and gave free hospitality and lodging to all gentlemen who came to the island.

Shortly after the first settlers arrived on the island in 1661, James Sands joined the settlers and helped lead the enterprise of settling Block Island. He was known to be intimate friends with Ann Hutchinson and Roger Williams, the first freeman on the island and the island's first representative to the Rhode Island Assembly, becoming the first statesman for the island. He was a brave, humane, and dedicated Christian, as well as an enterprising citizen. He devoted his house for the worship of God, and for many years it was attended every Lord's day.

Captain James Sands's wife, Sarah, was said to be a remarkable gentlewoman of sobriety, piety, and hospitality. She served as the island midwife and doctor all of her days.

Alexander was particularly impressed by stories of her caring devotion to all and by the lawful record she had made of the emancipation of her slaves.

When the two eased their mounts up to the grand stone house, the Sands's bondswoman, Nell, came to the door.

"Greetings, Nell," Alexander called out. "Is the good captain at home?"

"Mr. Alexander an' Nat'an," the servant answered. "Good to see you back home. Cap'n Sands be at de tavern at Harbor Bay. He may be on his way back shortly."

Alexander was amused. "Since when does our first warden frequent Harry's tavern?"

Nell smiled and shook her head, saying, "No, no. De cap'n got word dat Sam Williams and his mariners was drinkin' hard an' lookin' for some trouble. He went down to keeps de peace."

The three chatted briefly before saying farewell. As the two rode off, Nathan turned his horse eastward along the main cart path, which intersected the middle of the island, connecting the new Pier Harbor on the eastern shore to Dorry's Cove on the western shore.

Dorry's Cove was speculated to be the place where the Mohegan Indian war party landed in the early 1600s. The Mohegans were surprised by the island Manisseans and were driven across the island to be trapped and killed at the island's tallest bluffs. That was the place where Alexander now wanted to go.

Alexander abruptly called out, "Nathan, let's turn our mounts south to Mohegan Bluffs."

Nathan shook his head and smiled, calling back, "It didn't take you long to decide to go for a visit."

Alexander looked off to the west at the gathering clouds. "We may be in for some weather, and I don't want to miss a visit on my first day back. I promise to keep it a short stay, and then we'll look for Sands at the tavern."

The two rode south through the fields and meadows, past Sands Pond and on to the trail south of Pilot Hill, past the large Tug Hole until they reached the Indian trail, which circled the southeastern rim of the island.

Alexander set Nimbau on an easy gallop, and Nathan fell in behind, following the southern coastline east. Before the trail turned north, Alexander pulled his horse to a stop at the most spectacular stretch of the island's bluffs. As Nathan had often done before, he waited while Alexander rode down a short path to the ocean.

The young sea captain followed the narrow path south through the lush green grass and brush of the tall shadblow, low-lying bayberry and sweet greenbrier. Suddenly, the brush broke into a clearing surrounded by bright-pink wild beach rose bushes, which buffered a sheer drop of some two hundred feet. The jagged teeth of clay, rock, and dirt dropped straight down to a rocky blue-gray beach at the edge of an endless expanse of green and blue ocean. Beyond the rocky reefs, which had claimed an untold number of ships, there was not another body of land until one reached the continents of Europe or Africa.

Alexander looked down over the bluffs. He was greeted with the soft hooting of a barn owl nesting in the bluff clay, just below where he stood. He heard the flapping of wings, and a bank swallow flew past and headed directly into its own nest hole, off to Alexander's right. He breathed in deeply and smiled.

This had always been his most treasured place, particularly in the evening when it was a clear full-moon-lit night. He would ride to the bluff's edge and from this high vantage, with the moon's radiance reflected across the mighty ocean, he felt as though he were on top of the world. He found it breathtaking and awe-inspiring, without exception, whenever he stood out on this precipice. If ever there was evidence to him of the enormity of God, it was during these special moments. Once again, he breathed in the cool breeze and engaged in his quiet conversations with the Almighty.

There were times when he could swear he heard a voice crying out. The first few times he had heard it he found it a bit unnerving and considered that it might have something to do with the Mohegan warriors that the island Indians had fought and thrown over these bluffs. Yet the mysterious voice sounded more feminine, more soft and sweet, and over time, he had come to find it quite comforting.

Chapter Three

Alexander rode back from the edge of the bluff to find Nathan patiently waiting. When Alexander passed him, Nathan fell into line, and the two loped along the narrow trail headed north to the pier at Harbor Bay. Nathan spurred his mount and settled next to Alexander as they slowed to a walk.

The young black man broke the silence. "Captain, I can read, you know."

Alexander responded with a sigh. "Nathan, our voyage is over. We are no longer at sea, sailor. Please dismiss with the formalities while we are back on the island. And yes, I know you can read. Have you any other items of news for me?"

Nathan, in a rare display of impatience, snapped, "Alexander, I know you saw the posting back in Newport."

"No, I'm not sure I know what you're talking about," Alexander responded blankly.

Nathan sighed with exasperation. "The postings all over the port in Newport."

Alexander squinted, feigning strained thought. "No… no…. We were very busy unloading our cargo from India and filing our papers with the authorities. I must have missed them altogether."

"Well, let me repeat what it said, word for word: 'Ye able-backed sailors, men white and black, to volunteer for naval service in ye interest of freedom.'" Nathan paused and cleared his throat. When he continued, his voice quivered with a summoned courage. "Alexander, I want your permission to volunteer."

Alexander pulled on his reins and brought his horse to a stop. He cast his eyes down at the trail for a moment and then looked up at his friend. "Nathan, I know you're anxious, but I don't believe there is anyone more anxious than I. I await word from Hopkins of my assignment. You wouldn't want to lose the chance of our sharing in this fight together, would you?"

Nathan hesitated, weighing his words. "I know you don't agree with me, but it's been almost one year since Lexington, Concord, and Bunker Hill. One year! And good gracious, five years since our first patriot, Crispus Attucks, was martyred. You know as well that the Brits are pulling together a great army and organizing an assault. How can I wait any longer?"

Alexander chose to avoid the point Nathan was making, deciding instead to argue about something the two quietly disagreed on concerning the martyr Attucks. "We must be careful not to believe our own propaganda. You know that many believe Attucks to be just a rabble-rouser, a ruffian with no real patriotism in his bones. Many leading Sons of Liberty, including John Adams, have written so. I'm afraid it is so with many of the other blacks who have fought thus far—their motives are more for the thrill of retaliation against white men. I can't blame them for wanting revenge, but I don't believe their motives are pure."

Nathan's anger became visible, and he shook his head slowly as he listened. Alexander was surprised—and becoming annoyed—by Nathan's reaction. *Am I missing something?* he wondered. *Does Nathan really expect to win this argument?* As a slave owner, much as it was as a sea captain, Alexander had to maintain social order. If Nathan wanted to provide counsel, that was one thing, but a slave couldn't be allowed to win an argument. The imbalance of power would be an upset to everyone.

Nathan was, of course, more than a slave to Alexander. He was more of a friend—as close to being a younger brother as a Negro born into slavery could be. Alexander's convictions regarding freedom were deeply sincere, but the attitudes born of his father's handling of bondservants as he grew up still lingered. This was true even during Alexander's time at sea, where black and white seamen learned to coexist. As an officer, he could not allow the crew to make the decisions. Out on the open sea, the captain's supreme authority was critical to the ship's survival. The crew was dependent on his being the master, and this served to reinforce his bias back on land.

"You say Crispus Attucks was a fraud?" Nathan's voice bore a tone, at least to Alexander's ear, that bordered on insubordination.

Alexander's indignation grew. "Yes, and many others agree."

"Do you remember a sailor of your crew that sailed before the mast back in '69 by the name of Michael Johnson?"

"Yes...yes, of course. He was the large, strong, and capable seaman who sailed with us to the Virgin Islands on a molasses run."

Nathan probed further. "What else do you recall about him?"

Pleased to turn what appeared to be an escalating argument into reminiscing, Alexander said, "Well, he certainly was a courageous man who fought like the devil against the French privateers who tried to take our ship and cargo."

"Any other remembrances of him?"

"Of course, yes, indeed. He challenged me on several occasions over the treatment of the men."

"Was he correct?"

"Yes, I'm afraid he was. I was able to catch the bosun being heavy handed in his treatment of the crew. I still had to exercise my authority and punish Johnson for confronting me in front of the men, but he proved to be a man of conviction."

Nathan had the answer he wanted, and he rose up in his stirrups. "Well, my honorable Alexander, I must share with you that as I read the posting in Newport, a Negro man stood beside me, struggling to read it for himself. When I offered to help, we began to talk, and I found that he was a friend of Crispus Attucks and had sailed with him many times. In fact, he was in the pub in Boston with Attucks the day he was martyred. The truth is that Attucks did not sail under his slave name but under the name of Michael Johnson. Crispus Attucks—and your man of conviction, Michael Johnson—were one and the same person!"

Alexander's face dropped, and he struggled to recover from his surprise. "Well, I…I'm not sure about that, and who knows if the man you spoke with tells the truth? What I do know is that General Washington sent the blacks home from the military for just this reason last December. It was only when he struggled to raise the requisite army that he began allowing the Negro men to return and—"

"The point is," Nathan jumped in, showing no deference to his master, "these black men are patriots, much like me. Look at me, Alexander! Look at me! If you want to know why these men fight, look at me!"

Alexander was stunned by the directness and passion in Nathan's voice.

Nathan pressed on. "Attucks led those men into the street that day to serve justice. He and the four others who were massacred in Boston by the Brits were Americans, fighting for liberty. Then, just one year ago, at Lexington and Concord and Bunker Hill, men like Prince Estabrook, Lemuel Haynes, the man who shot Major Pitcarn—Salem was his name, I think—and other blacks were fighting for liberty as much as the white men they fought next to. These Negroes fight for a free America *and* for their own freedom and equality!" With these words, Nathan spurred his horse and galloped off.

Alexander felt like he had just slipped into one of the island's deep and slimy peat bogs. Nathan had surely gone too far; he had never been so direct with Alexander before. Still, Nathan needed Alexander's permission to volunteer and could not go without his blessing. Nathan also had promised Alexander's father he would always watch after his son. Young Nathan was a man of honor and was committed to keeping that promise.

A confounding blend of thoughts and feelings seemed to swallow Alexander up—anger, frustration, confusion, and questions of right or wrong conspired to suck Alexander under, and he had nothing to grab onto to pull himself up. "Lord," he whispered as he watched Nathan's steed round a distant bend, "give me wisdom and understanding."

Deep down, Alexander understood that what Nathan had said was true. Alexander agreed with many other Sons of Liberty, some of whom had even written articles stating that the freedom from British tyranny was meant for all men. But he also knew that slavery was not just an abomination brought on by King George: Many an American profited handsomely from the slave trade and would not let liberty from British tyranny and control over Americans' personal property stand in the way of their profits. Would freedom for all mean that slave owners would have to give up some of their property—bought and paid for in the form of African slaves—to earn independence from England? Would American commerce survive forfeiting one its greatest assets?

As Alexander tried to sort through his feelings, anger rose to the fore. He became incensed by Nathan's insolence and insult, just as an older brother would when being scolded by a younger brother. It burned even deeper with the indignity of a master being scolded by a slave. How dare Nathan challenge Alexander's motives? How dare Nathan think that his own passion for freedom was more than his master's?

Alexander snapped the reins and kicked in his stirrups to chase down Nathan. *I will have my final word*, he thought, and he quickly caught Nathan. Pulling his steed in front of Nathan's horse to cut him off, Alexander grabbed Nathan's reins and pulled the black man's horse to a stop.

His stern countenance left no room for argument. "Now you listen to me, you insolent bugger!" he shot at Nathan. "How dare you suggest that you or any other men under God have a greater interest in freedom for all men? Is there any man on this island that has done more for the welfare of its blacks? Have I not acted as a pastor and teacher to your brethren? Have I not jeopardized my career by refusing to captain ships for owners involved in the slave trade? Have I not politicked with the Rhode Island Congress to help draft laws to make the slave trade and slavery itself illegal? Have I not made every attempt to influence our congressional delegate, Stephen Hopkins, with my position on slavery as a part of American independence?" Out of breath, Alexander waited for Nathan's acknowledgement of the truth in all that he'd said, but Nathan simply stared back at him.

Alexander let go of Nathan's reins and straightened himself up in his saddle. "Now, with the Continental Congress dragging their feet and the English preparing to invade, I anxiously but patiently await assignment from Esek Hopkins. What more, I ask you, can I do?"

Nathan continued to stare blankly at Alexander. "Yes, Captain, I suppose you have done all you can do. I guess I could not ask for anything more. The trouble is, I ain't askin'. I ain't sure that all the white men—from Adams to Paine to Franklin to Stephen Hopkins—will make the black man free. The black man will have to fight even harder alongside the whites to get his share of this new land's freedom. You and all the others can't do it all for us."

Alexander sat back in his saddle. His own anger subsided as the truth of Nathan's words seeped through the cracks of his own deep-seated doubts. Still, there was something inside of him that had a hard time believing what he'd heard. He'd spent too much of his life thinking of himself as the great protector and defender of the slave. It was difficult for him to actually accept that the black man was capable of struggling to be free without the white man to do it for him. White men led the blacks into captivity; surely it would have to be the whites to lead them out. He now questioned all that he stood for.

His life experiences formed the way he thought the world was and should be. Now, he began to see a growing conflict: Could slavery be an obstacle to the cause of the colonies' freedom? Even as the Continental Congress met in Philadelphia, he knew there were Southern colonies—and interests from his own colony—that would stand against freedom for slaves as a part of American independence. Could the conflicting interests be so divisive as to derail a revolution? That possibility made him shudder. He tried to assure himself that even an issue as important as abolition should not stand in the way of freedom from England's tyranny.

Alexander tried to think of something—anything—that might put Nathan at ease. He took on a reassuring tone, saying, "Nathan, please. You know slavery is an abomination brought onto us by the king. Once we break ties with the king, it surely will be the undoing of this evil. I expect that you and many of your brethren will fight. I'm only asking you to be patient and fight alongside me. I assure you, it will be but a matter of weeks." Alexander was certain of Nathan's devotion to him and that he would be patient. One of the Scripture truths Alexander had always taught him was that patience was possibly the greatest of all virtues. That spiritual truth had born itself out in each of their lives, and it often held its own reward.

Now, Nathan sat in his saddle, quietly staring down and debating whether to argue any further. He knew full well, as did Alexander, that the blame for slavery could not be laid entirely at the king's feet. Nathan discarded his formerly argumentative tone and answered Alexander more calmly. "I'm afraid if freedom is formally declared, the politics of Philadelphia will not allow mention of freedom for slaves. There is not much I can do about that, but I can fight. My Negro brothers and I will fight twice as hard for two freedoms. But I suppose I'll wait. I promised Master Hawkins I'd see you don't do nothin' foolish. That's a job too big for any other man I know, white or black."

Alexander broke into a grin. "God bless you, Nathan Hawkins. I can't imagine fighting this revolution without you. Come—let us go cool our heads under the icy waters from the spring shed. Then we can go find Sands."

The two turned their horses onto the Spring Trail and trotted down to the harbor. They dismounted and scrambled down a short, steep path through the beach plum shrubs adorned with tiny white flowers. The path led to a shed with a large wooden spout from which icy cold spring water gushed.

They took turns drinking the pure refreshment and then gasped as they put their heads under its icy flow. Even during the hottest summers, the waters stayed ice cold. Alexander and Nathan often challenged each other to see who could keep his head under for the longest. The head-numbing pain was instantaneous, and neither ever lasted for more than a few seconds.

They returned to their horses and continued on the trail heading to the pier at Harbor Bay. Alexander quietly looked across the spring-fed pond that was situated at the edge of a thirty-foot bluff. The pond was filled with water-lily buds and was surrounded by swamp azalea, milkweed, and sweet pepperbush. Monarch and Viceroy butterflies danced across its smooth waters. Just beyond lay the rocky beach, the blue ocean, and a view of Clay Head on the northern end of the island.

Alexander was relieved the argument was ended, though he still had a lingering anxiety he could not shake. Every time he pushed himself forward with the primacy of his life's focus—American liberty—he was left with an unsettling feeling that something was left unattended, much like the feeling he got when leaving on a long journey and thinking that some detail had been missed—perhaps a lamp or a candle left burning. He would decide each time to simply live with the feeling, for the journey ahead was too long and too important to turn back for whatever had been left behind.

Chapter Four

It was turning damp and overcast as Alexander and Nathan rode into muddy, dreary Harbor Bay. They hitched their horses to the post right in front of Harry Littlefield's Spa. The tavern was little more than an oversized two-story shack. Alexander looked it over, amazed it was still standing. The tavern was sided by unpainted dirty brown boards—hardly a sufficient shell with which to protect it from the almost constant island winds. It was a drafty, cold building. During the winter, a big cast-iron, wood-burning stove left half the building too hot and the other half too cold.

As they hitched their horses to a post in front of The Spa, Alexander spotted their friends, the Indian Quepag and Simon Littlefield. The two men were walking down the dirty street toward them.

"Quepag! Simon!" Alexander called out to the tall, slender Indian and the short, stocky islander. "Good to see you, my friends. How has the island treated you in our absence?"

As expected, Quepag's expression did not change, nor did his pace quicken when he saw the two friends. He continued to slowly walk toward them, raised his hand, and gave a half-hearted wave. Simon Littlefield, however, exuberantly waved and ran to greet them.

Alexander thought back to his childhood, when the four friends had been very close. They had worked and played together, clearing the fields or tending to the livestock; clamming in the Great Pond at the center of the island; gathering seaweed and sea moss; and venturing out into the ocean to collect lobster or fish. For recreation, the four would hike the rocky bluffs located south of the Hawkins property and would climb down to the beach to throw stones or collect shells, driftwood, and flotsam that had washed up onto the shore. In the warm weather, they would swim in one of the many freshwater ponds around the island or near the beautiful length of sandy beach that stretched like a crescent moon along the northeast coast.

They'd loved to ride horses up to the section farthest north of the bathing beach to challenge themselves in the heavier surf. While there, they would pretend to be navy heroes fighting evil pirates in the tall green grass of the sand dunes and then would search for buried treasure in the dunes and the woods beyond. There were rumor and great speculation that pirates and privateers had left behind treasure after visiting the island. Certainly, some of them must have failed to return to recover their booty.

Simon reached them first and shook their hands. "Well, well, it is very good to see you both. I rather thought you might never come back to this island prison."

Alexander responded, "Simon, one man's prison is another man's heaven. I guess it helps to be away for so long to appreciate her value."

When Quepag reached them, he said, "You are back. It is much like you just left."

They shook hands as Alexander replied, "Well, it's been over six months. I'm glad you at least noticed we were gone. What's become of you both and our island since we've been gone?"

Simon responded, "Alexander, you know that virtually nothing changes on this island in six months' time."

Quepag added, in the slow and depressed-sounding tone that all island Indians seemed to share, "No, nothing changes much on this island. Still watching Wilson drink. The cod fishing is good. The corn season will be bad. A black slave landed on the island in the storm a week ago. Wilson claimed him, but he is still in irons." He paused to think and then finished, "Oh, yes, another just went off the bluffs—Big Jim. No, not much."

Alexander and Nathan looked at each other. Nathan replied, "Not much? Jim, eh? Jim was good. Was there trouble? Was he taking to drink?"

"No, Jim was at peace," Quepag answered. "There is a Mattanit spirit after our tribe. There must be."

Alexander was growing impatient with the pace of the conversation. "Quepag, I think we know which 'spirits' are involved. What do you say we find time in the next few days to clam and fish for cod? We can talk more then. Now, I'm anxious to catch up with our first warden."

Quepag's eyes brightened. "Yes, we can dig for *poquauhog* and fish *pauganaunt* together." With that, he nodded, said good-bye and walked away.

Alexander turned to Simon Littlefield. "Before sailing home I went to visit your sister, Caty, in Coventry, but it was clear that the Greene's house has been unoccupied for some time. Is everything all right with the general and his family?"

Simon chuckled. "I assure you, Alexander, that the British know better than to tangle with one Caty Littlefield Greene. The latest word we received was that Nathanael has been placed in command of the defense of Long Island. Caty took a schooner to Manhattan to join him several weeks ago and is staying with Henry Knox—against Nathanael's wishes I might add."

"As if General Greene didn't have enough on his hands," Alexander mused, "building fortifications while training and equipping a large army of farmers. Then again, she might be just the powder keg needed to defeat the Brits. And did I hear you say schooner? Your sister sailed from Newport, through the treacherous waters of the East River and onto Manhattan? This must be true love, as the Caty I knew hated even the calmest of water travel."

"Yes, she is rather fond of the general and can't stand to be apart, so she's willing to take the risk."

Alexander's tone changed to one of concern. "Word is the British fleet now anchored in Halifax is expected to sail for New York at any moment. I pray she is not there when they arrive."

Simon shrugged his shoulders. "You know well of my sister's reckless nature, occasional poor judgment, and headstrong spirit. She will do as she pleases, often ignoring the general's direct orders."

Alexander shook his head resignedly. "Yes, indeed. I know all too well. It would seem to be a common temperament for the women of Block Island." He turned to climb the steps of The Spa but stopped before entering to wait for Nathan. He looked at the island view to the north and mused that although he was closer in age to Nathan, he was very fond of Simon—he'd always felt a kinship to the eldest of the six Littlefield children. Alexander heard talk that Simon's mum, Phebe Ray, had conceived him out of wedlock but married his father, John Littlefield, before Simon was born. Simon never suffered from any stigma, as most islanders lived well by the Christian adage, "Judge not lest ye be judged."

Yet Alexander had heard the whispers. He himself had endured similar whispers about himself but always assumed it was people sharing their charitable concern for a boy growing up without his mother.

Back in the spring of 1761, as young Alexander stood graveside at Phebe Ray Littlefield's burial, he looked across the grave into the sad eyes of Simon and Caty. He felt as though he was experiencing the death of his own mother—a mother who died in childbirth but one he felt he had known and loved.

Those days following the funeral were a gloomy time for the friends, as the children bore each other's pain. But more often than not, it was Caty's bubbly spirit, quick wit, and cheery disposition that raised the spirits of the others. Even though Caty was the youngest of the friends, Alexander was fond of her, his feelings for her much like those for the younger sister he'd always wished for. Three years later, in '64, John Littlefield sent Caty to live with her aunt Catherine Ray in East Greenwich on the mainland. Alexander maintained contact with Caty, but her consuming fear of stormy seas caused her return visits to Block Island to be few and far between.

Alexander still was lost in thought as Simon clapped his hand on Nathan's shoulder, cautioning him, "Be careful. Sam Williams has been out fishing cod and horse mackerel and just returned as 'high hook'. He will be celebrating and be intemperate. I suggest you not go in. Still no Indians or Negroes."

Nathan shrugged. "I just spent six months at sea as an equal with white sailors. Let's see if this world can change." He smiled and ran up the steps to join Alexander.

They waved farewell to Simon and entered the building. Alexander was not a regular at the tavern and was so used to Nathan's company that he didn't give any thought to going into the building with him.

Upon entering, Alexander noticed the tavern was darker and dingier than he'd remembered. As his eyes grew accustomed to the dim light, he spotted First Warden Sands at the back corner table, sitting with several locals and keeping a watchful eye on the mariners. Sam Williams and three other mariners were at the table closest to the door. They looked as though they had been there for some time. Harry Littlefield was behind the counter at the far end, busily rinsing glasses in dirty water.

Alexander had forgotten the oppressive and distinct stench of The Spa. The odor was a combination of the salt air, the body odor of unwashed mariners, the spilled liquor on grimy floors, peat bog pull, and dried seaweed burned to heat the stove. If that wasn't bad enough, these odors were mercilessly augmented by the aroma of the tavern's standard meal: fish stew with calf's liver and fiddleheads. Both men winced as the full force of the foul air set upon them.

The Spa customers acknowledged Alexander—some with warmth, others with polite recognition. Williams and the mariners stared at Nathan with disapproving looks. Harry Littlefield immediately began a conversation with Alexander from behind the counter but neglected to raise the question of Nathan's presence in the tavern.

Alexander walked over, grabbed a chair, and sat down next to First Warden Sands. After exchanging pleasantries, Alexander addressed the first warden directly. "John, I understand that there is a town meeting soon. I have a number of items I would like to address with the town officers."

"Well, Captain," Sands replied, "we have a full docket to discuss and vote upon. However, the item of greatest concern is in regards to our friend Mr. Williams over there. He has petitioned for the release into his custody of a slave who washed ashore during that severe storm weeks ago."

"Have you checked with authorities on the mainland?"

"Yes, but there was no record of a slave ship in these waters. Of course, there wouldn't be, given that the slave trade is now illegal. However, he was found with a companion, murdered by a hatchet found in his own hand. We have to determine if the Negro can be safely released to Williams."

Alexander probed further. "What else will you be reviewing?"

"If we have any time remaining, we will be revisiting the town ordinance limiting the felling of trees, and we are also working on an ordinance to provide our slaves an incentive to earn their freedom. With all the independence rhetoric coming over from the mainland, our slaves are beginning to find their voice. Tell me, Captain, what concerns would you like to raise?"

"As you well know, John, given your leadership on the committee of resistance to the tea tax in '74 and your likely command of the Block Island militia," Alexander eagerly replied, "before I left on my last voyage I had pushed for the island's full and complete declaration of freedom from the king. However, on the long voyage, after much prayer and meditation, I realized just how precarious a position that would be for this small, defenseless island and our people. I'm more inclined now to recommend we maintain a position of neutrality—even though I know that many, individually and collectively, will do what they can to support the freedom fight."

Sands calmly responded, "Then you'll be happy to hear that was, in fact, the decision approved at our last town meeting. What else do you have?"

The young captain hesitated, surprised by the islanders' progress. "Well, very well. Yes, in addition, John, as you know, I am awaiting word from Hopkins for my commission to the new navy, so my time on the island may not be long. I would like your approval to rebuild the torch on Beacon Hill and to recruit men to set a constant watch."

"Alexander," the first warden answered wearily, "you know that with fewer and fewer occurrences of danger over the years, our lantern now stands neglected. There hasn't been any indication of raiding pirates or privateers for more than thirty years."

"What I envision, John, is our Block Island as the first location to spot the British Armada of troop ships as it sails from Nova Scotia and on to New York to squash this rebellion. I suggest that the island's lantern be the first signal light warning the continent that the king's army is at hand. On a clear night, our great beacon can be seen by all the islands in the region, and it could trigger a string of signal fires down the coast to New York and provide General Washington with as much warning as possible. I know of several men who would be eager to help. Do I have your permission to proceed?"

First Warden Sands stared off toward the front of the building, but Alexander knew he was listening. Finally, he replied, "Alexander, my good man, I admire your zeal, but I don't know if I agree with your sense of urgency. It will take the king's men many months—probably into the next year—to organize their expeditionary force. In addition, this is a significant decision, for wood and peat are very valuable commodities. With our forests almost depleted, we expect to completely prohibit the felling of any more trees. This is really not the time or the place for this kind of business. Besides," he continued, nodding his head toward the front door, "I think you have more pressing matters with your bondsman."

Alexander looked up and saw Williams and the mariners surrounding Nathan. Quickly, he stood up, knocking his chair over, and strode over to the group, just as the men were putting their hands on his friend.

"Now, now, there's been some mistake, mates," Alexander said in a level tone.

All four men now had Nathan in their grasp, but Nathan showed no fear; he just stood still, waiting for the right moment to battle. When the mariners looked around at Alexander, their swollen, bloodshot eyes set deep into their weather-beaten, drunken faces looked so demonic that it startled him. Suddenly, a bright flash went off in Alexander's head, and everything went black. Williams's voice echoed in Alexander's head as he drifted from consciousness: "We ain't your mates, Neighbor Hawkins!"

Chapter Five

"Hawkins!" Sands hollered in his face. "I'm afraid you've done your Negro a disservice! Many a man on this island has a growing resentment of the favors you've extended to that boy."

Alexander looked back at Sands, completely lost as to what Sands was trying to say to him.

Sands and the others at his table were lifting up Alexander and shaking him. Alexander's head throbbed, and he had no idea what had happened or why—and then clarity returned in a flash, and he jumped up, looking for Nathan and for Williams's men, but they all were gone. Through the grimy windows, he saw blurry figures wrestling about in the dirty street.

Alexander pulled himself from the islanders, bolted through the open door, and leaped from the stairs on to the pile of men. Though Nathan was at the bottom of the pile, he had already gotten in several good blows. The force of Alexander's leap scattered all of the men across the street. The mariners were drunk, so once Alexander and Nathan cleared to face off, they stood a decent chance against the men.

Alexander charged the mariners and went into a frenzy of punching and kicking, wildly landing many blows. Nathan freed himself from the group as their attention turned to Alexander. In that moment, Williams jumped up, grabbed Nathan around the neck, and put a knife to his face.

"Retreat, Hawkins, or I'll take a slice."

When Alexander saw the knife, he stopped immediately. "He's my property! Don't damage him, or you'll pay the price for it!"

"Samuel Williams!" Sands shouted from the top of the stairs. "You unhand that Negro! If you damage him, you'll have to answer to the constable and the town leaders."

Williams yelled, "He shouldn't have been where he was, and when we told the black bastard to git, he talked back to us. He deserves a good whippin'!"

Alexander's fists clenched as the other three sailors began to encircle him. He didn't think he could survive a fight with all three. Suddenly, out of the corner of his eye, he noticed someone stepping out from the side of The Spa.

Quepag walked forward and stood next to Alexander. "Williams, ya going ta have your men beat me, too?"

Williams paused and spit on the ground. "Quepag, ya foul heathen, I am tellin' ya ta step away. This ain't ya business."

The Indian stood there until Alexander demanded, "I'm the bondservant's owner, and I'll take care of any whipping that's required. Now hand over my Negro!"

They all stood silently for a moment, staring at each other, and finally Williams dropped his hand holding the knife to his side. "You baby this Negro, Hawkins. I don't trust you to do the right thing, but you can have him."

Just as Alexander started to breathe a sigh of relief, Williams hauled back his knife and stuck Nathan squarely in the buttocks. Nathan grimaced in pain and fell to the ground.

Williams and the three sailors then jumped into a nearby wagon and drove off. Sands called out to them, "You'll answer for this, Sam Williams!"

Alexander grabbed Nathan as he lay on the ground. He knew that the stab wound was intended to humble the slave, to embarrass him, and to remind him of his lowly position in life. He sensed that it was proving to be all too effective.

Alexander looked up at Sands and the islanders watching at the door. "Please get me something for the wound. I'll need some help moving my bondsman."

Nathan's face grew cold and angry. "The hurt from the wound I got today ain't nothing to the pain I just felt from the way you just spoke about me to those men."

Harry Littlefield threw a wad of cotton cloth down to Alexander, and Alexander began dressing the wound. Alexander took Nathan's outburst lightly. "Don't be so sensitive. For God's sake, I was trying to save you from even greater harm."

The black man grimaced but continued, "Maybe freedom means as much to me as it does to you! I ain't a free man now, so maybe it means more. You, of all people, got to stop treating me like a slave to others!"

Alexander paused from dressing the wound and replied with annoyance, "Nathan, I'm sorry I disregarded the town ordinance, but you need to gain your freedom first. You went in there knowing it was wrong, trying to be an equal."

The pain in Nathan's face was replaced by a quizzical stare. He pushed his friend away and said, "I don't need your help." He grabbed the dressing and wrapped it around the wound, then turned to limp back to the farm.

Quepag put his arm around Nathan's shoulder to assist him.

"Nathan, wait!" Alexander called after him. "Let me help you."

But Nathan, with Quepag's assistance, kept hobbling on, shaking his head.

Alexander had no idea why Nathan was so angry with him. He realized, however, that Nathan had been acting out his frustration with his position in life lately, and Alexander knew his friend was asking for trouble.

Alexander prided himself in always doing the right thing, but lately, his efforts had had quite the opposite outcome. Everything he touched seemed to wash away—like the sand fortresses he and Nathan used to build on Crescent Beach. As youngsters, they could spend hours crafting the elaborate structures, with moats and turrets adorned with seaweed flags, only to watch them pulled down by the rising tide, leaving nothing remaining of their labor.

He now felt shame in his own pride. He always thought of himself as somehow more righteous and better than the others who did not struggle morally with the evils of slavery. Now, the righteous work of his efforts to abolish slavery felt the crushing blow of a large wave, and it left nothing standing. The fortress of his convictions returned to the smooth sand of a world unchanged. He'd always felt his life would leave a clear and definable mark on this world and humanity, but his shame and embarrassment now made him angry and remorseful, the feelings building up within him until his body shook with emotion.

As he stood alone in the middle of the street, it began to rain. Alexander dropped to his knees and lifted his arms up to the sky in frustration. The sky opened up, and the rain began to pour. He called out from somewhere deep in his soul, "Nathan, don't go! Forgive me!"

With the realization that the damage was already done, he dropped his head and whispered to himself in disgust, "God, forgive the fool I am!"

~~~

Nathan limped home, hurting more from his friend's betrayal than the actual blade. *How could Alexander not understand after all this time?* He turned to Quepag to share his anger and
~~~

frustration. "I had to hear my own friend and brother say the very words I wanted to slap off the lips of those mariners."

"This is their world now, Nathan," Quepag answered. "The white men just let us live in it. You know Alexander tries, though. You know he cares for you."

Nathan felt sorrow as he realized Quepag was right. "Yeah, I'll forgive him. I guess I just come to realize that no matter how much he cares, a free, white slave-owner will never fully understand the feelings of a slave. What pains me the most was what Alexander said about me 'trying to be an equal.' I just realized for the first time that the freedom I want so bad is as much as I can hope for. Equality is something I may never get." This sad revelation hurt Nathan more than the pain stabbing him with each step he took. Even if he were to struggle to one day earn his freedom, he was sure to live in a world that would never consider him an equal.

Chapter Six

In the early morning, the Mohegan Indian Sachumjuia crouched behind the thick brush as he surveyed the property of the man named Sam Williams. The tall black man whom Williams had captured a week earlier and with whom Sachumjuia had fought was chained inside the small wooden shed. Williams and his Indian servant, Quepag, were not home. Sachumjuia stayed silent, deciding whether he should finish the fight with the slave.

Sachumjuia's thoughts turned back to the day in 1749 when he had first discovered his purpose in life. Each and every year since he had secretly returned to Manisses, he would pause to consider the powerful dream that had directed his life onto this strange path.

Late Autumn 1749

Sachumjuia sailed for several years with the pirate captain Giddy Gilcox on the pirate ship *Rogue Flattery*. When the British Navy chased Gilcox from the Caribbean up the North

American coast, it was Sachumjuia who had convinced Gilcox to stop at the island of Manisses. Once on the island, he deserted the pirates and ran to the tall bluffs where his forefathers had once fought. He gathered wood and built a fire. From a small pouch, he sprinkled a mixture of herbs, poppies, and gunpowder into the flames. They crackled and popped, developing a strong smoke that the Indian drew into his lungs.

He began to chant to the spirits. His chants were strained as he struggled to remember the words and the rhythms of the tribal elders. He wished that he had paid more attention to those men he used to scoff at. He was a hunter and warrior, just like his father and his father's father before him. Where his mighty forefathers had died in battle, he now desired to conjure up their spirits. It was a desire to feel close to them and to the heritage of his people—a closeness he had lost during his time spent out at sea. The Indian breathed deeply, closed his eyes, and chanted as best he could.

He began to feel himself rising up with the smoke and circling above the island. The freedom felt so good, but he had a purpose, and his voice screamed out for words of knowledge from the fallen warriors. All at once, the wind that was lifting him up died, and he plummeted to the ground. He could feel his body slam down hard, leaving him flat on his back.

From behind his closed eyelids, it became pitch black. But he was soon enchanted by the bright splashes that appeared. Colors shimmered like those colors of the rainbow but even deeper and more vibrant. He was in the midst of being mesmerized by the colorful display when a bright white light burned all the color away. In the light stood the form of a man, who eventually stepped forward to reveal himself.

The Indian wanted to speak and run forward to embrace the figure, who he believed was his father, but he could not move. As the bright light dimmed, he could see his father amid the bushes adorned with brilliant wild pink roses. His father picked one of the blooms from the bush and put it in his mouth. He chewed on the flower as if it were a fully satisfying meal. It appeared to be so satisfying, and with so many blooms around him, Sachumjuia wondered why he didn't eat more.

Suddenly, Sachumjuia felt a cold wind and harsh elements beat against him. He tried to ignore them and stay focused on his father. The cold wind caused the petals of the flowers to shrivel up and fall off the bushes until they were all bare. Finally, he saw the image of his father start to shrivel up in the same fashion as the flowers, and his body became like the petals. Bit by bit, his body fell to the ground with the rose petals until he was gone.

The Indian tried to reach forward and catch the falling petals, but he couldn't move. His arms were pinned to his body. Sachumjuia wrestled to loosen himself but couldn't until the petals all had fallen. He then tore his arms free to beat his chest. He struggled to scream out until a great wind surged from his lungs and a primal wolf scream escaped. His eyes bolted open, and he found himself sitting with crossed legs before the fire. Only now, a frenzied wind and rain was whipping up, and the burning fire had been scattered. Pieces of the wood were still burning all around, and many had blown right into the Indian's lap. He jumped up to brush the burning wood and ash from himself.

Sachumjuia's head was still cloudy from the smoke, so it took a second for him to recall where he was. Soaked by the heavy rain, he looked up from the fire and out over the high bluff. He saw something moving offshore. He was certain that it must have been their ship, the *Rogue Flattery*, but there were no sails aloft or even any masts left standing. She was moving slowly southeast, out to the deep water, and shrinking into the sea. Finally, she disappeared under the waves.

The question of what had happened to the ship did not even enter into his mind. The Indian began to jump and dance and chant again. These were not actions that came from anger or despair, but from exhilaration. He immediately concluded that his connection to the spirits had been made. His forefathers had heard his chants. They had not only provided him with a dream as an answer to the future course of his life but had made certain that he would follow their instruction by sinking the ship. Now, he concluded that he must seek out a wise man to interpret his dream so that he might fulfill his destiny.

Sachumjuia turned to head into the forest to find shelter from the elements but then stopped. His mouth fell open and his eyes widened. Stepping forward, he knelt down and reached out to touch something that he was not sure was real. Grabbing the stem, he pulled it from the bush and brought it close to his face. There before him in the soaking rain was the bright-pink wild beach rose from his dream. The sharp thorns from the stem confirmed that it was all too real. Beneath the pink flower, bright red blood dripped down his arm.

Chapter Seven

Sachumjuia pressed the medicinal salve he had mixed against the wound in his side, and his thoughts turned back to the present. He continued to stare at the shed that housed the black slave with whom he had recently fought. Each time he felt the pain, he became angry with himself. How could he have been so surprised? He must not let that happen again. The Mohegan replayed in his mind what had happened just days before. …

Sachumjuia finished his long trip in the Indian mishoon, paddling from the mainland to Manisses. He stored the small canoe and paddles in the tall grass, covered it with branches, and then climbed the short bluff. The brave had completed this trip dozens of times before during each spring season since 1749. When he reached the top of the bluff, he noticed a strange scent. As he sniffed the air, a bush to his right suddenly shook to life. A black man jumped out from the bushes to challenge him.

Sachumjuia swiftly and efficiently stopped the man with his hatchet, burying it deep into his chest. As he went to retrieve his hatchet, he was surprised by another, taller black man rising from the bushes, holding a spear.

Both he and the tall man ran to retrieve the hatchet. The black man was fast and quick with his weapon. He jabbed at Sachumjuia and then stabbed him in his side. Sachumjuia grabbed the shaft of the spear, pulled it from his side, and broke it across his own chest. The black man tore the hatchet from his dead companion's chest and ran off. Sachumjuia ran after him. No man had ever outrun Sachumjuia in the forest, but this man presented a challenge. The Mohegan warrior wondered if he was losing his skills or if he was simply tired from the long paddle.

Just as Sachumjuia was closing in on his prey, the black man broke out into a clearing. At the same time, Sachumjuia heard the sound of horses from the clearing, and he stopped. White men were there and one, with musket raised, climbed off his horse. He circled the black man as he yelled at him. Suddenly, he used his musket as a club to bash the black man's head, and he crumpled to the ground. Sachumjuia felt the urge to kill the white man, but this was not his mission, so he quietly retreated back into the forest to heal his wound.

Now, Sachumjuia had made his way to the white man's property to look for his hatchet and for the black warrior. As he looked in on his captured adversary, he debated whether he should finish the kill. That was his desire, but he also knew that killing the man was not really his purpose. As he wrestled with what to do, his thoughts again drifted back, twenty-six years earlier, when he had first learned of his purpose in life. …

Late Autumn 1749

The day after the *Rogue Flattery* sank off the south shore of Manisses, the first rays of the early sun awakened Sachumjuia. A bolt of light streamed through the thicket of trees and brush and through the branches he'd cut to cover himself near the cleft of a rock. The light struck him directly in the face, and the heat felt as if it were burning a hole in his forehead. He snapped awake, blinded and confused. The smoke he had inhaled the day before still lingered. Remembering the sight of the sinking ship, he pushed the branches aside and made his way back to the edge of the tall bluffs. Looking down, he saw a stretch of beach littered with debris.

He didn't know if there were any survivors, but he didn't really care—he had no emotional ties to any of them. They were not tribesman, brothers, or friends. He felt indebted to the captain, Giddy Gilcox, for setting him free and giving him the chance to exact revenge on white men. But there was nothing to tie him to the pirates, and except for the weapons and provisions, he saw no value in the treasure they gathered and hoarded.

The Mohegan was a warrior, and these men liked to fight, yet for him there was no purpose to it, save to vent his anger toward the whites. He was now certain his time had come to break away from Gilcox and his crew. So now, he had no feelings for whether these men lived or died. If any of the pirates survived, though, and lay in the sand below, he would go down and finish them off. He needed to make a clean start in order to pursue the meaning of his dream.

From his vantage point on the bluff, he could not see any bodies lying among the debris. He was just about to descend the bluff to sift through the wreckage when he spotted two men—one black, one white—coming from around the bend on the beach. From the way they were dressed, Sachumjuia could tell immediately that neither of the men were from the *Rogue Flattery*.

The white man came upon something that caused him to become very excited, and he called the black man over. Whatever it was, they wasted no time in picking it up and carrying it back down the beach. The Indian was curious to see what it was, but he heard a horse approaching and quickly ducked back into the forest—he did not want to be discovered. His plan was to search for a place in the forest where he could hide and set up camp. At night, he would venture out to find the Manissean Indian lodges. Even though the tribe was his longtime enemy, their sachem, Chief Penewes, was revered as a leader with great wisdom. If he was still alive, the Mohegan hoped to counsel with the sachem about his dream and its interpretation. The wild rose had told him that the answers to his questions were to be found upon the island of Manisses.

Sachumjuia spent the next few days on the island, where he uncovered a cave in the thickest part of the forest. It was at the lowest point of a hollow near the southern rim of the island, and it was obvious that no one ventured into the thick briers. The prickly underbrush seemed impenetrable and lay like a blanket across a quarter square mile.

Each night, the Indian would venture out and quietly gather information from the unsuspecting islanders, island Indians, and slaves. He stole into homes and into the town to listen to conversations, learning much about what was happening on the island. He then located the Indian lodges and hovels, called *puttuckakuans*, along with several *pesuponck*—sweat houses—scattered along the eastern shore of the Great Pond. He spent a few nights hiding in the shadows, gleaning information about the old sachem, Penewes. The sights, sounds, and smells of the Manissean cluster of hovels and tepees reminded him of when he was a young brave.

On this night, he watched as the Indians shared a dinner of succotash, clams, fish, and wild game. Piles of clam shells dotted the area. The tall Manisseans wore a mixture of white man's clothes and deer-skin garments. There were no bows and arrows, clubs, hatchets, or axes of stone to be seen. Sachem Penewes was indeed alive but was now blind and living alone in his lodge.

Sachumjuia quietly watched the chief's comings and goings and determined when he could find him alone. A young Indian boy would lead the old chief around each day and then bring him back to his lodge at night. Before the boy would leave for the evening, he would help the old man prepare for sleep.

Sachumjuia decided the time was right. At dusk, the Mohegan slipped into Penewes's lodge and hid, quietly waiting for the old man. Just as Penewes had done during the previous week, the sachem returned home, accompanied by the young boy named Quepag.

Chapter Eight

Late Autumn 1749

Sachumjuia watched how this young boy, whom he understood to be the chief's grandson, respectfully, tenderly, and patiently cared for the old man. The boy had been taught well and, even at this young age, appreciated the significance of the old man's life. They spoke at first in their native Algonquin tongue but then began a conversation in English, and Sachumjuia listened intently. They were talking about what had happened days earlier when the sudden storm had sunk Gilcox and the *Rogue Flattery*. He realized the two were saying something about the treasure his pirate companions buried on that day.

Sachumjuia did not care about such things. All the pirates cared about was treasure and rum and women, but he cared for none of it. His interests were not the silver and gold pieces the pirates fought and killed for. His desire was for freedom and vengeance and to retake what had been stolen from him and his people.

"Tell me again, Quepag," the old sachem said to the boy. "What happened the day of the storm this past moon?"

Young Quepag answered, "The Hawkins men were digging to bury the white woman, and I could hear others digging on the far side of the hill. I told the black men, but their ears were closed like poquauhog. They were stupid and tied me with a rope to keep me from running away. I was angry, so I called to you, Grandfather; called for you to do something to hurt them. Then the storm came. You sent the storm, Grandfather!"

Sachumjuia nodded his head as he listened. *It is this great sachem who brought about the storm! This is the wise brave who will help me understand my dream.*

"Yes, but Quepag," the grandfather interrupted somewhat dismissively, "tell your grandfather what you saw again. Quietly come and whisper it into my ear."

Quepag drew close to Penewes's ear and whispered; Sachumjuia strained to listen.

When the young boy finished, the old man straightened in his chair and frowned. "Quepag, you must not tell anyone what you have told me. I will set my mind on this through the night. You will wait for my answer."

"How long, Grandfather, must I wait?"

The old man reached up with both hands and cradled the boy's face, drawing it closer to his. He repeated, "Remember, tell no one of what you have told me. It is no matter of how long. You must wait until I come to you with my instruction."

The boy nodded his head. "Yes, I promise, Grandfather."

As Sachumjuia watched the boy lovingly kiss his grandfather good night, he felt unfamiliar emotions wash over him. His eyes began to tear, and he could feel sadness and something growing in his throat. He took it to be some strange spirit that was protecting the great chief, and he began to think it would be better for him to leave. As he waited for the boy to depart, the sensation began to subside. The experience, though, caused the brave to grow anxious about returning to his people and spending time with the old men of his tribe, sharing their rich lives. After counseling with Sachem Penewes, he decided he would steal a canoe and immediately paddle back to the mainland and seek out his people to reconnect with the Muckquand, the wolf spirit of his tribe.

The old sachem chief lay in his bed and continued to converse with his grandson. The boy carefully handled some of the old man's most treasured items—beautifully fashioned war clubs, a bow, knives, feathered caps, and animal skins. When he was done, the boy leaned over his grandfather and hugged him one last time before departing.

A wave of jealousy ran through Sachumjuia. He wanted something of what the boy had, but he struggled with understanding exactly what that was. He was just a boy! What could a powerful warrior want that a boy could have?

The cabin door closed, and the Mohegan waited until the boy was some distance away. Just as Sachumjuia was about to move toward the old man, the chief spoke in Mohegan Algonquin, saying, "*Wigun dupkwa*. Good evening."

The Mohegan stayed where he was, standing perfectly still. Then the sachem spoke in Sachumjuia's native tongue. *How could Penewes possibly have been talking to me?*

Again, the chief spoke up. "*Wigwomun*. Welcome. I have been waiting for you. You have come here to speak with me. I will be sleeping soon, so don't waste time. Step forward and we will talk."

Sachumjuia hesitated, but he could not wait any longer. He thought that even though the great sachem chief was blind, he must have vision exceeding the eagle and hearing greater than the wolf.

Finally, the Mohegan spoke up, speaking in English, with the accent of the natives of Albatross, his island home for many seasons. "Yes, I have come. Penewes, you are known to be a sachem of great wisdom. I am in need of your powers to tell me the meaning of a dream that has come to me in recent days."

"Yes, I know this already," Penewes said, "but where are you from? You do not have the tongue of the Nannhiggaeucks, or the Pequot, or the Mohegan. What is your name, and where are your people from?"

The Mohegan had not prepared himself to answer these questions, so he said the first name that entered into his head: "My name is Gilcox, and I'm from a tribe far to the south on the island of Albatross."

"You have traveled far, so tell me your dream."

Sachumjuia relayed every detail of his dream that he could recall. When he had finished, the old man lay quietly for a long time. The Mohegan was restless but sat in silence, waiting. Just as the Mohegan's patience had about worn out and he was sure the old man had fallen asleep, the sachem chief began to speak his interpretation.

"I know you come from a tribe of great warriors. Your father and his fathers before him were also strong warriors. At a time before you were even born, they fell, along with many others of their brothers, in a great battle. The enemy who did this thing is no longer your people's mortal enemy, but another enemy soon came to steal your attention and your vengeance away. The first enemy is still living, but the numbers grow smaller. Because of this great new enemy, revenge for this loss has never been completed."

Penewes paused as Sachumjuia's thoughts steeped in the wise man's words.

The sachem breathed in deeply, spread out his weathered hands, and continued. "The wild rose blossoms are your father's enemy. There are still enough to fill the wild rose bush. As with the rose that appears friendly, its beauty hides the sharp thorns underneath. Your father has come to you to seek out his revenge. He died at the hands of the paleskins in a battle, which was with honor. His forefathers died an anguished death, without food or water, hanging from a rock. Their death has never been avenged. The white men came and consumed your time and energy. They have distracted your destiny. You must now turn your attention back to your true enemy. He wants their death to be long and painful. You are to devour only one of the enemies during the warm season, while the beach rose first blooms. Each year you will repeat this until you have devoured every one."

The brave sat there, stunned. Penewes was telling him that it was now Sachumjuia's responsibility to complete the revenge of the Mohegans toward the Manisseans for their butchery of his forefathers at the island's tallest bluffs. This was something to which he would have to dedicate his life. If these were his father's words, then he knew he could not shrink from them. Just to be certain, he asked, "Could there be another meaning to this dream?"

The chief paused for a few moments before replying, "Dreams are sometimes difficult to fully know, but of this one I am certain. For people in this life with no peace sacrifice, revenge can never die. The past won't let it, and if people forget, the Wunnohquand peace spirits will remind them."

The Mohegan looked up at the old man. "Penewes, you are a wise leader. Do you look forward to the next life?"

"If it means I will be a young warrior again, then yes. I believe the next world may not be better, just another kind."

The Mohegan stepped forward and grabbed for his weapon. Then he thought of the boy and decided that shedding the old man's blood would not be right. "I want to repay you for so freely giving of your wisdom." He sat down next to the old man and leaned over to put his arms around his upper body. The Indian hugged the old man like the young boy had, but he pressed the sachem's face tightly into his chest. The chief struggled for a moment, but soon his body fell limp.

Sachumjuia left the cabin feeling proud and good. He had heard much from the great sachem chief and felt as though their two spirits had become as one. In his mind, the sachem had offered himself up as the first sacrifice to start the brave's new calling of eliminating the Indians of Manisses.

On his way out, he took one of Penewes's war clubs. He knew the old leader would have wanted him to have it to bring to life the dream he had interpreted for the warrior. Now he felt good that he had helped the old sachem to pass into the next life and proud that it had been such a peaceful transition.

~~~

The next day, the young boy Quepag came to wake his grandfather. He was anxious to find out if his grandfather had an answer regarding their secret. When he arrived, the old man lay there cold and still, with all but one of his treasured weapons under his folded arms.

Though Quepag knew his grandfather was gone, he was sure his spirit would return. His grandfather told him to wait for the answer concerning their secret. Now Quepag would do as the sachem chief instructed and wait with great anticipation for his grandfather's message. Quepag ran out to share the news of his grandfather's departure with the tribe.

The Manissean tribe agreed that the island spirit of "the little gods" had called Sachem Penewes home. The spirit allowed him first to gather those things he would need in the next life. They reasoned that the missing club was given as a gift to the spirit.

Later that day, the tribe prepared their chief's body for burial. The women also prepared eatables of various shellfish and stored them in earthen pots. This would be Penewes's food for his journey to another world.

The tribe's burial ground was known as Indian Head Neck along the edge of the Great Pond where the braves were buried upright in a walking posture, looking over the rich waters of the pond. They decided, though, that Penewes was deserving of a special burial place. They chose to bury him on the edge of the large freshwater pond at the northern point of the island. There, he could forever enjoy its cool, fresh waters, while his
~~~

spirit remained to provide the Manissean people with eternal guidance.

Just after dusk, they finished burying their sachem on the west bank of the pond. In his honor they built a raft, lighting it on fire and setting it adrift out into the pond. The tribe looked on. Beyond the burning raft, a fiery red and orange moon hung on the eastern horizon. The young grandson looked up, and there, silhouetted in the bright moon, was a large Indian brave with long flowing hair, raising a war club to the sky in tribute to the Manissean sachem. Quepag immediately recognized the club as the one missing from his grandfather's collection, and a smile crossed his face.

He smiled, for it brought him hope that his grandfather's spirit lived on. He was now assured that his grandfather would return one day to tell him what to do with his secret treasure, and his hope gave him great comfort.

Chapter Nine

Spring 1776

Alexander was tired. He had spent the last few days accomplishing weeks' worth of needed repairs and labor on the Hawkins farm. Though rewarding, the work was made all that much harder by not having Nathan there by his side. But Nathan's wound was on the mend, and so was their friendship.

As Alexander rode Nimbau, the old slave Stepney followed him on a mule named Dory. The two kept their rides to a slow walk and headed north up the center cart path to the meetinghouse located northeast of Fresh Pond at the center of the island. Other than a few of the larger farms and the buildings at Harbor Bay, most buildings on the island, including the schoolhouse, a pound, and a windmill, were located within two and a half miles of the Baptist church meetinghouse.

"Alexander," Stepney said, breaking the silence, "why are you takin' me to de town meetin'? You know I can't go in."

Alexander, startled from his deep thoughts, replied, "Yes, I'm sorry, Stepney. I guess in my exhaustion I forgot to mention the task I have for you. Do you know of anyone who has talked with the new African?"

"No, not dat I knows of."

"Yes, that's what I fear," Alexander continued. "I would like you to try to talk with him to see if you can get any answers. I'm afraid, under the circumstances, he will be turned over to the mainland authorities and may be put to death for murder."

"You know, sir," Stepney responded, "dat dere are many African tongues, an' dat was anudder life ago for me. I doubts I can talk to him, Alexander. Even so, I don't knows dat a deat' sentence is much worse den bein' a slave to Master Williams."

"Stepney, I know you and many of the Africans have learned to speak among the many tribes by using the pidgins you developed as captives on the long slave ship voyages, in order to communicate with one another. He is a silent man but perhaps he will talk with you. All I ask is that you try, and tell me what you can."

"Is it dat you don't believe he kilt dat ot'er African? Who else could have done dat?"

Alexander scratched his chin. "I surely don't know, Stepney. There are things that do not make sense. We should always seek the truth. You know what I always say…"

Stepney spoke the biblical adage that Alexander had tirelessly repeated over the years: "'And ye shall know de truth an' de truth shall set us free.'" He thought for a moment before commenting, "Though I don't knows dat it makes all dat much sense for me, bein' a bondservant an' all."

Alexander smiled in embarrassment and said, "I suppose that whether slave or free, the truth will make us honest men, my dear Stepney."

They started to see other islanders heading toward the meetinghouse, and Alexander exchanged greetings with them as they went along. When they reached the meetinghouse, there were already groups of islanders gathered and engaged in several conversations. He exchanged greetings with those he had not seen since his return. He spotted Williams, away from the others, standing with Quepag and the large African in fetters.

Alexander and Stepney hitched their mounts to a tree branch and went directly over to Williams's group. "Greetings, my friend," he said to Quepag. Nodding to the African, he asked, "And who is this imposing specimen of a man?"

Sam Williams immediately jumped in. "Hawkins, if you're looking for an apology, don't waste your time. I was tired and drunk, and your Negro angered me with his disrespect. He deserved what he got." Turning to Stepney, he continued, "You're a good slave, Stepney, but that boy of yours went where he don't belong."

Stepney obligingly answered, "Yes, Master Williams, but I wish you didn't have to stick him."

"He's my slave, Hawkins," Williams continued before Quepag could respond to the original question. "He ain't got a name yet, but he's a powerful worker, and he ain't caused no trouble."

"Indeed," Alexander responded. "We shall see what the town officers have to say."

He looked at the black man and extended his hand in friendship. The man looked directly into his eyes with no change in his stony expression. He did not reciprocate.

After an awkward pause, Alexander dropped his hand but continued to stare into the man's eyes. He noticed a clear strength and bearing.

"Now, Samuel, has anyone tried to speak with him?"

"No one is going to go near him," Williams answered curtly. "He seems friendly enough with Quepag, but I don't want nobody to hurt my chance to have this slave. Fact is, I think he's deaf and dumb. He don't act like he hears anything. But he works like an ox."

"Aren't you concerned that the leaders will turn him over to the mainland? That would mean almost certain death."

"Nah." Williams shook his head. "He's mine or he's no one's. If they say he's a killer and must die, so be it."

"Samuel, can I have a few words with you in private?"

As the two moved away, Alexander secretly motioned for Stepney to try to speak with the African. Stepney shrugged his shoulders and nodded his head.

When they were far enough away, Williams growled, "I don't need no preaching from you, Hawkins. Just tell me, is your boy Nathan going ta set Sands and the island leaders on me?"

While looking over Williams's shoulder to monitor Stepney's attempt to speak with the African, he said, "I have a mind to charge you reparations for the lost labor. Nathan, however, will not be bringing charges because even as a slave, he is a bigger man than you."

"Hogwash!" Williams shot back. "A slave is not a man, Hawkins. That's where ya cause trouble. You want ta treat them the same, and then they all start ta expect more."

Alexander responded, "That's where you're wrong. Our laws state that a slave is a man. He's not a free man like you and me, but he has rights, which include the right to life and rights to property. You can't be treating slaves worse than livestock."

"We've treated our slaves just fine, Hawkins. Look at Quepag. He's stayed with our family for a long time."

"I'm afraid you've had a poor history with slaves," Alexander responded. "Quepag is a different case. He's a paid servant who comes and goes as he pleases. For some strange reason, he feels a sense of obligation to you and your family—more like a brother."

"A brother?" Williams's voice grew in anger. "That Indian is indentured for crimes against my family. That's his obligation."

Just then, Williams caught Alexander stealing a glance over his shoulder and turned to see Stepney engaging with the African. He immediately ran over, yelling, "Hey, Stepney! You move away from him! What do you think you're doing? Don't get him all excited."

Just then, First Warden Sands came out of the building and began ringing the assembly bell. "Daylight's a-wasting. Let us call the meeting to order."

As the islanders filed into the building, Alexander pulled Stepney aside. The old slave whispered into his ear what he was able to glean from the African.

All the others had entered the building, leaving Sands waiting for Alexander. He and Stepney talked while slowly walking toward the meetinghouse.

"Now, Captain Hawkins," Sands called. "We have much business to transact. You know your bondsman cannot enter. I'm sorry, Stepney."

Alexander said farewell to Stepney and hurried into the building as Sands shut the door.

Chapter Ten

Alexander entered the dark church meetinghouse. He squinted and scanned the room to see who was in attendance. Almost all of the freemen residents of the island were there. He recognized the men from the most notable and longstanding island families, with the names of Sands, Littlefield, Ray, Rathbun, Dickens, Dodge, Briggs, Mitchel, Mott, Paine, Sheffield, Wright, and Rose.

The room was warm and dark, being lit by a solitary whale-oil lantern. The members of the town council sat in the front of the meetinghouse. Behind a large rough-hewn table, they discussed their agenda in whispered tones before the start of the meeting. First Warden and Moderator John Sands sat at the center of the table, with Walter Rathbun, Town Clerk, and Deputy Warden Caleb Littlefield sitting on either side of Sands. Town Councilmen John Littlefield, Edward Sands and Samuel Rathbun were seated at the far left of the table. At the far right sat the Town Treasurer, Nathaniel Littlefield, Town Sergeant, Oliver R. Rose, and Constable Laurence Tuckman.

Alexander shook his head in amazement to see Tuckman sitting in a position of authority among such notable islander freemen. He wondered if anyone else had come to learn of the secret of Tuckman's true identity. *Who would have thought that this man could have made this of himself?* Yet it didn't surprise Alexander that Tuckman had risen to this rank, thanks to his ambition and ability to politic.

Alexander was the only one on the island to remember Tuckman from a visit he made to the island years earlier. When Tuckman came to settle on the island, Alexander mentioned their first meeting, and Tuckman shared his life story, asking Alexander to pledge it to secrecy. Alexander kept that pledge, and he never shared it with anyone else.

Tuckman's birth name was actually Lough Taugger, being part of a clan from Ireland's smallest county, located in the central region of Longford. He was a square-shouldered block of an Irishman, who at sixteen had been thrown into a British jail in Ireland. His crime: fighting to retain his family's property after the English landowner evicted them.

Like many of his brethren, he was considered by the English as suited only for a life of servitude. The young American colonies were in dire need of laborers, so many Irish and Scottish prisoners were sent as indentured servants to serve out their prison sentences in the New World. Tuckman's period of indentured servitude was to be eight years. The first four were spent on a Rhode Island plantation, but his papers were subsequently sold to a Connecticut farmer. He spent the remainder of his term in the county of Fairfield, on a farm north of the seaport, Bridgeport.

While he was a servant at the Rhode Island plantation, he cared for and raised a new breed of champion saddle horses called Gansett Pacers. On a rare excursion to Block Island, he delivered a horse to the Hawkins family. The Irishman followed Alexander, the young, proud owner of this beautiful animal, on his first ride before finalizing the sale.

The two galloped down to the southernmost region of the island, which was filled with rolling hills that gathered into a lush hollow. They followed a trail along a tree-lined ridge overlooking the entire island. It was spring, and migrating raptors were soaring above the hollow, riding the turbulent island winds.

Tuckman was taken with this majestic bird and its distinctive white markings. The raptors put on a show—the gray-backed males performed a strange looping sky dance before him. He watched as these birds of prey swooped down into the grassy areas and easily picked up small vermin and snakes.

The beauty of the hollow stunned him. He looked over a shiny silver pond that lay to the west amid the shadblow, in their short-lived white bloom. Closer to the ridge, a patchwork of dark greens flowed from the arrow wood, pokeweed, and greenbrier shrubs, mixed with amber fields of aster, milkweed, and goldenrod, beneath the vapors of soft white shadblow. This tapestry of wildflowers rolled and waved like a flag in the wind, spilling over the high bluffs down to a purple stone and golden brown sand and looking out over a thundering blue-green sea. The sight made him pine for his homeland.

His home county in Ireland was full of woodland patches dotting the rolling countryside and rivers winding their way slowly through the fields. Yet it was on the few trips he made as a child to the southern coast of County Cork that he fell in love with the rugged seaside. Even then, he dreamed of one day making that place his home.

The beauty of the island and the memories of his beloved Ireland were too much, and he broke down and cried. He committed to himself that when his period of servitude ended, he would come back to make Block Island—and this place, in particular—his home.

Years later, he was a free man who had changed his name to Lawrence Tuckman. His sandy brown hair and lack of the freckles typical of the Irish allowed him to pass himself off as an Englishman. Only when his beard grew out would the telltale red hair of his ancestors expose him as Irish. In spite of the popular facial hair fashions of the day, Tuckman always kept himself clean-shaven.

He made his way back to Block Island and eventually persuaded Alexander's father to allow him to acquire a small plot within the very hollow that had brought him to tears.

The Irishman ingratiated himself to the islanders by teaching them improvements to their potato farming, which greatly enhanced the size and quality of their crops. His familiarity with the peat bogs of Longford also helped the islanders to maximize their harvest of peat for heating fuel from the numerous tug holes on the island. His place within the community of islanders steadily grew to the point where he now was an elected town official, serving as constable.

~~~

Alexander looked for a place to sit on the wooden benches. He spotted his friend, Benjamin Beach, waving to him and made his way over. The two shook hands and embraced.

"Good to see you, my friend," Alexander said in a hushed tone. "How is your sister?"

"It's good to see you as well," Beach answered. "I'm fine, but my sister is still dealing with her disappointment. Where is your father?"

"He's resting, exhausted from trying to keep up with me since my return."

First Warden John Sands stood up abruptly and pounded his gavel on the desk to sound the start of the meeting. He announced, "As many of you know, I will be sailing to the mainland tomorrow to represent the island in the General Assembly. I have also been asked to take command of the Block Island company of militia. Given these increased responsibilities, I will have to put the gavel into the capable hands of one of my fellow officers. Constable Tuckman has requested the honor of acting as moderator, and Deputy Warden Littlefield
~~~

has agreed." Handing the gavel over to Tuckman, he acknowledged, "Constable Tuckman, the meeting is yours."

Tuckman anxiously took hold of the gavel saying, "Thank you, First Warden, and we pray Godspeed for you in your many responsibilities." He then proudly and firmly rapped the table, as if testing out his newfound power.

As the gathering grew silent, Alexander continued to converse with Beach. Tuckman called out, "Let us come to order. Captain Hawkins, since your jaw seems so thoroughly exercised, would you open our meeting in prayer?"

A mild laughter filled the room while Alexander sheepishly stood up. The group became quiet as all closed their eyes and bowed their heads.

Alexander prayed, "Our heavenly Father, we thank thee for all that we have and for all thou are. We turn to thee now, asking for thy great wisdom and counsel during these proceedings. May thy truth guide us to thy righteousness in all our decisions. Amen."

"Now," Tuckman immediately began, "this meeting was called to address the matter of the new Negro who washed onto our shores. We do have several other items on our docket tonight, if time allows, so let us move quickly ahead with the most pressing matter. Mr. Williams, will you bring the African forward and state your request."

Williams and Quepag escorted the African to the front of the room. As they came forward, one of the islanders called out, "What is the Indian doing here in our meeting?"

"Yes, I am sorry," Tuckman quickly responded. "I should have noted. We have allowed Mr. Quepag to stay, as he seems to be a soothing influence on the savage. He is simply here to maintain our safety. Now, Mr. Williams?"

Williams faced the crowd and cleared his throat. "As you all know, this African showed up on our island over a week ago. There has been no claim ta him, so I claim him as my slave. He's a good worker and has been gentle and peaceable this whole time."

"Yes, indeed, Mr. Williams," Tuckman responded, "but what are we supposed to do about the other African found murdered by the very bloody hatchet found in this man's hand? Many here are still concerned for their safety and have expressed a desire to have him put off our island."

"Well…" Williams stumbled to respond. "I don't know for certain what happened, and nobody else here does neither. I think it was that he was defending himself. All I know is that he hasn't shown no violence since."

After a moment spent looking across the assembled men, Tuckman answered, "Well, Mr. Williams, I have spoken with the town officers, and we have agreed that without any compelling evidence to the contrary, and for the safety of all those on this small island, he should be put off to the authorities on the mainland. However, we have likewise agreed to leave this to a general vote. Do you have anything else to say?"

Williams stood quietly for a moment. Suddenly, he turned toward the African and menacingly yelled "*Ahhhhhhhh!*" while clapping his hands and making threatening gestures in the stoic man's face.

The meeting erupted as everyone there recoiled in surprise and fear. Tuckman immediately began pounding his gavel, yelling, "That will be enough, Mr. Williams! Control yourself!"

Williams stopped, pointed to the African, and yelled, "You see? He didn't even flinch. There ain't no violence in him. He's my slave, so let me have him."

Once again, Tuckman pounded the table and said, "Samuel Williams, that will be enough. Please control yourself and take your seat. We shall see how convincing your argument has been." Turning to the crowd, he continued, "Unless there are any other questions, we shall have a vote."

Chapter Eleven

While the meeting progressed the Mohegan, Sachumjuia quietly hid outside in the moon shadow of the church meetinghouse. As he peeked through a gap in the boards, he could see the freemen of the island deciding what to do with the black man. He was still wrestling with the desire to kill the man, but now it appeared that the islanders were going to take the decision from him and send the African off the island. The Mohegan reluctantly reminded himself that his revenge against the black man was not a part of his purpose in life.

His mission for this spring was done. Sachumjuia had killed the island Indian named Big Jim. He had been the first one to come along the Indian trail on the southern rim of the island. This black man being tried had taken away Sachumjuia's hatchet. Without his hatchet, he had to use a stone on Big Jim, but it still went quickly.

He wanted to retrieve his cherished hatchet, but there were always too many whites around to steal it back. He had gone for too many seasons without being detected by the islanders to risk being discovered for a hatchet. His work was done, and he'd be satisfied to return to his mainland camp without it.

As Sachumjuia crouched in the dark, he wondered, as he had many times before, if the vision of the life purpose to slowly eliminate the Indians of Manisses was true. Had his spirit father really visited him? Had he really understood it correctly? Perhaps the sachem Chief Penewes misinterpreted his dream. It was becoming tiresome to paddle out to the island each spring to kill only one island Indian. The Mannissean tribe would not last much longer, though. He thought back to the time, so many seasons ago, when his destiny was confirmed for him in the year of 1749. …

~~~

That first canoe trip back to the mainland after the *Rogue Flattery* sank and after the sachem Chief Penewes's burial was a long one for the powerful brave. He had underestimated the distance and the time it would take to reach the shore of Rhode Island. Pulling himself up onto the rocks of Manutuck, he breathed deeply. *Yes!* He remembered the salty seaweed smell of his old shoreline. It excited his senses to think of spending time back with his Mohegan family, and he became even more anxious to find the tribe. A desire to rekindle the cold embers of his national pride pulsed through his veins.

Based upon what he had seen and heard on the island, Sachumjuia knew the white man would still have a strong presence on the mainland. He clung to the hope that his nation would be free and intact, but by the looks of the Manissean tribe, his Mohegans might well be an even smaller shell of their once great nation.

Working his way through the areas of Quonochontaug and Misquamicut, Sachumjuia crossed the Dawcatuck River into the land of Quinnetucket. The few Indians he came across were not his people but some of the Nipmuc. He was glad these were not his people, for they were dirty and ragged and
~~~

wearing mostly white man's clothes. He felt ashamed and was tempted to kill them for embarrassing all natives, but he decided to leave them alone in their misery. The dirty stragglers pointed him back north to the Quinnetucut River Valley and what had been the Mohegan capital of Shetucket, where the tribe was now making their camp once again. With every step, the brave grew more anxious about the condition in which he might find his people.

He was familiar with the land and was surprised at how easily it all came back to him. As if it had been only a full moon ago, he crossed the same land he had hunted as a young brave.

He saw more and more signs of his tribe as he neared the Mohegan camp. Rather than being excited, though, this worried him. His people were always known to live in great numbers, leaving little evidence of the camp's approach. Even when the whole tribe moved their camp, there would be little trace of them left behind. It seemed that his people had become sloppy, and this told him that they no longer cared as much as they once had.

What is it my people don't care about? he wondered as he moved farther inland. He figured they didn't care about the spirits of the trees and the waters and the mountains and the animals, as they once had. His people were dishonoring what was not theirs, and the brave was sure the spirits would pay them back for this dishonor. It also meant they didn't care if other peoples knew where they were. Had they given up on the idea that they could maintain their own world, and did they not care if the white man found them? This meant they were handing over their freedom as a separate and united people. The carelessness said to the outside world, "Come, because we cannot stop you, and we don't care anymore."

He decided that they could not care much about their heritage and their forefathers and their rituals, songs, dances, and chanting. Were there enough elders living to keep their past glory alive?

The prodigal Mohegan stopped by a stream and knelt down to drink. The cool refreshment tasted much as he remembered, and it caused a hope to rise up within him. If the water tasted the same, then maybe things could be the same. He himself had turned from the traditions and was led away off on his own. Hope grew that he could lead the others back to care again.

Sachumjuia pressed on. He saw much of the game and wildlife he'd hunted years before—deer, bear, and fowl—along with the juicy wild fruits and nuts. He was tempted to gather some food, but he didn't want to delay. Certain the Mohegan camp was over the next hill, Sachumjuia broke into a run. Climbing the hill at a frantic pace, he reached the top, exhausted. He looked down to see smoke rising from the trees below along the riverbank. This was the place the Mohegans often set up camp, so he was encouraged that they had not been forced from their land.

The brave's energy was almost spent, and he breathed heavily. Seeing the camp put him at ease. He took his time climbing back down the other side of the mountain, though he was still anxious about who and what he would find.

Many of the brave's closest warrior brothers had died, first fighting against white men, then with the white men against the Pequot, the Narragansett, and the Abenaki. He did not know if any of his closest members of the tribe would have survived his ten-year absence. The grandmother who had raised him was sickly even when he left, and he was sure she was gone by now. Would he know any of the remaining tribe, and would any of them know him?

Slowly, he snuck into camp undetected, surprised at how easily he gained entry. The sun was just disappearing behind the mountain, creating a twilight that allowed him to move freely around the lodges.

His fears had been well founded. The tribe looked as though it was only women and children. Where were all the men? Perhaps the warriors were off hunting or fighting, but somehow the condition of the tribe he saw before him told him that wasn't so. The camp looked dirty and disorganized. He recognized a number of the women who were there and felt sure some of the older women would recognize him.

The brave continued to search until he came upon a large longhouse of logs with smoke coming from a central chimney. Finding a gap between the logs, he peered in. Inside, the men were smoking and drinking from brown jugs, stumbling about, and behaving foolishly. Some were off in a corner throwing dice—the small white boxes with spots—as the pirates often would. He recognized some of the men, but they no longer carried themselves as Mohegan braves should. Like the pirates, the Indians were yelling and often fighting after they threw the boxes on the ground. Many were dressed in the white man's clothes; few had the markings of a Mohegan warrior brave. His anger boiled up, and he decided right at that moment he would give these men one chance to prove themselves.

Sachumjuia stood up and pulled his hatchet from his belt. He ran his fingertips over the blade as he planned what to do next. How could these braves prove themselves to him, and he to them? He decided to make himself a target by breaking into the front of the longhouse. If these men could stop him or wound him before he passed through to the back door, he would stay. Either the warriors would kill him, or he would convince them that they must follow him back to their glorious past. If they could not stop him, and he exited the back of the longhouse without any wounds, he would simply continue on, never to return.

There were places deep in the White Hills of Taughannick where he could camp and never be discovered. He would seek out a handful of men and women worthy enough to maintain the ways of the Mohegan forefathers. Together, they would start a new tribe to keep the traditions of the Mohegan people.

The brave walked around to the front door of the longhouse. Several children playing alongside a nearby hut in the growing darkness looked up for a moment to watch the strange brave, but they soon returned to their play. Sachumjuia stood still for a moment, then stepped back several paces. He asked his forefathers for strength and drew in a deep breath. Lifting his hatchet over his head, he bolted into a run, emptying his lungs with the war cry of the wolf.

The men in the house all went quiet and then lifted their heads at the powerful roar. Even in their drunkenness, they would know this was the first sign of attack. When the door exploded with Sachumjuia's impact, they all fell back to the sides of the building.

The powerful brave moved steadily but swiftly through the longhouse, and as a man would stand to confront him, Sachumjuia dispensed with him. In their drunkenness, the men scrambled for weapons, and a few fired shots and threw knives, but all missed and only harmed some of their own. By the time the brave reached the other end of the longhouse, he had killed four men and left several others injured.

He quickly took his final two steps, throwing himself against the rear door and through it. Outside, he stood for a moment and looked himself over. He could not find one scratch on his body. He could hear the men behind him begin to gather themselves and their weapons to charge out the back door. When they made it outside, they could only fire two shots before this "ghost" disappeared into the woods.

Several of the braves recognized the warrior and called out his name. They had been certain of his death long ago, and along with his death went the last hope of regaining the abounding freedom the Mohegan wolf clan once had. His fight for revenge and freedom made him a hero, and now this brutal visitation set the lore for his legend.

The brave ran and ran to his new home, deep in the hills of Taughannick. It was there he would build a new life and carry out the destiny that his spirit father revealed to him on the island the Indians called Manisses and the white man called Block Island.

~~~
~~~

As the islander freemen prepared to vote, Sachumjuia decided to leave. It was evident to him that the new black man would be put off the island, and the hatchet would go with him. He had already spent too much time on the island. This season was complete, and he only wanted to return to his mainland camp.

The Mohegan quietly slipped through the forest toward the great bluff. First, he would pay his respects to his forefathers, and then he would take the long paddle home once again.

Chapter Twelve

The air in the church meetinghouse was growing hot and stuffy. Alexander collected his thoughts as the crowd in the room murmured before the vote. He tried to put the pieces of information together in his mind. The African had not killed his brethren; of this, he was certain. Just as Tuckman was raising his gavel to call for the vote, Alexander stood up and blurted out, "Yes, Laurence, I do have a question."

The constable was a bit startled but replied, "Yes, Captain Hawkins, please go on."

Alexander waited a moment as the crowd grew silent, then simply asked, "Where did the hatchet come from?"

Murmuring rippled through the meeting, and Tuckman rapped his gavel on the table, clearly surprised by the question. "Alexander, the African was caught red-handed. The bloody hatchet you see here on the table was found in his very hand."

Alexander worked his way from his seat and stepped forward toward the table. He held up the hatchet for the others to see. "Yes, but I ask, where did he get it? We all assume that the two black men washed ashore from a slaver illegally operating in these waters. Somehow, they were able to survive stormy seas while naked and chained with heavy irons. We found their irons, which matched their chafed skin. I'm quite certain that the last thing a desperate and chained man, escaping from a sinking ship in the middle of a terrible storm, would do is grab for a hatchet. So, I ask, do any of you recognize this hatchet? Have any of you lost this sharp tool? If not, where did it come from?"

The crowd sat quietly for a moment until Tuckman responded, "Alexander, it is a fair question, but I'm afraid it does not provide us with any answers."

The sea captain continued, "Well, let me just add that my man, Stepney, who we all know to be as honest as the day is long, actually spoke with the slave in a common tongue."

The crowd murmured again, and Tuckman pounded the table, saying, "Quiet, please. Alexander, what did he say?"

"Stepney was only able to understand a few words. Apparently, he is the son of a king—"

"Captain, that has no bearing here," Tuckman immediately interjected, pounding the table again. "We do not recognize a slave's past. Is there anything pertinent to his defense?"

"Yes, I'm sorry," Alexander continued. "The man claims he did not kill his comrade but that it was a man he referred to as the 'long hair'—someone who looked something like our friend, Quepag, but much bigger, with long black and white hair. I would suppose that this hatchet is of Indian origin. So I would conclude that this man did not murder his comrade. It would seem as though an Indian took the African's life."

"This all may be true," Tuckman rebutted, "but we know there is no one on this island who fits that description. None of our Indians have the striking hair as you have described. If this man is not the killer, then who is? If the African stays, how can we be certain that we will be safe?"

"I suggest we ask Quepag," Alexander answered. "After all, he has spent the most time with the African. Does he think this man is a killer, and if not, then who else could it be?"

Tuckman turned to the Indian and asked, "Mr. Quepag, we don't normally recognize Indians in our meetings, but under the circumstances, we will make an exception. What is your opinion of the African's disposition? Is he dangerous?"

Quepag paused, then slowly answered, "He is strong, but he is good. I see no danger to the people on the island. I believe the real killer is the same Woonanit spirit who is killing off our tribe."

The meeting erupted with challenges to Quepag's claim. Many islanders were upset with the island Indians' growing use of alcohol; they believed that alone was responsible for the Indians' dwindling numbers. The islanders found the excuse of an Indian "spirit" killing the Manissean Indians offensive and preposterous.

Tuckman pounded the table. "Exercise control, people!" Turning to Quepag, he continued, "Your claim is another matter. I think we all know which 'spirits' have wrought havoc on your people."

Suddenly, Williams interjected, "It must have been Big Jim. He went off Mohegan Bluffs about the same time I discovered the African. Big Jim must have tangled with the other African, killed him, and fell off the bluff."

The constable turned to the Indian again and asked, "Mr. Quepag, what are your thoughts on Big Jim? Could he have done it?"

The crowd murmured, but Quepag shook his head. "That is not Big Jim's hatchet," the quiet Indian said. "Big Jim did have hair, but it was not long and black and white."

"Well, I'm certain it was longer than yours, Quepag," Williams added.

The crowd began talking to each other while the town officers quietly discussed the information among themselves. Tuckman rapped the table again. "Quiet, please!" he barked. "The officers have agreed that, at this time, there is no way to know. Big Jim was already laid to rest in the burial ground near Fresh Pond a week ago. The African's story seems consistent with the circumstances." He turned to Alexander. "Captain Hawkins, do you have anything else to add before we vote?"

Alexander was not convinced it had been Big Jim, but he was convinced that the African was not the killer. He decided he would make a stand, though it might be at great risk to his own reputation. That still small voice from within was telling him he needed to intervene on this man's behalf. Feeling a strong sense that this man had a reason and a purpose to be on the island, he mustered all the certainty he could and said, "I, for one, will not vote to send him to the mainland and to what would be almost certain death for this man. I trust Quepag's opinion about his character. I see an honest bearing in the African's eyes. I am willing to risk my own personal reputation that, under Sam Williams's and Quepag's care, this man will not cause any trouble to our islanders."

With that, Alexander sat down. Tuckman took another look to John Sands for guidance. Sands only nodded to encourage the constable in his authority. Tuckman shook his head and looked over at Alexander sternly. "That is a strong commitment, Captain. If he stays, we will hold you accountable for his actions." Turning to the crowd, Tuckman said, "Now, I ask for a verbal vote of yea for the African to be put off the island."

Tuckman allowed a few moments to pass. Only a few islanders voiced their vote of yea.

The constable and the other town officers looked at each other in surprise. Tuckman followed up, asking, "And now, let us hear those who vote nay."

Once again, the moderator allowed a few moments to pass while a large number of nays rang through the hall.

Tuckman shook his head in surprise. "My goodness! The nays have the vote. The African stays. Mr. Williams, you must maintain the African in fetters until further notice. Your slave and Quepag are now excused from the meeting."

As the three left building, the constable rapped the table once again, saying, "Given the lateness of the hour, we will not have time to properly address our other matters. However, I have just two items that I will now mention as, hopefully, one consideration." Tuckman placed several papers in front of him and cleared his throat, "As we all know, an ordinance was enacted back in '21 to limit the felling of timber. In recent years, this has gone largely ignored and once again we face a scarcity of timber. We now propose to reinstate this limitation to preserve our timber and fencing stuff, which means limited building materials for homes and fences.

"Further, our slaves and bondservants have been growing restless about gaining their freedom, with the news of emancipation laws coming over from the mainland. I propose for future consideration that each master offer freedom to his slaves as a reward for tasks involving the clearing of fields of stone—stones that will be needed for building homes and fences. I leave that proposal with you to meditate upon and for further consideration at our next meeting. Now, unless there are any other urgent matters, I make a motion to close our meeting."

After a brief closing prayer, the constable declared the meeting adjourned and banged the gavel on the table with relish and authority.

The islanders began to file out of the building. Alexander felt good about the results of the meeting. The African's life was spared, and the islanders were beginning to talk about slave emancipation. As he exited the schoolhouse, he spotted Williams standing in the moonlight with the African and Quepag. "Congratulations, Samuel," he called out as he approached them. "I guess you have your slave after all."

"Yeah, I guess I owe ya, Hawkins," Williams said grudgingly. "But don't look ta me thinking, like the other islanders, that ya're all better than anyone else."

"Williams," Alexander said, shaking his head, "you don't owe me anything but this: You now have a moral obligation to treat this man with dignity and respect. If I ever hear that you have been abusive, I will do all I can to correct it."

The mariner only grunted in response.

Alexander smiled at the African. He was somewhat expecting the big man to thank him, but the slave did not respond. Then Alexander realized that the slave likely had no idea of what had transpired in the meeting.

Turning to Quepag, Alexander reached out and shook his hand, saying, "You take care of our friend, and we'll find time tomorrow for some clamming in the Great Pond."

Quepag smiled. "Tomorrow will be a good day for poquauhog."

Chapter Thirteen

Early July 1776

Alexander stood on the end of the porch of the Hawkins home looking over toward the crest of the hollow. A month earlier, he had been excited to finally receive his commission into the fledgling American Navy. He was to depart soon to assume his new position, yet he felt conflicted. There was still so much business to tend to on the farm before departing. Financial conditions had worsened. His father's health and mind were rapidly deteriorating, and the slaves would have to manage on their own as best they could. For this departure he did not know if or when he would return.

The most pressing problem was that the British embargo had interrupted their ability to export their products, and as a result, the world's demand turned to other suppliers. The whole island economy was coming undone.

On that morning, before reporting back to the mainland and the shipyard south of Providence, Alexander rode to the

Mohegan Bluffs. He chose to ignore the trails and instead rode south of Fresh Pond and past Paine Farm.

He slowly guided his horse through the heavy growth of shadblow. The shrubs had grown so thick as to create a tunnel of foliage, and Alexander had to hug the horse's mane to ride through. The thick brush ended abruptly, opening up to the large Paine Farm fields of butterfly weed, asters, hawkweed, and milkweed. The fields flittered with swallows, as well as butterflies and dragonflies. Alexander swatted and slapped away at the large green darners and mosquitoes as he rode on. On the other side of the field, his horse waded through one of the few above-ground streams on the island.

Alexander's ears perked up as he recognized the familiar melodic sound of the song sparrow. Pushing on, he passed through some of the richest moist-shrub habitat on the island before finally arriving at Mohegan Bluffs.

At the edge of the precipice, he looked out to his right and stared over the vast ocean to meditate on the Holy Scripture he had read the night before. Saint Paul had written: "If God be for us, who can be against us?"

Alexander climbed off his mount and considered God's Word as he continued to stare to the southwest, toward Long Island and New York. This is where the battle lines had been drawn. There was no need for the warning lantern-fire after all. General Washington and General Howe both knew—through informants and by direct communication—that they would meet in New York. Earlier in June, British general Howe had begun sailing from Halifax, Nova Scotia. He had heard word that Washington was digging in for Howe's imminent arrival.

Alexander closed his eyes and listened for the familiar, sweet, comforting sounds from the bluff top. Soon, that surprising deep peace rolled over his body like a warm ocean wave. As he turned to climb back onto his horse, that peace was shattered. His serenity and confidence crumbled, and his knees were weakened at the sight that appeared before his eyes. Fear ran down his body and spilled over the edge of the bluff, down the rock and clay face to the stone and sand beach, into the water, over the waves, and out to the deep blue-green to meet the sight of what looked to be the greatest British armada to have ever sailed.

Alexander whispered under his breath, afraid that they could hear his fear, "By God, how will we ever defeat them?"

The ships that carried the English Army and Navy to squelch the colonial rebellion covered the entire expanse of the eastern horizon. The mass of white sails was a reflection of the soft white clouds overhead. But these sailing "clouds" were full of the king's fury, and they grew menacingly larger as they sailed toward Alexander. It was the most overwhelming sight he had ever witnessed!

His initial impulse was to duck and hide from the armada, as if it were a sea monster that would reach out and snatch him from atop the bluff. He turned to the saddle for his musket but realized he had left it at the house. He even started to search for rocks at his feet to hurl at the enemy before realizing his folly.

Perhaps the rocky reefs below that had claimed so many ships in the past might reach out and grab the lead ship of the armada. Then, one after another, each ship would be sucked down, and it would all be over. He stopped to shake his head at his foolish wishful thinking.

As the patriot Paul Revere had done over a year earlier, Alexander wondered if he, too, should mount his horse to swiftly ride and get the word out that the British were on their way. He then reminded himself that this was no secret—the British *were* coming, and Washington knew it.

Alexander knew the greatest event of his lifetime—and many a lifetime before and after—was unfolding before his eyes. This awesome show of power and might reminded him that an American victory would not be possible without God's blessing and divine intervention. The Scripture verse on which he'd meditated earlier now came back to him and spoke to him clearer than ever before: "If God be for us, who can be against us?"

Alexander had always been sure of the righteousness of the fight for American independence, but he now prayed it would prove to be true at *this* place and in *this* time.

Realizing there was nothing within his power to be done, he straightened up, let go of his feelings of helplessness, and took in the majestic sight. As the great fleet passed right in front of him, it swung around, heading toward Long Island. It was breathtaking to see the great man-of-wars, along with the large troop ships and supply ships that seemed small in comparison. It truly was a staggering display of power and efficiency. Uniformed sailors were scrambling on each ship, attending to every detail. The men, equipment, and powerful weaponry made Alexander shake his head in disbelief.

Alexander watched as some of the English sailors up in the highest yardarms of the British ships spotted him. They pumped their fists and jeered at him. He knew that many British found the Americans and their cry for liberty offensive. To the British, the Americans were crude, second-class subjects to the crown who dared to question His Majesty's authority. The British were anxious to put the lowly colonials back in their place.

Alexander's face turned red with anger, yet he could only wonder how Washington would ever defeat this great force. Amid the fear and sadness it dawned on him that there could be a positive outcome to the sight before him. With the British attack finally about to be realized, how could the Continental Congress not resolve to make a full declaration of independence from the king?

Alexander's commission from Esek Hopkins as a navy captain had come in late May, and since then he had been working feverishly to pull a ship and crew together. He set up his headquarters at a shipyard located south of Providence on the west bank of Narragansett Bay. This location enabled him to gain access to regular communications to and from the Congress in Philadelphia.

Commodore Esek Hopkins's brother, Stephen Hopkins, was the Rhode Island delegate to the Congress. Alexander had worked closely with Stephen Hopkins to push through legislation banning the slave trade in Rhode Island back in '74. It was Alexander's close relationship with Stephen Hopkins that influenced Esek to commission Alexander as a captain in the new American Navy.

Esek Hopkins grew to trust Alexander enough to assign him to receive the communications from Philadelphia and then personally deliver them to the commodore. Hopkins would allow Alexander to read the communications, and the two men would often discuss the contents.

Alexander's access to this information allowed him to keep abreast of the struggles in Congress. After a year of dragging their feet to make a formal declaration, a committee of five had recently been assigned to produce such a document. When he heard who made up the committee, he could not understand why it was Virginian Thomas Jefferson and not family friend Benjamin Franklin who was to draft the document. Alexander was skeptical that the delegate from the largest slaveholding colony in the Americas was the right man to see that a document for independence would include freedom for slaves.

Jefferson was a large slave owner himself. Virginia had already shot down emancipation legislation that Jefferson had drafted a year earlier. With the pain of his failed attempts to legislate emancipation in his own colony still fresh in his mind, would the Virginian even try to address the issue in this declaration of freedom?

Now, with the power and might of the entire British kingdom descending upon them, the colonies would have to make a decision. All of the minor points and distractions would have to be put aside. American liberty and self-determination were at stake.

Alexander found renewed energy as he continued to watch the armada pass by—the fleet of ships still covered the entire northeastern horizon. He turned to climb on his horse, and as he put his foot in the stirrup, he heard a wagon at the far end of the path to the bluff.

Chapter Fourteen

From the other side of the tall, thick brush, a deep, gravelly voice bellowed out, "Hawkins, ya there?"

It was the unmistakable voice of the crusty old mariner Bertram Spats. Alexander wondered what Spats could possibly want with him.

He rode out to greet Spats, saying, "Yes, Mr. Spats! To what do I owe this honor?"

"There's no honor intended," Spats replied. "I'm doin' ya a favor, is all. When I was on the mainland your Negro, Nathan, gave me a letter ta deliver ta ya."

Alexander's interest grew. Nathan knew he was due to return that very day, so why would he have sent a note? "Did Nathan mention it was urgent?" he asked.

As Spats rummaged through a box behind the oxcart seat, he replied, "Your black pressed me ta take it, and I give in. Here—here it is. Now take the damn thing!"

Spats handed the letter over—it was completely soaked. Alexander took the corner of the letter between his thumb and index finger and held it out while it dripped. He looked back at Spats and shook his head, saying dryly, "Thank you, Mr. Spats."

Spats scowled. "Well, is ya goin' ta open it?" Now that Spats had delivered the letter, he seemed to think he had a right to know its contents.

Alexander shook the letter out, and the seal came undone. "Yes, perhaps it has something to do with the king's parade now rounding the island."

Spats spoke while Alexander read. "I seen the sails as I rode up here. It looks like King George's plannin' a big party. If he thinks all them ships is going ta scare me, he's daft! Now we will see if Washington has the stomach ta stand and fight!"

The old mariner continued to talk as Alexander struggled to read the ink that had begun to run on the wet parchment. He looked at the date and said, "This date is over three weeks ago. Have you been holding this that long?"

"I only had it for three days," Spats said indignantly. "Your Negro said something about it bein' delivered ta Hopkins by mistake. I'm guessing it made the rounds a bit."

"Yes, I'm sure it did, both over land and *through* the sea, it would seem." Alexander struggled to read the blotchy parchment while Spats impatiently waited for his report.

The communication, from Stephen Hopkins, explained that he was writing directly to Alexander to make him aware of some disturbing developments at the Continental Congress. The Southern colonies threatened to block a vote for independence if the declaration dared to make any reference to freedom for slaves. The Southern colonies were soliciting support from Newport's wealthy slave traders to put further pressure on the delegates to compromise on this critical point.

Alexander paused to consider the note's implication. How could a new land, birthed for freedom of men, not extend that freedom to the black man? Up to this point, Alexander had trusted in the quality and morality of the men he knew in Congress to address this issue when the time came. With the great British armada pressing in, he feared that Congress might compromise on slavery for the sake of gaining the unanimous vote for independence.

He read on to find that Stephen Hopkins was asking him to use whatever influence he had with leaders in Rhode Island to prevent those in Newport from siding with the Southern colonies. If there were any influence he could bring to bear, now would be the time. He expected a final vote within a few weeks—perhaps even days—from the date of the letter.

Alexander realized that the time had already passed to act on Hopkins's request. The thought came to him that he must go to Philadelphia himself and plead with the delegates to include freedom for the black man in the declaration.

He pulled himself up into his saddle and took one last look over his shoulder beyond the bushes and out to the end of the armada sailing past. He knew he would not have to outrun these ships, but the time to act was *now,* and he decided right then that he would travel as hard and fast as his reliable stallion, Nimbau could take him until he reached the courthouse of Philadelphia.

The young captain wasn't sure if he was really convinced that the Congress would deal with this evil, or if he was willing to compromise in order to gain what he yearned for most.

Spats could wait no longer. "For bloody sake, are ya goin' ta keep it all ta yaself? I don't have all day. I ain't no plantation owner. I got a livin' ta make!"

Alexander shook his head again. "I'm truly sorry for interrupting your busy schedule, and I am most grateful for your service, but the letter was written to me in confidence."

The old codger shot back, "Well, I could have opened it myself anytime, but I decided it best ta wait ta deliver it sealed up."

Alexander wondered how he could argue with such "rational" thinking and relented. "Of course, sir, and I'm truly grateful for your consideration. The letter has to do with the American declaration for independence from the king and whether it should include freedom for slaves."

Spats immediately responded, “Why, one’s got nothin’ ta do with the other! I don’t need mainland patriots ta decide I’m free from the king and then tell me I got ta give up my property.”

“Mr. Spats, as I recollect, you are not a master of slaves.”

Spats was not amused. “No, I don’t need any more mouths ta feed. And last time I checked, the Hawkins family had plenty.” The old mariner rambled on regarding the Hawkins family, and Alexander’s mind drifted off. Spats pulled him back by asking, “Ya listenin’ ta me, Hawkins?”

Alexander was embarrassed. “Yes, I’m afraid you make a good point. One day I plan to right the wrong of Hawkins slaveholding, but for now, I am in need of transport for a swift crossing to the mainland.”

Chapter Fifteen

Two days later, Alexander sat slouched in the saddle atop his powerful black stallion—he'd transported faithful Nimbau from Block Island over to the mainland. She was not the fastest, but she was strong and durable. The two rode hard on this unusually cool and damp July morning. As he patted the side of her glistening thick neck, the blast of the horse's breath shot out her open nostrils. The sight reminded him of the spray of the sperm whales that so thrilled him on many a voyage.

His mind was suddenly brought back to the present and back to the decisions that weighed heavily on his mind. He reflected on the events that brought him here to the Pawcatuck River crossing into Connecticut.

The captain stared south, toward Rhode Island's salty marshlands of tall brown cattails mixed with the slender green reeds, to the inlet from Long Island Sound. He was conflicted once again. It had been more than two days since he had spotted the British armada and since then, with every step he took toward Philadelphia, he had challenged himself. His convictions had stabbed at his mind on the sail from

Block Island to the mainland, then on the ride to the shipyard near Providence, again upon reporting to the commodore's office, and now, once more, as he prepared to take the ferry barge that crossed from Rhode Island to Connecticut.

Alexander was convinced he must weigh in on the decision of slavery, but he also knew there was much to do in preparation for his command on the eve of this campaign. Soon, the whole British Navy and Army would be encamped on American soil. Each time, he responded by convincing himself that the slavery decision was just as urgent. If a declaration was formally made without including freedom for slaves, a great opportunity would be lost. How long would it be before it might ever be dealt with again?

Alexander assured himself that once he crossed over into Connecticut, there would be no turning back. He became angry with himself for having so much doubt—so much waffling, as well as questioning whether anyone would care to listen. He knew down deep that his greatest desire was to be at the shipyard to complete his command and prepare to engage the enemy.

Riders and carriages were beginning to queue up for the ferry barge, but he wasn't ready to do so himself. He moved Nimbau off the Boston Post Road over to a stone wall, some hundred feet to the north of the road. Dismounting, he let the reins drop to the ground. Nimbau grazed as Alexander sat on the wall to rest and make his final decision.

The captain ran his hands over the stone, noticing how well the wall was built. Most stone walls were crude efforts, with stones simply piled one on top of the other. This wall, however, was arranged with mortar sealing it together. The wall was the southwest corner of the Hollard plantation. Alexander's family had socialized with the Hollards years ago. Now, however, the fields on the other side of the wall were unkempt and overgrown, giving him some idea of the condition of the family and their plantation.

It dawned on him as he sat there that much of his desire to go to Philadelphia was because of Nathan. There was no clearer picture in his mind of a black man being equal in every way to any white man he knew. Did he want to prove to Nathan that he cared as much for slave freedom as he did for American freedom? Was he going for the right reasons? And still, there was that same nagging voice that kept telling him to leave the world as it was—years of slave and master relations would not easily be undone.

It further dawned on Alexander that his current struggle was much the same struggle as this new nation would have to face. If the declaration did not include black slaves at this critical time, when Americans could rally around freedom, then *when*? He realized that the conscience of a new nation, founded upon liberty, would eventually be faced with a great decision. He had a vision of the fledgling nation being torn in two by that decision and possibly undoing all they would have fought for.

Was that inevitable? Could the truth be that the national conscience would not be ready to deal with such a task until the country was mature enough in its own independence? He thought he had his answer for a moment but then thought again how much better off a newly established nation would be if this issue were settled from its start, leaving one less great struggle in the nation's formative years. How much pain, anguish, and division could be avoided? Alexander had never felt so torn and confused in his entire life.

An old black man, selling potatoes and onions from a cart by the road, noticed Alexander and came walking over. He startled Alexander from his deep thoughts by saying, "Beggin' your pardon, Master. Is you all right? Can I help you wid somet'in'?"

"Why, no…no…" Alexander struggled to regain his composure. "Thank you, my friend. I'm just resting and admiring this wall."

"You seems to be troubled about somet'in', Master. You sure I can't gets you somet'in'? I does have some mighty fine onions to he'p take your tiredness away."

Alexander really didn't want onions, but he thought he would do the old man a favor, so he agreed to purchase two. The old man rambled off and soon returned. As he handed the onions and took the coin Alexander offered, he said, "So you like de look an' feel of dis here wall? It was part of de Hollard plantation when it was built."

"Yes, I thought so," Alexander replied. "I was familiar with the family. Say, can you tell me what's become of them?"

"Well, Master, you's askin' de right person! I was owned by Master Hollard, and I done built dis here wall."

"My goodness! I am Captain Hawkins of Block Island. What would be your name, sir, and how is the family?"

"My name be Caesar, an' I's sorry to say dat de family was hit wit' hard times. Dey sold der land an' moved west to New Jussey."

"Is that correct? With the fine work on this wall, why did your master not take you with him to New Jersey?"

"Master Randolph was good to me an' always kep' his promises. He told me if I's ever to complete dis wall around de acres an' acres of dis plantation, he would make me a free man. I's don't t'ink he ever t'ought I's could do it, but after twenty-eight years, I's done it, an' Master Randolph gives me my manumission papers." He paused as he reflected. "You knows, I didn't really wants to leave de family. I's started out to builds de wall for my freedom, but dere came a time when I almost enjoy buildin' de wall."

Alexander smiled at the man's sentimental notion. "Well, yes, of course, but you must take enormous pride in not only this great accomplishment but even more so in your personal freedom."

Caesar hesitated a moment and then responded, "Well, Master...may I's take de liberty to talk trut'ful?"

Alexander shook his head in wonder, realizing that for the black man, after decades under slave formality, old habits were not easily broken. "Why, of course, Mr. Caesar, please. We are both free men."

"Master, you looks to me to be a fine Christian man who loves his God an' Savior."

Alexander was quick to agree. "Why, yes, Caesar, I do. Indeed, I do."

"Den Master, you knows at some time I learnt dat even a slave can be a free man!"

Alexander nodded in pious agreement but thought to himself that the slave was given to a good but somewhat naïve notion. Alexander had held Sunday services for the slaves on Block Island. He had taught this gospel of freedom found through Christ to the slaves, but he was never sure that he fully believed it. He tried to clarify by saying, "Yes, our God gives us freedom of mind and spirit, but men can take away our physical freedom. Without that, we truly are not free men at all."

"Well, Master, I knows dat I never felt so free before or since, after I gives my life over to my Savior. As for bein' a free man, I guess it don't matter much if people still treat you like a slave."

Alexander was confused, so he probed further. "Caesar, are you telling me you don't enjoy life any more as a free man than you did as a slave?"

"I guess I gots de chance to go some places an' do some t'ings I couldn't before," Caesar allowed, "but even when I shows people my papers, most don't treat me no different. Fact is, many is suspicious an' treat me worse 'cause dey t'ink I'm lyin' to 'em. I woulda gone to New Jussey wit' Master Randolph if he didn't say he can't afford me no more. He was a good master, and I knows many dat suffer under bad ones. As for me, de peace I have in my heart is de same, slave or free!"

Alexander considered what the black sage had just said. It was the first time this idea had really caught hold of him. Whether freedom for the slaves came now or some time in the future, how long would it take before people's notions of the differences between blacks and whites would actually change?

A sense of peace swept over Alexander, and the urgency that he felt was beginning to seep away—it would be a long road ahead. His conversation with Caesar had brought him the wisdom for which he had been praying: Slave freedom was just as important as American independence. He would ride to Philadelphia and do what he could because it was the right thing to do. But the struggles for freedom, American independence and slave emancipation would require time before each freedom could be fully realized. And both would require time for old notions to wear away. Ultimately, he had very little control over any. He would do all that he could, however, with those things over which he did have some control.

Alexander concluded the conversation by saying, "Thank you, Caesar, for your kindness and wisdom. Would you mind keeping me in your prayers?"

He somewhat expected Caesar to be surprised that a white man would ask a black man for prayers, but Caesar responded, "Sometimes it's dose dat seems to need it least is de ones dat needs it de most. Go wid God's blessing, Master!"

Chapter Sixteen

Alexander climbed back on Nimbau, exchanged farewells with Caesar and then galloped back up to Boston Post Road. When he reached the road, he could see that the ferry barge had returned. There seemed to be a commotion, and a few people in and around the ferry were cheering. The ferry gate opened, and a rider bolted from the ferry and rode hard straight for Alexander, yelling as he went. As the rider came closer, Alexander recognized him as Hopkins's courier, Joe Wilcox, and Alexander waved him down. The courier was slow to react and rode a hundred feet farther down the road before he pulled his horse to an abrupt stop, wheeled about, and galloped back to Alexander.

The man was excited and short of breath. He dug into his satchel as he apologized, "Beggin' ya pardon, sir. The great news has come!"

"What news is that, man?"

Wilcox's voice rose as he said, "Sir, the news we all been waiting for. The Continental Congress has voted unanimously to declare American independence from England!"

How long had Alexander waited to hear these words? He'd always anticipated that a wild sense of celebration would overwhelm him upon hearing this news—certainly it would be a day filled with excitement and joy. At that moment, however, he felt nothing. He asked with some urgency, "What of the question concerning slave freedom? Was that part of the declaration?"

Wilcox gave Alexander a quizzical look and handed him the communication, struggling to think of an answer. Alexander grabbed the sealed envelope, broke the seal, and read it. It was a brief note from Stephen Hopkins to his brother, Esek:

Brother,
On this day of July 2, 1776, the Congress of these new United States of America unanimously voted to declare our independence from the king and from the English Parliament. We are now a free and independent nation! May God bless and protect us in the struggle ahead.

Your brother,
Stephen

Alexander read through it twice and then quickly asked the courier, "What of the declaration document itself?"

"Sorry, sir, it was still not signed when I left the afternoon of the second."

Alexander shot back, "Did you see it? Did you have a chance to read it?"

The man struggled to understand why Alexander was not overjoyed with the news. "Yes, I'm not much for readin', but I was able to see a draft that had several sections crossed out. They was still making final changes."

"Did you hear of anything in the document referring to abolishing slavery as a part of American independence?"

Wilcox thought a moment and replied, "Yes, yes, I did hear of that. Fact was, there was a great argument over them slaves.

The argument was threatenin' to divide up the Congress and kill the vote for independence."

Alexander's eyes grew wide as he concluded that they must have agreed over freedom for slaves and voted to declare independence. The excitement he had always anticipated began to rise up within him.

The courier continued, "The draft I seen had strong words about slavery. Now...what was it that they said? Yes, it was sayin' that the king was wagin' cruel war against humanity. Yes, a cruel war against humanity. I liked the way that sounded."

Alexander's excitement was growing in anticipation of the realization of all that he had hoped for.

"But those words was crossed out in the draft, and that was the declaration they was votin' on."

Alexander's growing excitement suddenly burst. His shoulders slumped over, and he dropped his head in disappointment.

Wilcox waited in silence, confused by the captain's behavior. He finally asked, "Sir, would you be deliverin' this communication to the commodore, or does I?"

Alexander simply handed the parchment back to the courier and said, "Thank you, sir, and Godspeed."

With that, Wilcox saluted, turned his horse, kicked in his heels, and sped off.

Alexander had his answer. Tomorrow would be the fourth day of July, and he was sure that the delegates would have signed the document by the time he would arrive in Philadelphia. He turned his horse around and headed east, putting the stallion into a slow walk. What could he have done differently? Who had he really failed? More than for anyone else, this ride to Philadelphia had been for Nathan. Did he really want to prove to Nathan that he cared about the plight of slaves? He'd only proven to himself where his priorities lay. Perhaps he was not the freedom zealot he had always thought himself to be.

Alexander held an image of himself as the champion of freedom, but had that been more important than the cause of freedom itself? Alexander shook his head and shuddered at the clarity of the question and its troubling answer. In a world of compromise, he must be true to his convictions. He could not single-handedly abolish slavery, just as he could not single-handedly fight this imminent war for freedom. At that moment, the young patriot decided to put both in God's hands. The battle for the two freedom struggles would continue, but he had a clear answer as to where his priorities must lie—at least for the time being.

Captain Alexander Hawkins had his commission to an old and decrepit brig that needed to be restored, and he had a crew to train. He shook his head and shoulders to throw off the disappointment that had grabbed hold of him. His purpose was now made all too clear, and with God's help, he would be true to it. Alexander snapped his reins, spurred the stallion, and barked, "Yah!"

Nimbau jumped forward with a vigor and energy that shot right up through Alexander's own body. Preparing to win American independence would, for the time being, be his sole purpose. He would do everything he humanly could to see this victory through. He now knew that the gnawing in his stomach regarding slave freedom would not leave him, and just knowing what it was brought him some relief.

That disturbing feeling of something left unattended took hold of him again—a lamp left behind, still smoldering. He shook his head. *No, I am too far down this path to turn back now.* There was little he could do about it but trust that God would see to it that the lamp did not burn down or destroy all that remained behind. God willing, the lamp would one day no longer be a threat but a light to ignite another freedom fire.

Chapter Seventeen

September 1776

Alexander sat at his desk and looked through the dirty window at his ship, the *Adrian*. Quill in hand, he recorded every detail that needed attending in order to be fully ready for his new command and the *Adrian*'s first mission.

His ship was an undersized and aged brig with a length of seventy feet and a beam of twenty-two feet. It carried sixteen six-pounder, straight bore guns. The *Adrian* sat languishing under repair in Providence. She was a Spanish ship Alexander had renamed for the Dutch explorer, Adrian Block.

The captain took full advantage of the time in dry dock to make design revisions that considerably improved her stealth. Adding a false narrowing to the bow and increasing the size of her masts also added sail. He considered increasing her arsenal but decided to maintain her guns at sixteen, favoring speed and maneuverability over firepower. The repairs and design work dragged on for what seemed an eternity to Alexander, but in August 1776, she was commissioned the US brig of war *Adrian*.

Alexander was aware that the other captains in this new navy did not share Hopkins's faith in him, and his commission was viewed with skepticism. Their circle was small and elite, and Alexander had not paid his dues to become a member. He was fully aware that he needed to earn their approval and respect, so he accepted his assignment to the old brig without complaint. The young captain understood the other officers only accepted him based on the likelihood that the whole affair would be over before his ship would be seaworthy enough to sail.

Alexander, however, threw himself into the project, working at a fever pitch, overseeing the repairs and even lending his brawn when necessary. He planned out every detail thoroughly, first by handpicking the crew and then by securing all the materials, supplies, guns, and munitions. Resources were scarce, but he relentlessly scavenged, bartered, requisitioned, and even stole whatever was needed. These minor obstacles were not going to deter him from entering into this monumental struggle for freedom—and so he pressed on.

While he cajoled and threatened the shipyard to complete the repairs, he drilled his crew on a smaller craft, the schooner *Stalwart*. His drills became live exercises designed to wreak havoc with Tory shipping and disrupt the operations of ships of the British Navy already in northeast waters.

They would steal into northeast ports, quietly cut anchor lines, and make off with bigger and bigger vessels. Privateering and downright pirating would provide the majority of vessels for the burgeoning American fleet. On both sides of the Atlantic, ships would be overtaken and commissioned for service in the fight for American freedom. Not only were the ships themselves valuable, but their cargoes were also used to either finance the war effort or to enrich the privateers.

In July, the greatest British expeditionary force ever assembled had arrived and encamped on Staten Island to begin the

Northern Campaign. The war had begun in earnest, and the British, under General Howe, were now prepared to rout out Washington's misfit army.

Alexander resisted the doubt that seeped into his mind. How could they dare to stand up to such a formidable force? The American Navy was little more than a handful of vessels. At the moment, the whole navy was composed of the flagship, *Alfred*, and the brigs of war, *Columbus* and *Providence*, along with a dozen or so smaller vessels. The captains from the merchant ships and experienced privateers captained the ships, the most notable being Fleet Commanding Officer Esek Hopkins, along with Captains Dudley Staltonstall, Abraham Whipple, John Paul Jones, and the Philadelphian, Nicholas Geste.

Alexander went over to the window, still absorbed in thought. As the *Adrian* sat in dry dock she resembled one of the great beasts the whalers would drag onto the shore. Like those black behemoths, this ship had been split open and layers of fat stripped off its carcass. Now, she was all buttoned up, with the last of the tarred caulking rope hammered between the hull's planking, making her watertight. There remained only the painting and finish work to her bow, and then she'd be ready for launch on her shakedown cruise, sailing through Narragansett Bay, out into the sound, and back.

Alexander was eager for command, and it showed in his zeal. From the small three-room shack that he had commandeered as his headquarters on the shipyard, he personally oversaw every detail of the *Adrian*'s repair and outfitting. Hopkins encouraged him to set up his office at the stately house that served as naval headquarters, but he had declined. Alexander already alienated many of his peers by his efforts to undermine the slave trade. Now, his decision to be physically removed from his peers made for one more reason why the other officers had trouble accepting him.

Still lost in thought, he sat back down at his desk. He was suddenly startled by a knock on the door. Nathan—now assigned as Alexander's personal attaché and quartermaster—

entered with raised eyebrows and a slight nod over his shoulder, as if to say, "Heads up! Ranking officer on deck."

Nathan squared to attention and saluted, announcing, "Captain Geste to see you, sir."

Surprised, Alexander jumped to attention, sending the parchment, quill, and ink flying. None of the other naval officers had ever visited him here. Whenever he was needed, a messenger was sent to escort him to meetings at the headquarters. As he hurriedly tried to straighten up the mess, it occurred to him that if any of the officers were to visit him at the shipyard, he would have assumed it would be Geste.

Nicholas Geste was a young and clever sea captain, well known for smuggling valuable cargo past the British tax ships on behalf of wealthy New England traders. Alexander had only met him on a few occasions, and he wasn't sure if he could be trusted. Even so, Geste appeared to be genuine and congenial, while not taking himself too seriously.

Geste had a military bearing. He was smartly dressed in his full uniform of blue coat with red facings and red sash cuffs, flat yellow buttons, a red waistcoat, and blue breeches. Alexander felt a twinge of jealousy. He had only recently ordered uniforms from Providence for himself, his officers, and the crew—it had required his selling some of his personal assets to finance the purchase—and it would be some time before they arrived. To Alexander, it was money well spent to provide the requisite attire that would be the final element in turning his crew into a cohesive fighting force.

Geste saluted Alexander, politely ignoring the disarray he was in. "Captain Hawkins, it is a great pleasure to see you again. How goes the battle?"

Alexander wiped his hand on his breeches, leaving a large ink smudge. He returned the salute, leaving another smudge on his forehead. "Captain Geste, the pleasure and honor is all mine." Extending his hand, he said, "Please come in and have a seat."

Geste looked down at Alexander's ink-stained hand and replied, "I hope you won't take offense if I don't return my hand."

Alexander sheepishly withdrew the handshake and pointed toward the seat, saying, "Not at all. I'm sorry for the state of my appearance, but I do hope to make it up to you by offering something to drink."

"Yes," Geste responded without hesitation, "a brandy would be most welcome."

Alexander flinched but turned immediately to his quartermaster. "Nathan, a brandy for the captain."

Nathan stared back at him as they saluted, and from behind Geste, he rolled his eyes, shrugged, and lifted his palms up.

Alexander just waved him out, feeling completely embarrassed that he should have made it clearer that his offer was intended for coffee or tea. A strict rule under his command was that no liquor was to be found with any officer or crew anywhere in the vicinity of the *Adrian.*

Alexander looked at Geste and saw a faint smile cross his lips. Of course, Geste knew this rule. This clever officer had a reputation for being a playful joker, and now Alexander realized he was pulling his leg. They both knew Nathan would likely not find brandy to serve Geste in the few short minutes they would be together. Alexander felt embarrassed, but he sensed Geste was trying to teach him a valuable lesson. Alexander needed to stand up for himself and not be intimidated by his navy peers.

Chapter Eighteen

Nathan left the captain's quarters and headed straight for the outside door. As he reached for the handle, he stopped and shook his head. A sense of angry indignation flared up. *No, I'm not going to waste my time—or any of this navy's time—tracking down brandy for this pompous officer! Our orders have been clear from the beginning.* The young quartermaster returned to his desk to complete the pile of work that lay there. As he sat down, he shook his head. *I'm surprised at you, Alexander Hawkins*, he thought. *You have always been a captain of principle, but now you seem so easily intimidated. It ain't like you. I'd just as soon face a navy reprimand then go against what you always taught me.*

While in his early twenties, Nathan had sailed alongside Alexander for six years on merchant ships, honing his nautical talents across the seven seas. Nathan didn't necessarily care to spend his life on the open sea, but he wanted to experience life beyond slavery and Block Island.

When Alexander told his father that he had decided to follow a career on the sea, Nathan convinced the elder Hawkins that he could keep an eye on his son, and at the same time, his ship service could pay some debts the farm had with the shipping company. This was a common practice of slave owners—to offer their slaves' labor to settle their debts. In turn for Nathan's promise, Alexander promised Nathan's mother, Molly Mum, that he would see to it no harm would come to her son.

During their time out at sea, Alexander quickly rose up the ranks, while Nathan spent his time as a very capable and reliable common seaman. On his final two voyages, Alexander captained ships to the Mediterranean and India. His talents were evident, and it was expected that one day he might become one of the top captains of the merchant fleet.

During this period at sea, Nathan watched as Alexander was put under tremendous pressure to captain ships engaging in the slave trade. Some of the most active trading of slaves was done out of Newport, Rhode Island. Alexander refused to be a part of it and was able to convince the owners of the ships on which he worked to engage in trade that would be more profitable in the long run.

Nathan was extremely proud of Alexander as he became a staunch advocate of abolishing the slave trade within Providence Plantations and Rhode Island. He even testified before the legislature on several occasions. This, however, did not sit well with the other heads of shipping, who relied heavily on slave trade as an integral part of their overall business. They put pressure on their peers, and Alexander Hawkins's value as a merchant sea captain began to decline.

During those years, both Nathan and Alexander had come to understand that the logical beginning to the eventual abolishment of slavery would have to be the establishment of an independent nation—a nation based upon the principles of self-government, respect for human rights, and personal freedom. But in the meantime, a major step could be taken by making the trafficking of slaves in and out of the country illegal, thus cutting off its very lifeblood.

Nathan had followed Alexander through the course of these events, and the two often talked of the future. Alexander and a growing number of patriots were proving themselves to be exceptions to the rule, believing wholeheartedly that change was possible. Nathan and many of the slaves put great confidence in those white men who advocated change. It was a confidence placed in Alexander's strength of character, faith in God, and dedication to the cause of freedom.

Recently, however, Alexander seemed willing to make small compromises on the matter of slave freedom in the pursuit of American independence. Alexander's exchange with Captain Geste seemed to be one more case of a subtle compromise on his convictions. Though this could never tarnish Nathan's devotion to Alexander, it caused him to doubt all men's true convictions.

Was the freedom from British rule going to be enough to satisfy Alexander and the others who now claimed to be sympathetic to the cause of slave emancipation? Would freedom for the black man become an afterthought that would dry up and blow away on the winds of victory against the crown? Nathan began to wonder just how much Alexander was willing to compromise.

~~~

In the captain's office, Alexander wondered about the purpose for Geste's visit. Though his tone was conversational, there was something Geste seemed anxious to convey. After the small talk petered out, he finally got to the point. "Hawkins, I have very little time—I must join our commander in Philadelphia immediately. As you know, the Continental Congress is questioning Commander Hopkins concerning the *Glasgow* affair."

Alexander knew all about the fiasco. On one of the first naval engagements of the war, the *Providence*, under Hopkins's command, had cut off from engaging the British ship *Glasgow*.
~~~

It was a most unfortunate beginning for an undermanned fleet already lacking in confidence against a superior navy. The courage of Hopkins, as well as that of the entire fledgling navy, was now under fire in Philadelphia.

"I believe Hopkins when he said it was due to poor wind," Alexander said solemnly.

"Yes," Geste quickly asserted, "these proceedings are a terrible sham and a complete embarrassment to true patriots. The real crime is in tying up such vital resources at this crucial point in time. Here we are fighting amongst ourselves, when we have our hands full with an enemy ready to overwhelm our fledgling revolution.

And make no mistake about it, Hawkins: I was there just days ago. I assisted Washington and his army in retreat from Long Island onto New York Island. It was a miracle that they escaped, but it was not a pretty sight. I'm afraid if someone does not respond quickly, then all may be lost."

Alexander felt sick at what he heard. "What can be done? Our hands are tied. Can this navy do anything without the Continental Congress's approval?"

"No, I'm afraid that any action now will not be sanctioned, but something must be done. Who is willing to risk life, limb, and career for the promise of freedom? It may be too much to ask of any man." Alexander pondered the increasingly obvious message that Geste was trying to convey. As he did so, Geste pulled out a dispatch and placed it on the table. "Hawkins, I have recorded my thoughts and concerns, and I leave them here for your own education." As Geste rose to leave, he offhandedly mentioned, "I have voiced the same concerns to Lieutenant Colonel John Mead in command of the garrison at the township of Greenwich. My friend Mead agreed that whoever felt compelled to act in support of Washington's troops would do well to be in contact with him, Horseneck being a fine staging point to gather more men and munitions."

The two men stood and saluted. Alexander came around his desk, saying, "Thank you, Captain, for this education.

I pray God's strength for you, Hopkins, and the others in Philadelphia. Godspeed."

Geste grasped Alexander's hand with both of his and looked straight into his eyes. "Hawkins, I see great things for you. Godspeed to you as well and strength in whatever battles you fight."

Just as Geste went to the door, Nathan knocked, entered, and snapped to attention. He began nervously to repeat Alexander's standing orders. "Sir, I regret to inform the honorable officer that no liquor or alcoholic drink shall be found on navy—"

"Well done, seaman," Geste cut him off. "You have passed my test, and I hope the rest of our navy will act upon what is right and noble. That honesty of heart and conscience, along with a few miracles, will be what it takes to win our great struggle. Carry on!" He started to leave but stopped short of the door and, with his head down, quietly said, "I believe it would be best if we could agree that this meeting never took place." With that, Geste exited, leaving the two men to breathe a sigh of relief as they both slumped against the furniture.

Alexander felt overwhelmed by the challenges Geste had just laid before him, but curious, he reached across the desk and picked up the parchment pouch. He broke the silence with "Nathan! Paper, ink, and quill. We have much to do in a very short time."

As Nathan ran out to collect the writing materials, Alexander opened the dispatch left on his desk. It was not a complete document but only notes that read as follows:

Continental Army soundly defeated at Brooklyn Heights. Washington has escaped from Long Island and is now secured in lower Manhattan Island.

Troops appear ragged, outmatched, and their will to fight on has ebbed to a very low point despite Washington's valiant attempts to rally them.

Army in desperate need of muskets, munitions, and bayonets!

British fleet stays anchored south of Guannis Bay, being held back by the battery at the southern tip of New York Island.

British and Hessian troops are mobilizing in Brooklyn on Long Island for the assault on New York Island.

Munitions and bayonets stored in great quantities within the township of Greenwich at a location known as Coe's Cóbh on the River Mianus.

Lieutenant Colonel John Mead of Greenwich is prepared to aid in any attempt to supply the Continental Army on New York Island.

Alexander put the note down and paused to consider its full meaning. The standing orders from the Continental Congress and his mentor, Esek Hopkins, were clear—all naval operations were on hold. Hopkins himself was, in essence, on trial for his apparent "unwillingness" to engage the enemy, as well as for his perceived inability to control the actions of those under his command.

Alexander was faced with a perplexing dilemma. He wondered if he should risk his commanding officer's career by acting singularly on his own initiative. To take on this mission would certainly further undermine Hopkins's authority and jeopardize his command. If the mission were to fail, the blow to Hopkins's career—as well as his own—would be particularly devastating. The decision to proceed based on trusting Geste's assessment was risky, but without action he feared that their freedom struggle might soon come to an end.

A fearful notion entered his mind. *Was it possible that it all could be over by the time we reach New York Island anyhow?* That very thought resolved his dilemma. He could not turn his back on this revolution for the sake of anyone's "career," nor would he allow it to end before doing all he could do to secure victory.

Freedom was worth sacrificing everything for. At the moment, the choice became all too obvious.

Alexander decided that the men of the *Adrian* would beg, borrow, and "procure" all the munitions they could possibly lay their hands on. Alexander could put a small squadron together and sail down the coast to Horseneck, pick up whatever munitions they could spare, and continue on to lower New York Island to deliver their cargo.

God willing, they would return the same way without so much as seeing the enemy. The one remaining question in Alexander's mind was whether there was a way they could accomplish this mission and still not do further damage to the career of his commander and benefactor, Esek Hopkins.

Alexander warmly remembered a beautiful time on a magical island and the life he was willing to sacrifice, all with a hope that one day he would see his dream realized in its full glory. He felt the familiar twinge of pain for the love he had already sacrificed. In his mind, he might have already given the ultimate sacrifice...but how much further was he willing to go?

Chapter Nineteen

September 1776, two weeks later

The pungent odor of spent gunpowder hung in the air. The crew of the American Navy brig of war, *Adrian*, scrambled about, shouting in the chaos of the shipyard. Their ship had returned to the bay just the day before, was tested, and quickly outfitted to be ready for her first assignment from the navy command. It now appeared it was not only the American patriots who could steal vessels right from under their enemy's nose.

In the cool September dawn, the morning mist mixed with the steam of the men's breath and the smoke from musket discharges. Captain Alexander Hawkins calmly stepped through the fog to the edge of the breakwater. He raised his pistol and effortlessly pulled the trigger at their escaping vessel. *Bang!* The shot echoed across the water.

The sound, the smell, and the feel of the charge felt so good. In the midst of the chaos, a calm sense of pleasure warmed Alexander on this cold morning. He figured that this exhilaration was akin to how a prisoner felt when first released. The captain caught himself lost in reflection and reminded himself of the urgency at hand. Looking about, he realized that his crew, too, seemed to be enjoying themselves entirely too much. They were acting more celebratory than vengeful.

Alexander reached out and grabbed the arm of his first mate as he ran by, almost taking him off his feet. "Mr. Capen! May I have a moment with you, please?"

Capen, initially annoyed by the interruption, realized who had grabbed him and quickly pulled himself together. "Yes, yes, of course, Captain. Shall we continue to fire upon the ship?"

"No," Hawkins replied. "Spread the word to cease firing. The *Adrian* was out of range minutes ago, and if anyone is watching, I'm sure the theft of our ship is beginning to look suspiciously faked."

Musket fire continued to randomly fire around them as Alexander yelled above the fray, "Have you sent word to the acting navy command?"

Capen jerked as a musket fired behind him but responded, "Yes, sir! As soon as the action started, we sent a man off with your message."

"Very well," Alexander commended. "Round up the men and have them clear for action aboard the *Stalwart* so that we may be off before any response to my note can make it back from Providence."

The first mate acknowledged the order, but Alexander continued, "And Mark, tell the men to try to *act* as though they are angry. For heaven's sake, it should at least give the appearance that the Brits have just stolen their ship."

Capen smiled. "Captain, it's hard not to feel a bit giddy. For your crew, this war has finally started!" The first mate wheeled around and began to bark out orders to the men to hold their fire and make their way to the schooner.

Alexander breathed in the pungent smell of the gunpowder. It smelled different this time. He had grown up with this smell, but now he took notice of it, perhaps for the first time. He wondered if everything would seem new to him now.

The crew streamed through the fog past their captain, making their way to the *Stalwart*. Their ship, the *Adrian*, was shrinking as it sailed south through Narragansett Bay. A smile broke across the captain's face as he jogged behind the last of his crew to board the schooner.

Captain Alexander Hawkins had just sent an urgent message to Providence, explaining that Tory British sympathizers were absconding with the *Adrian*. Now, on his own authority, he was in hot pursuit, commanding the nimble schooner of war, *Stalwart*.

Alexander gathered most of the crew. Some were unaccounted for, including his lieutenant and quartermaster, but the *Stalwart* could not accommodate the whole crew anyway. They immediately weighed anchor from the shipyard just south of Providence and were quickly in full sail. They navigated through Narragansett Bay, and once out in the open water, Alexander looked to the southwest through his spyglass. There she was. Only the *Adrian*'s topsails were trimmed. He scanned the horizon to the east and spotted two smaller vessels in full sail headed west, straight toward the *Adrian*.

Capen approached Alexander and asked with a slight smile, "Clear for action to prepare to engage the enemy, sir?"

"No, Mr. Capen," Alexander replied. "I'm sure that won't be necessary. If we do come under fire, it could only be by those vessels from Block Island. Those surly islanders might be out to finish off my family and make claim to the Hawkins's island property. Let us make haste straight for the *Adrian* so we don't give them the opportunity. What say you?"

"Aye, aye, sir!" the first mate responded and started barking out orders looking quizzically back at his captain while scratching the back of his neck.

The captain smiled, realizing Capen was wondering if what his captain just said about the surly islanders stealing the Hawkins's property had any truth to it. It was meant to be a joke, but now the captain himself paused to consider the possible truth behind the humor.

Chapter Twenty

Although the wind from the southeast was strong, the *Adrian* slowly loped along under minimal sail. On board the *Adrian*, the rest of Alexander's missing crew, along with a few Block Island recruits, had removed their phony British uniforms and disguises and were enjoying recounting the excitement of their successful mission.

Lieutenant Fulton and Quartermaster Nathan had led the showy assault. They made sure there were adequate witnesses who would assume it was a Tory plot. Therefore, Captain Alexander Hawkins was now doing his duty by retrieving his stolen ship.

The *Stalwart* swiftly caught the sluggish *Adrian*, and soon, both ships bobbed in a light sea. A longboat from the *Stalwart* was lowered and both Alexander and Capen were transported to the *Adrian*. As the captain boarded the brig, he was greeted by the lieutenant and quartermaster with salutes followed by handshakes.

Alexander addressed the acting command. "Well done, Mr. Fulton and Mr. Nathan. Your first command was quite successful, but I'm afraid you must now turn the vessel back over to the 'enemy'—namely, me."

Fulton responded with a conspiratorial smile. "More than happy to give up command, sir."

"Well, Mr. Fulton, let's just say it is a transfer of command. I believe you are now required to command the *Stalwart* on this mission. Please see to it...and Godspeed."

"Right away, Captain!" Fulton exclaimed before climbing down to the waiting boat.

"Alexander," Nathan spoke, "I expect you want me to join Mr. Fulton?"

Alexander knew that Nathan strove to escape his captain's—and master's—long shadow, but he responded, "No, Nathan, that won't be necessary. I'll need you here aboard the *Adrian*."

Nathan opened his mouth to argue, but Alexander quickly gave him a look that silenced him, ending the discussion before it started.

The transport rowed back to the *Stalwart* as two small, two-masted packets sailed up to complete the squadron. Mostly sailors from Block Island manned the ships. The islanders sailed and fished from their open two-masted boats, called *double enders*, yet they were accomplished men of the sea and extremely capable sailors. Alexander had arranged for two coastal packets through friends in Newport, and his island neighbors were happy to man them for this mission.

Alexander called out from the bridge of the *Adrian*, "Ahoy, islander vessels! Do you sail under a flag of friend or foe?"

The captain of the packet *Betty T* called back, "We sail under the flag of island neutrality. A Block Islander is first and foremost a free man! We responded to a request from a fellow islander to assist in the transport of goods to New York Island. We await your orders, Captain."

"Henry Beach, rest assured that you and your men will be rewarded handsomely one day for your part."

"I won't keep my breath waiting for my reward in this life!"

Alexander smiled and turned to the other vessel. "And what of the *Just Wind Travails*? Is she prepared to sail into this freedom affair?"

A gruff, somewhat angry voice shot back, "When a Block Islander sends a request for assistance, a fellow islander responds. A Block Island man is a free man, and we take no orders from a Hawkins—but we can be instructed!"

Alexander shook his head as he smiled, trying to think of an appropriate reply. "Russel Whitfield," he finally called back, "you are as stony hard as the island we love." Then, addressing the rest of the squadron, he shouted, "If you are all so inclined, follow in my wake!" He turned to his first mate. "Full and bye, Mr. Capen, full and bye."

Capen repeated the order, and the *Adrian*'s crew, together with the islanders, sprang into action. The four vessels set sail and awkwardly organized themselves into a line, with a course heading due west into the Long Island Sound.

Alexander found himself in command of his own small squadron, consisting of the brig *Adrian*, the schooner *Stalwart*, and the two smaller island packets. He felt secure that they could carry out their vital mission without jeopardizing the integrity and authority of their navy leaders. With stores of rifles and munitions in their holds, they sailed to meet Lieutenant Colonel John Mead at Elizabeth's Neck in Greenwich, Connecticut.

As Alexander stood on the quarterdeck, in a fog of his thoughts concerning all that needed to be attended to, he looked heavenward and shook his head. Somehow he knew, at this very moment, that he was fulfilling his real purpose in this life. If he had doubts before about going ahead with this mission, they escaped him now.

~~~
~~~

His squadron sailed under a steady breeze from the southeast, heading along the Connecticut coast to Greenwich. The *Adrian* led the way, with the schooner and the packets struggling to keep up. The sun had recently risen after a cool, clear moonlit night on the Long Island Sound. If the wind kept up, the squadron would reach Elizabeth's Neck by morning light.

Once beyond New London, they took a more southerly route to avoid the mysterious waters known as the Devil's Belt, which ran along the Connecticut coast from New Haven to Fairfield. Beyond Fairfield, Alexander's concern began to ease that they might run into the scoundrel HMS *Rose*, a Royal Navy frigate. As if reading his captain's mind, Capen spoke up. "No sign of the HMS *Rose*, sir."

Alexander coolly replied, "Yes, Mr. Capen, I wouldn't expect so. The *Rose* is likely sailing around lower New York Island, supporting the British invasion. She won't be giving us any trouble in the sound."

"I am aware of her reputation," Capen added. "I don't really know much about her or her captain and crew, but I, for one, hope she drifts a little too close to the New York Island battery and Washington blows those buggers from here to hell!"

"I'm afraid, Mr. Capen," Alexander replied, "that her captain is a little too clever for that, but it would be welcomed news."

The HMS *Rose* was a sixth-rated ship of the line, carrying twenty-four guns. She sailed under the command of James Wallace and had patrolled the waters off the northeast coast for years, wreaking havoc on colonial shipping and decimating the economy of Newport and Rhode Island. It was because of the HMS *Rose* that Americans first petitioned their legislature to create an American navy. The *Providence* was the first ship commissioned into service.

After dismissing the first mate, Alexander's concern drifted to the next crucial objective of their mission—finding Greenwich at Elizabeth's Point and locating Lieutenant Colonel Mead. The *Adrian*'s crew had done all they could to load up with muskets and munitions. If the weapons they now carried, however, were all they could deliver, then Alexander questioned whether they should take the risk at all.

Rumor had it that the wealthy colonial landowners in Greenwich were secretly producing weapons, with great quantities stored up for the area's defense. The local Greenwich garrison's hands were tied by a decree forbidding military expeditions unless by the authority of the Continental Congress, the General Assembly of Connecticut, the County Congress, or the Greenwich Committee of Safety.

At a tide mill in an area known as Coe's Cóbh at the mouth of the Mianus River, patriots were secretly producing and storing weapons. Alexander was growing anxious again, and when he felt this way, he would find himself in silent conversation. He asked for providential strength and wisdom, acknowledging his own weakness and self-doubt but having confidence in God's power to accomplish his will.

The captain took a deep breath of the cool, salty air and opened his eyes. Whether his contemplations were brief or lengthy, or whether they ended quietly by his own final thanksgiving or abruptly by some attention to duty, Alexander would always feel reassured and more confident afterward.

Chapter Twenty-One

The following morning, Lieutenant Fulton had transferred back over to the *Adrian* and was now piloting the lead ship of the squadron. Alexander had brought him aboard for his familiarity with all of the Long Island Sound, including the East River and the waters around New York Island. His expertise made finding Elizabeth's Point in the dawning light relatively easy.

The ships all came leeward as Captain Hawkins called out, "Lieutenant, drop anchor and lower a boat! Call the shore party to attention and prepare to go ashore. We will take the boat and circle the point to look for a sign from Mead. You will take command of the squadron."

"Yes, sir!" Fulton replied, and then turned to pass on the captain's orders.

Alexander, Nathan, and an attachment of men boarded the small boat lowered by the crew to sail around the point. Alexander hoped to see an indication that someone would be there to meet them. A wispy serpent of smoke rose from the trees just beyond the beach. Thinking it was a sign of a small fire, they started for shore. The tide was low, and the beach long and gradual. Barely a ripple of a wave lapped up onto the sand.

The shore party took the rigging down and rowed the boat onto the soft sand. After climbing out of the boat, they waded through the shallow water and pulled the boat up to the brown beach. Without a sound, Alexander signaled the men to proceed up to the tall grass beyond the beach. Quickly, they moved from the beach, still looking for a sign of anyone to meet them.

Alexander huddled the men together and spoke in a hushed tone. "Men, it is unlikely there will be any trouble, but be on guard. Truth is, it may be difficult to make contact with Mead. The militia in Greenwich may be bracing for a British attack, and we don't want to be mistaken for the Brits. Be prepared! Now let's make our way into the woods toward the smoke." He then turned to Nathan, singling him out, and said sternly, "Sailor, you stay well behind me. Now let's move forward."

Nathan's scowled. The comment hadn't been intended as hurtful, but when Alexander heard the snickering from the other men, he realized that he might have embarrassed his quartermaster. He hissed, "Quiet! Let's move into the woods without a sound."

The shore party readied their weapons and headed straight for the smoke. Once in the woods, they walked right up to the fire. A rusty pot hung over the flames; it contained what appeared to be beans boiling at the bottom. The men looked around quietly, wondering where the inhabitants of the camp were, all the while trying to fend off the vile smell coming from the pot.

"Good gracious," Nathan said as he waved his hand in front of his face, "this is one way to defend against the Brits." The men started to chuckle, but Alexander raised his hand to signal quiet.

They were all somewhat blinded by the bright morning rays reflecting off of the smooth water and golden-brown sand.

Their eyes strained as they adjusted to the dark shade of the trees. The small campfire made the dark shade of the woods that much blacker. The silence was abruptly broken by the words, "Kin I he'p ya?" The whole party ducked and scrambled from the invisible enemy, yet no one knew where the voice had come from—and then it came again, "Ya's lookin' fir Mead?"

The men focused on the direction from which the voice had come. There, sitting up against a mossy tree, was a man so dirty and discolored that he blended in perfectly with the bark and moss. He was eating his meal off a large piece of bark with his dirty fingers.

"Good God, man," Alexander let out, "you are a clever one! Scared us half to the grave." He paused to wait for a response, but the man just shrugged and kept eating. Alexander took a step closer. "Yes, I'm looking for Lieutenant Colonel Mead. Where shall I find him? Our business is most urgent."

The man wiped his fingers on his beard. "Men'll be 'long sho'tly. Todd gone rode ta git 'em when he seen ya boats."

"Very well," Alexander responded. "We will wait here." After a brief pause, during which the man continued to eat, Alexander asked, "What might your name be?"

The man was in the process of licking the bark but stopped to say, "I's told names ain't nessity, but I's called Threadneedle."

Mead's doing his part to maintain secrecy, Alexander thought, *even though this man seems to have missed the point*. "Threadneedle?" Alexander said conversationally. "Sounds like a good name for a patriot."

"Me mum was Pequot an' me pa an Englishman," Threadneedle responded absently. "And I's dunt care one way tanutter 'bout Kang Georgy. He don't bodder me. But Mead asks me a favor, an I's does it."

As Threadneedle spoke, he shot suspicious glances at Nathan, seeming nervous about the black man's presence.

Alexander was completely repulsed by this man. He was a dirty, foul, disgusting creature. Alexander didn't want to be influenced by his physical repulsion of the man, but he was growing wary of trusting Threadneedle.

Threadneedle prattled on until they heard the sound of horses approaching. The shore party circled together and braced for the unexpected. Through the trees, they saw four horsemen led by a colonial officer decked out in a heavy blue wool coat with red facings and topped by a three-cornered cap sprouting a long feather. Two colonial soldiers and a civilian dressed in animal skins followed behind.

Alexander turned to Threadneedle for confirmation that this was whom they were waiting for, but Threadneedle paid little mind to the men on horses. Alexander took this as an indication of safety, so he stepped out from the trees to wave the men on. The officer rode up and dismounted, and the two men exchanged salutes.

Alexander offered his hand, but before he could introduce himself, the officer cut him off. "Captain, let us limit our conversation to what is most imperative." He seemed particularly uncomfortable and clearly wanted this meeting to be as short as possible.

Alexander responded in kind. "Of course, sir, I await your instruction."

Mead—or at least, that's who Alexander assumed he was, based on the officer markings on his uniform—outlined new information that would alter their plans. "Quite honestly," the officer said, "under the circumstances, I didn't expect that Captain Geste could convince Hopkins to allow someone to carry out this mission though something told me that I should keep a man posted, just in case."

"Well, sir," Alexander interjected, "the truth is that this mission has not been officially sanctioned."

"Yes, yes," the officer jumped in. "Then we have a mutual understanding." He looked around anxiously, as if he thought they were being watched. "There have been significant developments that will likely alter your plans," he continued. "General Putnam has been sending us regular reports. He has just reported that General Washington has evacuated lower New York Island and retreated to a northern part of the island known as Harlem Heights."

Alexander felt encouraged—this could make their mission that much easier. Once through the Long Island narrows and into the East River, they could sail north and not only avoid the enemy but also avoid the treacherous waters of Hell Gate.

Chapter Twenty-Two

Hell Gate. The name itself caused Alexander to shudder. He had tried not to think about facing the challenge of this waterway, with its converging tides and swirling currents. The passage was known as a graveyard to ships and sailors alike, and he did not relish the thought of captaining a ship through it for the first time. The Dutch called it *Helegat*, or "Bright Passage," due to the way the sunlight played on the churning waters, but to most sailors, it seemed more like a passage through the gates of hell. Learning that he could avoid that trial, Alexander began to breathe a bit easier.

The officer, however, was quick to sober him with a bit of bad news. In support of the British invasion of New York Island was a battery of cannons and mortars erected at Hallet's Point on Long Island. The battery was used to breach the American fort, located directly across the East River at Horn's Hook.

Alexander listened with interest but struggled to understand the pertinence of the information. "Yes, sir, but Hallet's Point is south, on the other end of Hell Gate. My intentions now are to sail north between Montresor Island and Morrisania up to the Harlem River."

"Yes, of course," the officer continued, "but we have just received word from fishermen that the British have moved their battery one mile north and have fortified a position on the northern shore of Long Island at a point known as 'the pin-folds', directly south of Morrisania. The battery consists of two twenty-four pounders, three twelve pounders, and three long twelve pounders. They have the range to easily cover the two-thousand-yard width of the waterway. Certainly, the English realize how important cutting off this supply route would be toward completing a stronghold on New York Island."

This raised the risks dramatically, and Alexander could envision how desperate the situation was becoming—and how urgently they must act.

"If you and your men choose to continue," the officer went on to say, "there will only be one opportunity while… ahem…" The officer paused for emphasis. "*Mead* might not be looking."

Alexander narrowed his eyes. Was this man trying to be clever? If the reference to "Mead" was intended to clarify the officer's identity, it had failed; it only served to make Alexander even more unsure of whether this person was Mead.

The officer didn't seem to notice Alexander's confusion and continued outlining the strategy. "Take your force across the way to the immediate northern shore of Long Island and wait there until dusk to return. When back at Elizabeth's Neck, head just a bit west and north of here to the mouth of the river known as Mianus. Sail upriver for a short distance. On the west bank, you'll see a large stone building with a cupola and a weathervane on its peak. At your return, the tide will be rising so your ships can anchor fairly close in. There will be men in jolly boats to meet you and ferry the cargo to your ships.

"I have circulated a request for volunteers from the Greenwich garrison at Horseneck to act as marines. These men have had their hands tied by bureaucrats for too long, and they are eager to fight. I expect a good response. We have some whale boats outfitted with swivel guns. The men will use these boats to sail to the northern shore of Long Island and then follow the coast west. They'll come to shore just east of the British encampment."

Alexander struggled to keep up with the officer's directions as he envisioned the route in his mind.

"Before the British will be able to fire on your ships," the officer went on, "the marines will have attacked their fortification from land. If the battery still manages to open fire upon your squadron, I suggest your lead ship fire upon their position to draw any return fire while the other ships slip through to deliver their cargo."

Alexander listened intently while waiting for an opportunity to ask questions. But when the officer finally paused, Alexander didn't know where to begin.

"One final warning," the officer added before Alexander could form a question, "*when* the cannon fire begins, the HMS *Rose* is almost sure to join the fray. She has been patrolling up and down the North and East Rivers. Any questions, Captain?"

Alexander stared off across the water at the squadron, trying to take in all that the officer had just said. His focus on the desperateness of Washington's situation was replaced by his concern for the men. There was something about the way the officer had emphasized "*When* the cannon fire begins" that struck Alexander and caused him not to fully grasp the officer's mention of the HMS *Rose*. He knew he was expected to respond quickly and confidently with a snappy salute, but he simply and deliberately said, "I understand, sir."

His thoughts were on the men, wondering whether all were willing and able to take on this increasingly risky and dangerous mission. He decided that once they reached the northern shore of Long Island, he would pull the boats together to allow the men an opportunity to reconsider their involvement.

Without another word, the officer and his men were off, galloping away, leaving a cloud of sand and dust.

The troubled captain ordered his shore party back to the boat, and they shoved off from the sandy beach. As they rowed toward the *Adrian*, Alexander looked over his shoulder to see Threadneedle watching them. Alexander raised his hand in farewell, and then saw the woodsman, too, raise his hand. But rather than returning the farewell gesture, the man put his index finger out and pressed it against one nostril. Blowing hard, he cleared the other nostril of all its contents. Alexander turned away in disgust. He tried not to be insulted by what was certainly the dirty man's complete lack of social skills.

The group returned to the *Adrian* at anchor amidst the makeshift squadron. Alexander reassumed command and addressed the lieutenant. "Mr. Fulton, set a course due south. We shall spend the day anchored off the northern shore of Long Island, waiting for darkness."

"Very well, Captain," Fulton replied, and turned to repeat the orders. The men jumped into action, and soon, all four vessels were headed for the opposite shore of Long Island.

Alexander stood at the bow of the *Adrian*, gripping the cap rail tightly. The normally self-confident and steady Alexander Hawkins felt an unfamiliar anxiety—an anxiety that grew to anger. He thought he had given over his anxious feelings to God's control. Now, he felt his confidence being pushed aside by his fear, much like the waves that crested before his ship, pushed aside by the bow's progress through the water.

At the beginning of their mission, he'd felt a sense of losing a grip on the events unfolding before him. He didn't like that feeling, but for the first time, he realized to what extent he would have to be willing to relinquish control to his God.

Captain Hawkins stared ahead toward Long Island. He could not seem to escape his doubts, and he questioned where these ships, these men, and this revolution would all end up.

Chapter Twenty-Three

On the northern shore of Long Island, near the mouth of Oyster Bay, Captain Alexander Hawkins had the ships drawn in and lashed together. From the quarterdeck of the *Adrian*, he addressed all the men at once. "I have learned that there has been a battery placed between ourselves and our destination. This will likely mean engagement with the British. This mission was originally presented to you as a delivery of arms, but it now appears to be one of great danger. At this time, before we proceed any further, I want to offer to anyone—particularly you islander volunteers—the chance to return home. Some of you, I know, are willing to fight for your personal freedom, but I also know that some may struggle with relinquishing allegiance to the crown. Now is the time to decide to go forward or go back. There will be no judgment placed on any man's decision."

Several men began shouting to go on. Soon, the rest joined in the chorus until the men on all four ships were shouting and cheering. Alexander tried to speak, but the sailors shouted him down. His face turned red with embarrassment at the over-whelming show of patriotism.

Out of the cheering, a chant began to swell from the sailors until all cried out the familiar rallying cry of the young revolution: "We have no king but Christ!" Alexander realized that each of these men had already come to grips with his decision to face the consequences of the rebellion.

This was exactly what the navy crew had signed on and trained for, but the islanders had not formally signed on for continental service. That did not mean, however, that they—to a man—didn't want freedom from England, and given the opportunity, that they would not enjoy the chance to join in to have at their British rulers when the opportunity arose.

As the sun set, the captain led his crew in prayers of thanks-giving and for God's blessing on their lives and the mission.

With the bosun mate's call to quarters, the makeshift squad-ron headed back north to the Connecticut coast. It would be a cool night, with a light chop to the sound supplied by a good easterly breeze. While out on the open water, Alexander would often feel a sense of sadness but would soon be rescued by that silent conversation, reassuring him that he was not alone.

Locating Elizabeth's Neck again, the squadron sailed around the point. Slightly to the northwest gaped the mouth of the Mianus River. Soon, they would be up the river into Coe's Cóbh to complete their final preparations for the *Adrian*'s date with destiny.

Just as the Greenwich officer had said, jolly boats were waiting with crates and kegs. Along with them were the three whaling boats, of the kind used to row out from the great whal-ing ships in chase of their mammoth prey. Each whaling boat was outfitted with swivel guns and, between them, held some thirty Greenwich militiamen. Alexander surmised that some must be capable sailors, for there were no civilians among them.

The four vessels anchored, and Alexander instructed Nathan to oversee the transfer of the munitions from the boats. Earlier, while on the northern shore of Long Island, the crew had transferred most of the cargo on the *Adrian* to the other ships. This exchange was based on the Greenwich officer's indications that the *Adrian* would have to engage the British battery, allowing the other ships through to deliver the cargo. He had decided that his ship's role would be to provide clear passage for the others, and he determined that the *Adrian*, along with the militia, would seize control of the battery and take what munitions and supplies they could carry. What they could not take, they would render useless to the British, creating a safe passage for the revolutionaries.

His one hope was that with the East River now protected by British guns, the HMS *Rose* would be on the other side of New York Island up the North River. The wind and weather being right, she might never be made aware that the fight was on.

Alexander called over to the whaling boats to introduce himself. "I...uh...we...uh..." he stammered, suddenly remembering the need to remain anonymous. "I am this ship's captain. I need to speak with whoever is in charge."

A figure stood up, framed in the moonlight. "That would be me, sir—the detachment's lieutenant. I am awaiting one of the jollies to transport me to your ship."

"No, wait there," Alexander quickly interjected. "I'll come to you." A small skiff was lowered, and two men rowed Alexander to the whaler. He wanted to go to them in order to size up the quality of these new recruits. When they arrived at the whaler, the two officers quietly saluted and shook hands. The captain took a quick look at the men, replete in their splendid, clean uniforms and shiny new muskets with sharp bayonets, and he wondered if any of them had ever seen action.

"Lieutenant," he said, looking the officer in the eye, "your men are obviously honorable patriots, but if they have not yet seen action, they are certain to see it this very evening. Are you positive they are up for the task?"

"Yes, Captain," the lieutenant assertively responded, "you are correct in your presumption that these men are fine patriots and dedicated soldiers. They have pushed themselves in training for this very opportunity, and I guarantee they will fight with honor and distinction." Then he added wryly, "May I ask how many sea battles your crew has fought?"

Captain Hawkins smiled and nodded his head. "Yes, Lieutenant, I'd say we will all have earned our rations by the morning's light. Now let us make our plans and be on with it before any word gets out ahead of us to give the British warning."

The lieutenant joined Alexander as he returned to the ship, and they huddled over a candlelit map to coordinate their attacks.

"My squadron will give the militia until midnight to sail across the sound," Alexander detailed. "Your men will follow the northern shore west, past Throgs Neck and into the East River. From there, you will pass to the western side of Flushing Bay and go ashore near the area known as New Town. Then, follow the shore northwest on foot until you are within striking distance of the British battery at the pinfolds. Your Greenwich force will then wait for my squadron to arrive. At precisely the first sound of the British guns, your militia is to attack in full force. I assume we are in agreement that, in all likelihood, the British battery will be manned with men more prepared to fire cannons at ships than to fend off a land attack of any significance."

The two men quietly studied the map for a moment longer until the Greenwich lieutenant said, "Agreed. I understand. It is a good plan, and we Greenwich men will do our part."

"And so shall we," Alexander concluded. "This shall be a glorious night. Godspeed, Lieutenant."

The lieutenant took the skiff back to the whaler, and Alexander could hear him in the distance, outlining their mission to his men. While Alexander's ships were still taking on the munitions, the Greenwich garrison paddled the three whalers to open water and set sail for western Long Island.

Alexander watched the three whalers sail off, their white sails illuminated by the full moon that hung high in the night sky to the east. The conditions seemed to be perfect for the mission that lay ahead. Alexander watched the activity continue and realized the mission was actually going to happen. It was all he had dreamed of and hoped for. He thanked God for the arrival of this day and what it represented for the miracle of revolutionary freedom—a freedom of which he suddenly felt most certain.

Chapter Twenty-Four

Nathan saw the look on the faces of the Greenwich men. He had seen it in Threadneedle's eyes too. In fact, he had seen it a thousand times before—that strange mix of surprise and disdain. Generally, regardless of a white man's feelings on slavery, none of them wanted to see a black man doing anything beyond "slave's work". Though inadvertent, Alexander wasn't helping matters as he continued to treat him over-protectively, more as a young sibling than as a man

As Nathan traveled in the skiff from boat to boat, overseeing the transfer of the crates and kegs, his frustration with Alexander grew. His captain had embarrassed him on Elizabeth's Point. When Alexander told him to stay behind him, how could his captain not realize what message that would convey to the other men? The men made sure he heard their snickering comments. Yes, Alexander was fulfilling his promise to Nathan's mother, but he clearly didn't understand how demeaning it was.

Nathan was conflicted. He loved Alexander and wanted to be with him, but he was a grown man now and wanted to stand on his own two feet. He always felt like Alexander's younger brother, and he resisted the idea that he could never be anything more than that. At the same time, he reminded himself that he was very fortunate to have been born into the Hawkins family. The freedoms he enjoyed were much greater than those of other slaves. His freedoms led to his desire to pursue even greater freedom for himself and for his black brethren. Nathan's thoughts took him back to his childhood on Block Island...

~~~

They were a small group of friends. Nathan always stayed close to Alexander and their friendship extended to the Indian boy Quepag, Simon and Caty Littlefield, and the Beach children, Rebekah and her younger brother, Benjamin. The Beach family had young slave children their age, but they were not allowed to play with them.

All of the children regularly competed in games of sport. Benjamin Beach and Caty Littlefield were the youngest and struggled to keep up with the older children. Rebekah had inherited a strong competitive spirit from her father and felt inclined to step in to compete where her brother could not. Quepaq was a natural athlete but lacked any real competitive drive.

Although the youngest of the group, Caty Littlefield's strong personality, gay spirit, and clever mind often put her at the lead in the group's play. Nathan was several years older but found himself infatuated with this bright, friendly, and spirited young girl. All of the group enjoyed young Caty's antics and would often find her leading them on an adventure.

Her favorite game was "Puss in the Corner," and she would make the six friends play it for hours. It was a game for five players but required so much running that one of the players would look to be replaced regularly, keeping all active and involved. Both Rebekah and Caty were smart, headstrong,
~~~

competitive Block Island girls who could ride, run, hunt, and fish as well as the boys.

At times during the cold, wet seasons, the island would seem like a dark, damp prison as they pined for the adventure and excitement of the mainland. Yet there was a sense of timelessness to the island, with little of the rigid structure they heard was imposed on the children across the water.

Horseback riding was one of the great pleasures—and necessities—of Block Island. Even at a young age—with the boys in their continental breeches and stockings adorned with bright knee-buckles, and the girls in their gracefully flowing riding dresses, and Quepaq in his animal skins—they would race around the hills, through the ravines, and on the beaches. They knew every trail, field, wall, and pond across the island.

Young Caty's imagination brought wonder to everything that might go unnoticed by the others, wonders to be found in the dunes and the beaches running into the edge of the ocean. The shapes and vast colors of the wet stones, the vegetation clinging to the rocks and pilings, and all the creeping, crawling crustaceans found in the clear water became treasures of play. Wrecks littering the shore stirred their imaginations with all that had happened to these ships and men before the powerful sea threw them upon Block Island's shore.

When her father sent Caty to live on the mainland in '61, the group sorely missed her inquisitive, adventurous, and imaginative free spirit. Nathan, in particular, had quietly shared with Alexander the disappointment he bore for the loss of the lovely girl he fancied but could never have. Alexander convinced him that it was better she was physically removed from the island than to have her there but so inaccessible.

With Caty gone, Rebekah became more aggressive and competitive, as if she had to prove the strength of all the women on the island. When the friends were younger, Rebekah would easily be the victor in games of competitive sport. She was not a graceful winner and would playfully taunt the boys. Eventually, as the boys grew older, they easily surpassed

Rebekah in strength and skill, but due to Alexander's and Simon's gentlemanly nature, and Nathan's and Quepaq's subservient positions, they would continue to let Rebekah win at the end of the day.

Eventually, though, Nathan grew tired of losing. He decided that he would no longer pretend he was something less than who he was and began to regularly upstage Rebekah. This infuriated her. She never really warmed to Nathan as a friend, but for lack of playmates on the island and in order to play with Alexander, she accepted him.

As time marched on, Rebekah discarded the boyish image of her youth and adopted the gentler feminine ways of a young woman. Still, she could never accept Nathan's relationship with Alexander. The differences were too much a part of the fabric of their lives. For Rebekah, like many other slave owners, accepting a slave as more human than she believed would have a devastating effect on what she wanted to believe about herself

Nathan was keenly aware that the Beach family had always been different from the Hawkins family in their treatment and attitude toward slaves. The Beaches' relationship was like a few slave other owners on the island and many over on the mainland. Values and beliefs varied widely with each slave-holding family. The Hawkins and the Beach families personified the differences found in New England society of the day.

It was true that all slaves had some individual legal rights, protected by local authorities, but those officials would rarely involve themselves with an owner's right to manage his personal property. Each slave-owning family would make up their rules based upon their own values and beliefs.

Nathan had to agree that the Beach family treated their slaves humanely and cared for their physical condition, but there was no doubt that their slaves were acquired for service to the family and to the farm—that fact was paramount. He had seen instances when a slave could not fulfill his or her economic purpose; then there was little emotional attachment.

To Nathan, the Beach family's slaves were treated more like their cherished horses. Yes, there was level of devotion and other emotions toward them, but any good horse could not be afforded too much liberty. If a horse came up lame, then no matter what the emotional attachment, it would be discarded.

The living conditions for the Beach slaves were also typical of most other New England slaves. They slept on the dirt floors of the farm barns and sheds, using straw as mattresses. They owned very little for themselves beyond the tattered clothes on their backs. Most of the slaves were required to grow their own food or scavenge for it. The house slaves often had a higher standard of living than the field slaves and were even allowed to eat what was left over from the meal prepared for the family. On special occasions, they were given uniforms that they wore proudly. Some even lived within the family home, although down in the dirt-floor cellar. In the cellar, they had some heat in the winter, unlike the crude shacks or barns where field hands lived.

Nathan felt proud and particularly blessed that the Hawkins family, like most islander families, treated their slaves better than those on the mainland. He was like a member of the family. While his living conditions were certainly below the whites' standards, they were far and away better than those of some others on the island and most on the mainland.

Nathan and his parents, Molly Mum and Stepney, lived in a simple building erected just for their housing, with a crude stone fireplace for heating and cooking. Whatever they could make or find for furnishings was considered their property. These belongings came from rummaging through island dumping areas, from the Hawkins family hand-me-downs, or from scavenging shipwrecks. Typically, Molly Mum cooked food in large quantities in the main house to feed all on the farm.

It was still by no means an easy life for the Hawkins slaves. Joseph Hawkins was a hard taskmaster and a strict disciplinarian. Nathan knew well of Master Hawkins's harsh punishment, be it for sleeping late, or taking extra food, or for simply displeasing his master with lack of effort. Any one of these could get him a whip of the switch or the loss of a whole day's food. Yet each slave felt that punishment was dealt fairly, even equally, among free and slave.

While Joseph was recognized as a good and decent man, he believed wholeheartedly in the system of slavery. Even with his strong conviction that the slaves were his personal property, he treated them humanely and gave them many of the same rights and responsibilities he gave to his own son.

Nathan appreciated Alexander's influence on his father's treatment toward the slaves. Even as a young boy, he knew Alexander never felt comfortable with the system of slavery. In fact, subjugation and servitude of any kind caused a passionate desire to well up within Alexander to break the chains of human bondage.

Over the years, Nathan came to grips with the fact that slavery would not just suddenly disappear. In the meantime, he would do what he could to influence change. Even though Nathan felt a strong desire to come out from under Alexander's shadow, he also knew it was only because of that shadow that he might ever have the chance to stand as a free man.

Chapter Twenty-Five

Nathan's mind turned back to the many details that still needed attention. Once more, he boarded the skiff to visit the other vessels and go over the final details of their mission. While on board the *Stalwart*, he looked over the cargo they were storing, and what he saw caused him concern.

Just then, Alexander came aboard, and Nathan approached his captain and saluted. "Captain, do you see what I see?"

"Well, I'm hoping, based on what I saw of the cargo on the other ships, that this ship is loaded with muskets."

"I just completed checking all of the ships, and I'm afraid not," Nathan reported. "The holds are mostly filled with crates of bayonets. Yes, there are kegs of powder, primer, and musket balls, along with a few crates of muskets, but mostly there are crates and crates of bayonets. Certainly, many more bayonets than the muskets we carry. Even more bayonets than can be used to equip the muskets we brought from Providence."

Alexander's temper began to rise. He called down to the nearest jolly, "There! You men from Coe's Cóbh! Who is in charge?"

One of the men looked up to Alexander and responded, "No one is in charge. Fact is, we ain't even here!"

The other men with him began to laugh, but Alexander cut them off. "I'm in no humor, man! We have patriots in desperate need of our help, and I'm afraid there has been a terrible blunder."

The men immediately sobered up, and the same man replied, "Beggin' your pardon, sir, but we all have the same orders. What you have here is all that we were commissioned to deliver."

Alexander turned back to Nathan and lowered his eyes. "Nathan," he said, shaking his head, "what possible use could all these bayonets provide without the muskets to attach them to? They would seem to be useless ballast that will slow us down. I've a mind to take the vast majority of them and drop them to the river bottom."

Nathan noticed that the activities on all the ships had grown quiet as the men heard the commotion and stopped to listen. "Captain, it doesn't appear to be right, but it seems to me that the whole mission, the reason we're here, is based on faith—faith in Geste, in Mead, and in General Washington. From the beginning, we have only responded to the needs they have outlined, without any firsthand knowledge. If this is the cargo they say needs to be delivered, then why should we question them now?"

Alexander dropped his head and said slowly, "Nathan, your thinking is so clear, your approach so accurate, and your wisdom so profound. This, and the fact that you are years my junior, is what I find so irritating." He looked up at Nathan with a smile, and they both broke out into laughter. Immediately, all the men resumed their work to complete the finishing touches before they were to sail.

With the cargo stowed away and the jolly boats now tied to the salt works dock, the Coe's Cóbhers slowly faded into the dark thick woods.

"I wonder where those men are headed," Alexander said to Nathan.

"I spoke with one of them," Nathan answered, "and he said that they were going to hike a mile north along the river to the Mianus Tavern. That's where they tied their horses and where they told their families they would be spending the evening."

The captain signaled to the other vessels and gave orders to clear for action. The *Adrian* was soon under sail, with the sloop *Stalwart* and the two islander vessels following behind. The small squadron slipped quietly from Coe's Cóbh and out the mouth of the Mianus River.

When ships cleared for action, whether to prepare to set sail or to prepare for battle, there always was a great deal of noise. Yet this time, Nathan noticed there was an eerie quiet to their work—a quiet partly due to the orders they were given to maintain silence so as to slip through the Long Island Sound waters with little notice. If they could catch the British sleeping, they might be able to sail far across the 1,500 yards of their line of fire before being discovered. But Nathan saw that the quiet had a double edge to it. It also caused the men to grow anxious and introspective, increasing their tension.

While Nathan himself was excited, an ominous chill still managed to shake his body. There was no doubt in his mind that their mission would be successful, but he was just as certain that a heavy price would be paid.

The black sailor looked up at the full moon, now high in the night sky. He felt good that their humble little squadron would have a brilliant light by which to navigate. Then he gazed over at the other ships and across the Long Island Sound to the northern shore of Long Island. He realized that if he was able to see the shore so clearly, the moonlight also made their ships clearer targets for the big British guns. His anxiety grew.

~~~
~~~

Captain Alexander Hawkins slowly but anxiously paced the quarterdeck of the *Adrian*. Sweat beaded on his brow and above his lip. His long brown hair lay damp from sea and sweat. He wished he could strip off his heavy wool coat, but it was his uniform, and he wouldn't dare enter into battle without it. He looked over at Lieutenant Fulton, who continued to act as pilot. The lieutenant seemed completely at ease, and Alexander was determined to show just as much confidence for the sake of leadership.

Fulton's role became increasingly important as the squadron sailed from the Long Island Sound through the narrows of Throgs Neck and spilled into the East River. Even though the light was adequate for navigation, Fulton knew where the deep water was and which shallows to avoid. The rest of the squadron stayed on the *Adrian*'s course and followed in her wake.

With Flushing Bay to their south, they planned to sail around to the north of Hulet Island. Just to the northwest of Hulet lay two small islands known as the Brothers Islands, and Alexander chose to sail through the channel between the Brothers. This route would leave the shortest distance of the roughly two thousand yards to which they would be exposed to the British battery before entering the northern channel and the cover of Montresor Island.

If and when the British started firing their guns, the *Adrian* planned to break off and engage the battery, just as the officer "Mead" had recommended. The other three vessels would continue to follow the course mapped out, heading northwest into the channel, which led from the East River to the Harlem River. Upon arriving at Harlem Heights, they planned to anchor and begin ferrying the supplies to the New York Island shore.

From Harlem Heights, Washington's troops were certain to spot the vessels flying the rebel flag—a pine tree embroidered under the motto "An Appeal to Heaven"—and send a detachment to help unload the munitions and transport them back to the encampment. His hope was that upon their return, the

Adrian and the Greenwich militia would have overwhelmed the battery to make for a safe sail back home.

As the *Adrian* approached to the north of Hulet Island, Alexander, in a loud whisper, relayed his orders to his lieutenant. "Mister Fulton, pass the word to the crew to quietly clear for action and prepare for battle. Have the gunners man their gun stations on the port side. See that all are primed, loaded, and secured in their breeches."

Alexander's tension grew as they rounded Hulet Island and headed for the channel between the Brothers Islands. There was little sound, save for the flapping of sail and the creaking of timber. He looked through his spyglass, anxiously anticipating the sighting of the first guns of the battery.

The captain tried to imagine how the British battery would be set. Certainly, the guns would be splayed in a large arc around the pinfolds and at the edge of the short bluff that sloped down to the water's edge. There would be very little beach. Alexander looked for the Greenwich whalers and spotted the three boats close to shore at New Town. He breathed a sigh of relief. Surely the Greenwich militia was in position at this point.

Once through the Brothers channel, Alexander veered more to the southwest and let the others head northwest, as they had planned. He was going to assume the British would be on their toes, so he made certain the *Adrian* would be in position between the battery and the rest of the squadron. If the British did fail to engage, then he would fall in behind the islanders and follow them north to Harlem Heights.

As they broke through the channel, Alexander spotted the first guns in the battery. They were clear as day, sitting up on the bluff—black, shiny, and in perfect position to fire across at passing ships. Alexander's anxiety grew. *If I can see them so clearly, then the Brits most certainly can see us.* He shook his head, surprised at how their course had brought them so much closer to the battery than he had envisioned from the map.

Through his spyglass, he could see that the guns were not trained in their direction, and he felt a moment of relief. Also, he could see no activity or lights burning beyond the fortifications built up along the edge of the bluff. As they began to sail west—now in full view of the British position—the steady wind, which until then seemed to have no limit, was suddenly and completely cut off. The sails that only a moment earlier were full and stretched taut were now limp and lifeless. Alexander could hear whispered curses ripple through the crew. For a moment, even he was unsure of what had happened—or what they should do.

His pilot, Fulton, quickly looked around, cursed, and then reported, "Captain, my memory had slipped regarding the wind in the East River. Those British buggers knew enough to place their guns at the pinfolds because Hulet Island can act as a perfect foil to the wind and set us adrift. We must try to move ourselves more north or south to regain the wind."

One by one, each vessel followed suit, with their sails limp. The strong current and converging tides pulled all four vessels west and south, toward the treacherous, choppy waters of Hell Gate.

The men maintained their quiet, but Alexander could see the strain on their faces from the growing anxiety. They needed wind desperately, but until they caught a gust, they were drifting directly into what looked to be a British crossfire.

Alexander lifted his spyglass and realized that the whole string of cannons were not arrayed in an arc as he had thought; they were all pointing north to one location—the location for which they were directly heading. For the first time, he could see flames flickering from behind the fortifications, and the painful realization hit him that his squadron had fallen into a trap.

The captain felt a sharp pain in his stomach, followed by a sudden sense of nausea. The feelings of fear and trepidation from several days earlier rose up again. The thought of Captain Geste immediately came to mind. He knew down deep within himself that he could not trust this rascal. Now he was sure that Geste had set him up for disaster.

A sense of doom began to overwhelm him, and Alexander quietly whispered, "God save us."

Chapter Twenty-Six

The captain's mind raced to find a solution to prevent the *Adrian* from entering the British crossfire. He called to Fulton, "Send the bosun forward to let go the anchor immediately!"

Fulton did not hesitate and, rather than relaying the order, raced forward himself. Reaching the cathead, he pulled free the ring stopper, letting the heavy iron anchor fly. It dropped into the East River with a loud splash. For interminable seconds, the heavy cable shot through the hawse pipe until the anchor suddenly grabbed fast to the bottom. The ship came to a violent stop, sending the crew stumbling forward. The line held fast as the stern slowly swung around. The ship arched slightly north, where she started to find some wind.

When the captain saw the sails start to fill, he gave the order to axe the anchor line. The ships following behind had drifted too close to each other, leaving the *Stalwart* struggling to avoid the *Adrian*. The collision was unavoidable, and she smashed her port bow into the starboard of the *Adrian*'s bow. Following in line, the two islander vessels' bows glanced off the stern of the vessel directly in front of each of them.

In the next instant, the *Adrian* righted herself and pointed west, wind filling her sails. The other three vessels were bounced into a more northerly course and also caught some wind. Alexander raced from the stern to the bow to check their bearings and to see how the other ships had faired from the collisions. He saw all four ships were on course with full sails. *Only by God's grace!* None of the vessels seemed to have suffered major damage, and the three cargo-laden vessels sailed on as though nothing had happened.

The calm was broken, however, with the British guns opening fire. The *Adrian* had avoided sailing into the center of the crossfire, but the guns that were pointed northeast—in their direction—had opened upon them. Alexander counted the bright flashes and large concussions: *one, two, three, four, five, six.* Large geysers of water erupted all around the ship. Again: *one, two, three, four, five, six.* More geysers shot up from the water until—*CRACK!* The main mast topsail had taken a direct hit, and splinters rained down on the crew. The vibration sent a large fracture ripping down through the main mast, yet she somehow held, and the main sail appeared fairly intact and still operable.

"Clear to fire!" Alexander ordered. His lieutenant, in turn, echoed the order. Alexander then bellowed "Fire!" and the lieutenant again repeated the order. When the guns fired, it was as if the *Adrian* herself had exploded.

From the bow to the stern, the *Adrian*'s eight guns unloaded their balls. The guns held to their breeches, and the ship rocked back from the force. The crew watched and hoped.

Through his spyglass, Alexander spotted the first three shots as they hit the bluffs in ascending order, sending big clouds of dirt and rock into the air. The next five shots hit squarely among the British guns that had fired upon them, disabling several. The crew let out a roar. This was the first damage they had inflicted upon their enemy.

Alexander then noticed the bright flashes to the east of the battery and remembered the Greenwich men. It dawned on him that these poor fellows might also be entering into a trap. As his gunners reloaded, the British were recovering from the *Adrian*'s first volley and setting the sights of their other guns on the *Adrian*.

Alexander saw the militia on the top of the bluff valiantly charging the British position. It looked very much as though the battery's right flank was left completely unguarded. Suddenly, to the captain's horror, he saw a bright flash, and a loud roar echoed across the water. A half-dozen militiamen suddenly disappeared into a cloud of fine red mist. Hidden cannons filled with canisters of grapeshot unloaded at a frighteningly short distance and chewed through the valiant men as if they were parchment.

The shock of this sight caused Alexander to lose awareness of the battle before him and the fact that the British had restored order. Now, with guns aimed, loaded, and ready, the British fired randomly and found their mark.

"Captain!" Fulton anxiously yelled, as if to awaken Alexander. "Cannons ready to fire!"

The great concussion and gruesome scene stunned the Greenwich men. They stood in apparent disbelief, splattered with blood and pieces of the remains of their mates while the British continued to fire on them. Alexander feared that if the British had the men—or the nerve—they would charge with their bayonets and end it right then. The Greenwich men struggled to find their bearings amid the continuing gunfire.

"Captain!" Fulton shouted again, just as a British twelve-pounder slammed into the stern and opened a hole in the captain's quarters. Several men caught debris and were left stunned and bleeding. Alexander finally awoke to his own battle and ordered, "Fire!"

Once again, the *Adrian*'s cannons let fly with impressive accuracy, upending many of the British guns that had just found their range.

Above the din of the battle, Alexander shouted to Fulton, "Trim the sails and set the bearing for northwest at two o'clock.

On my mark, you'll come about and bear southeast, straight for the middle of the battery!"

The order confused Fulton, but he immediately repeated it to the deck crew. He seemed to know that Alexander was determined to support these desperate Greenwich men and was going to risk doing so from close range.

The British camp was in disarray. The battery was undermanned, and the *Adrian*'s cannon fire had already taken out quite a few men. Although the militia attack was proving to be a devastating failure, it served to occupy a handful of the British. They pinned down the Greenwich men under musket fire while they reloaded their deadly cannons with grapeshot. Each time a man stood up to attack or retreat, he was immediately shot down.

The *Adrian* came about on her captain's mark and now, with a good wind, was bearing down straight for the center of the battery at the pinfolds. The British saw the brig bearing down upon them and struggled to turn their guns toward the ship. Panic overcame them—the ship loomed so close to shore that it must have appeared as though she would actually climb the bluff and run over them. She continued to draw closer and closer to shore, testing the nerve of the entire crew, until finally, with no more than a few hundred feet between the *Adrian* and the British battery, Alexander ordered, "Come about now!"

As the ship swung parallel to the shore, Alexander ordered, "Guns one through four—*fire!*"

In a steady sequence, each cannon unloaded and demolished a gun in the battery, killing or maiming many of the Brits. The British battery fired everything they had, but the *Adrian* was moving too fast and too close. The crew held their collective breath as they ducked, certain that they were to be blown into the next life, but every shot fell behind the racing ship or sailed right over her.

As the ship passed farther east and lay squarely in line with the British position that pinned down the Greenwich militia, Alexander ordered, "Guns five through eight—*fire*!"

The guns let loose and explosions erupted all around the position. "Come about in a tight radius, Mr. Fulton," Alexander ordered. "Present our starboard guns primed and ready to fire."

Alexander gave the order, "All guns—*fire!*"

The *Adrian* jumped back from the force of the guns all firing at once. The resulting devastation left the British camp in total chaos.

The captain next ordered, "Heave to, Mr. Fulton. Lower a longboat. You will take command of the *Adrian* while I lead a party of a dozen men ashore to join the attack."

After gathering muskets and pistols, the shore party quickly descended into the longboat. Nathan jumped aboard to join the shore party. Alexander cursed and ordered him off, but he refused to leave. With no time to waste, the captain gave orders to shove off.

"Damn you, sailor," he said to Nathan with a scowl. "I made a promise to Molly Mum that I would not put you in harm's way."

"And so you have not," Nathan responded. "This was my choice. Besides, I made a promise to your father. Do my promises mean anything less?"

Alexander shook his head in frustration and worked his way to the aft of the boat. The men settled into the boat and pushed off from the ship. A momentary silence fell over them, save for the sound of the men straining at the oars and the oars slapping the water. The silence was broken by the *Adrian* as she continued to fire randomly into the battery to keep the British scattered.

"Men," Alexander said gravely, "there will most certainly be musket fire exchanged, as well as grapeshot to rain down on us, but we must push forward and rally the Greenwich men! Nathan, you will act as my second, reloading my weapons. By God, you will stay behind me, and when I order you to stay put, you will do so. Do you understand?"

"Aye, aye, Captain."

Musket fire began to pop in the water around them. As they approached shore, a cannon went off, and a canister spray erupted off the port bow, shattering two of their oars. About fifty feet from shore, one of the sailors, young James Martin, took a ball to the thigh.

A few strokes later, when they judged the water to be about waist high, the captain told the wounded man, "Mr. Martin, stay with the boat and keep down. Do what you can to help gather any wounded." He then ordered the rest of the men into the water and to spread themselves out as they attacked.

Chapter Twenty-Seven

Back on the *Adrian*, Fulton struggled to steady the ship and maintain her position. A strong current was bringing in the rising tide, and the wind blew directly off her stern. The ship's gunners continued to reload and fire, inflicting some damage, but more important, they continued to disrupt British efforts to reorganize. Here and there, where guns were still operable, the British returned fire on the *Adrian*. The ship sustained damage from several direct hits, but none of them was crippling. One shot opened a hole in the forecastle and another glanced off the bow well above the waterline, leaving a dent and cracked boards. Most of the British attention was now on keeping the Greenwich men at bay and fighting off the small force attacking from the river.

The Greenwich militiamen were still frozen in their places. The pattern continued—every time a man made a move, he would immediately be cut down. Their lieutenant was shredded by the first canister blasts, leaving the remaining men leaderless. From their position, they could see Captain Hawkins and his crew rowing to shore. They surely saw Alexander yelling and pointing his sword in their direction but seemed unable to make out his instructions.

Alexander left orders that as soon as his boat made it to shore and the party had reached the base of the bluffs, the *Adrian* was to unleash a volley into the enemy position, keeping the militia pinned down. After the first volley, the ship's gunners were reluctant to fire upon them. The Greenwich men were so close to the enemy position that they feared dropping some of their balls right on their own militia.

The time had come, and the *Adrian* let fly a full volley. The balls dropped all around the British, and the earth shook. The militia, too, was shaken, but when the smoke cleared, Alexander and his team charged up the bluff. He was yelling in the militia's direction, pointing his sword at them and swinging it toward the British. All it took was for one Greenwich man to stand up and charge, and the rest followed.

With the militiamen's blood-curdling screams and their fearsome, needle-sharp bayonets before them, the concussion-shocked British fell back to a defensive line within the battery stockade. Another group of British continued to rain down fire upon the captain and his team. Several men around Alexander were cut down.

With Nathan constantly reloading two muskets and two pistols, Alexander offered up a steady stream of fire. They were scrambling up the rocky bluff when Alexander spotted a lit cannon, ready to fire down upon them. As he ducked behind the rocks, he screamed for his men to get down. The blast seemed to crack open the very air and shake the entire hill. The rocks around them smoked from the pelting of hot lead. A moment later, Alexander raised himself up, shot a man at the cannon, reached for the second musket, and continued fire as the others scattered.

Looking back, he saw Nathan unscathed, but several others behind him lay across the rocks, covered in blood, their bodies torn open. "Nathan!" Alexander commanded. "Stay where you are!"

Nathan obeyed with reluctance, tossing Alexander a loaded musket and pistol. As Alexander reached the top of the bluff, the few remaining British fell back to the center of the battery. The eight men left were anxiously struggling to reload. As the Greenwich men charged, the British threw down their weapons but not before a few were run through with Greenwich bayonets.

We have done it! We have captured the battery! Alexander thought as he stood in amazement and exhilaration.

Alexander had left further orders that upon his securing the battery, he would signal from the tip of the pinfolds by waving his sword. Alexander's signal would cease any further cannon fire from the *Adrian* and would also tell Fulton that it was safe to send more men to retrieve the wounded. After that, they would gather any British supplies worth salvaging.

With the fighting now stopped and the British prisoners secured, the only sounds were the moans of the wounded and the crackling of a few fires. As Alexander raced back to the tip of the pinfolds to signal the ship, he glanced to his left and noticed an odd sight.

Standing there, peacefully warming himself over one of the fires, with a horse at his side, was a civilian—a dirty, moss-colored man with a bushy beard. Though the man seemed familiar, Alexander paid him no mind; he was anxious to signal his ship.

When he reached the signal site, he drew his sword and with great excitement, pointed to his wounded men and then to Nathan just below him, and yelled, "Men, the battery is ours!"

Alexander was sure that aboard the ship, the crew had their attention focused on the pinfold point. Their guns were primed, with torches raised, awaiting the order to fire. He could imagine them holding their breath in anticipation of the triumphant sword to be raised. When Alexander began waving his sword, it took a moment, but soon he could hear his men aboard the *Adrian* erupt into wild cheering.

It was only at that moment that Alexander realized who the stranger was who warmed himself by the fire. "By God!" Alexander screamed out. "It's the traitor, Threadneedle, from Elizabeth's Point!" He shook his head in disbelief. *But how could he have gotten here before us to warn the British of our plans? I knew he was not to be trusted.*

As he spun around to order Threadneedle's capture, a bevy of cannon fire thundered over the water. He wheeled back and was stunned to see the HMS *Rose* broadside to the *Adrian*, rocking back, with her starboard side covered by smoke. Looking to his right, he saw the twelve-gun volley rip into his ship. Every shot found its target on the unsuspecting *Adrian*. She erupted into smoke and fire, triggering several of her own guns, pointed at the battery, to fire.

Alexander's despair for his ship was short lived. One of the *Adrian*'s rounds erupted in the earth just behind him and sent the helpless captain flying almost fifty feet through the air and dropping him into the East River.

Chapter Twenty-Eight

From his position in the rocks, Nathan had followed this chain of events with the same disbelief as Alexander. When he looked to Alexander to gauge his captain's response at this sudden turn, he was shocked to see the man catapulting through the air. The concussion of the hit, as well as this terrible sight, left Nathan breathless. Although stunned, he followed his friend's flight, expecting to see poor Alexander dashed into pieces.

Nathan's adrenaline took over, and without a thought, he took several quick strides over the rocks and leapt into the water. He reached Alexander within seconds. His friend and captain was floating face down in the water, the flesh on his back exposed by the explosion. Fortunately, Alexander was not far enough out to be caught in the strong current. Even so, Nathan struggled to keep Alexander's head out of the water while dragging him toward shore.

Nathan spotted the longboat and headed straight for it. When he reached the boat, he found the wounded sailor, Martin, still there. Martin was in tears, staring out at the *Adrian* still being pummeled by the *Rose.*

"Help me, Martin!" Nathan screamed. "I have the captain here, and he's hurt."

Martin steadied the longboat and grabbed his captain's shoulder, helping to pull the large, wounded man into the boat.

The captain lay unconscious as Nathan feverishly studied his wounds. There was more left of him than Nathan had expected to find. When Alexander began to cough up water, it gave Nathan hope that his friend would be all right. Suddenly, he turned sick when he saw that Alexander's right arm below the elbow was gone—the wound had been hidden by the torn remnant of Alexander's coat. The cut was clean, as if done by a surgeon, but it represented to Nathan all that had been lost in just the last few minutes.

Nathan grew faint, and something in his mind and soul broke. A great victory had so suddenly turned to disaster. In an instant, his world was shattered. In desperate confusion, he told himself that he had to restore order. But how? What could he do? The only thing to come to his dazed and delirious mind was to find Alexander's arm—to put everything back together. In his confusion, Nathan turned and dove into the water, intending to retrieve the severed arm.

He began to swim down into the murky, turbulent water of the East River. The water offered virtually no visibility, but he began sweeping the water with his hands, desperately trying to locate the missing arm. Soon, he found himself being pulled down and away from the shore into the powerful, choppy current of Hell Gate. His entire body was twisted and turned until he lost all perspective of up or down.

Nathan was running out of breath and began to panic, but then, in the midst of this tumultuous ride, he felt a warm sensation sweep over his body. Surprisingly, his thoughts went back to the sunny summer days in his youth, playing with Alexander in the enormous surf of Block Island, with the large waves crashing down upon them, turning them over and over. The powerful force of each wave would drive him down to the bottom and kept him under. The momentary sense of panic at that time was brief, as every time he would spring to the surface, laughing in exhilaration over the wild ride.

Now, Nathan gave up his panic and enjoyed the wild ride, feeling peacefully assured he would come to the surface. He smiled and began to laugh.

~~~

"Nathan!" Martin screamed after him. "Where in the hell ya going? We got ta git! The captain needs ya! Nathan!"

The sailor lay in the boat with his captain as the sounds from the battle continued. He looked for Nathan to surface, but the black man never came up.

Somehow, he knew he would never see Nathan return. He turned his attention back to the captain's wound, wrapping it with a piece of his torn shirt and applying his belt as a tourniquet to stop the bleeding.

The *Adrian* continued to take round after round from the *Rose*. The ship was engulfed in flames, but a few of the *Adrian*'s crew held their stations and returned fire. Finally, the American ship started to list and to slowly sink.

Martin watched, weeping and anxiously waiting for someone to join them. As things grew quiet, he heard musket fire erupt again within the battery and was certain British reinforcements had now arrived. Martin climbed out of the boat and into the saltwater. The cold water chilled his skin, and the salt burned his wound.

He took the bow rope of the longboat around his shoulder and proceeded to half-swim and half-crawl along the shallow water's edge, heading east, back to the Greenwich whaleboats they had passed earlier. Once out from under the battery, he climbed back aboard and awkwardly paddled east along the coast.

The three Greenwich whaleboats were still anchored there. Martin hoped that some of the militia would have escaped but
~~~

realized they would have already arrived there if that were true. Weakened from loss of blood and physical exertion, Martin had no strength left to transfer Alexander to the whaler. He simply tied the longboat to the stern of one of the whaling boats, climbed aboard, cut the anchor line, and set sail back for Greenwich. As they slowly sailed east, Martin could hear the captain call out for Nathan.

Martin strained under the pain of his wound to single-handedly sail the whaleboat. He finally called back to his captain, "He swum off, Captain. Black Nathan's gone."

Chapter Twenty-Nine

When Alexander finally awoke several days later, he was soaked in the sweat of a broken fever. His body was trembling—it had been the trembling, combined with the noise around him that brought him back to consciousness. His mind was swimming as he struggled to make clear his situation.

The room was very dark, and he was lying in a bed. There were candles and lamps burning. He heard whispered voices and started to make out a shadowy group of people gathered to his left. *I must be home in my bed with my family*, he thought.

When his eyes began to clear, he realized that the group all had their backs to him and seemed huddled together over something. They appeared to be struggling with something they were working on.

Alexander heard muffled cries, which grew louder and more panicked. As he looked over, his eyes came into clearer focus, and he saw James Martin's face. The sailor's eyes were bulging open and a hand was covering his mouth. The sight of the young sailor brought forth a foggy memory, and he thought, *Yes, I ordered the injured Martin to stay in the boat. But what for?*

Alexander thought he heard the name Molly spoken, and he called out, "Molly Mum, what is going on here?"

A woman broke from the group and came over to him. "Goodness, you are awake, sir."

The woman was certainly not his housekeeper. In his hazy state, the woman looked much like Rebekah Beach. "Rebekah?" Alexander asked. "Is that you? Where am I?"

"I'm sorry," the woman replied in a kind voice, "but I'm neither Molly nor Rebekah, although I can understand your confusion. My name is Holly. You are at the Bush family farm. Earlier this morning, some fishermen found you and this gentlemen in two boats tied together. They saw your wounds and brought you up the Mianus River to our house in Coe's Cóbh. We've done our best to nurse you two with compresses of oils and herbs. We've cleaned your wounds and changed your dressings, but it became obvious that a surgeon was required. The surgeon just arrived, and he is doing surgery on your friend to save his life."

Alexander struggled to comprehend. "Surgery?"

The woman dabbed his forehead with a wet cloth. "Yes, the poor young man's leg had turned green all the way up to his hip. Unfortunately, the rum has not proven to be very effective, and he has suffered through the operation."

Alexander's mind began to clear, and he now understood that they were in the process of sawing off Martin's limb. His heart began to pound, and he struggled with the confusion in his mind. What had happened? Why were things so terribly wrong?

The woman caressed the side of his head, and when he looked up, he saw his Rebekah. Alexander passed out as his mind went back to the last time they were together…

~~~

On a shiny late-July day, Alexander strapped the afternoon meal Rebekah had packed onto his young stallion, Nimbau.
~~~

The two then rode north up the center cart path, toward the east beach, past the Great Pond, with Fort Island on their left, across the Indian Head Neck, and through what had been the Thomas Terry property. He couldn't help but recall the stories of the infamous island settler.

In Terry's short residence on the island, he was known for his great self-possession, shrewdness, and daring, unexcelled by the bravest. He was one of the six men who built the barque in Braintree, Massachusetts, and sailed it down to Taunton to pick up the other settlers and their cattle, to sail on to Block Island in 1661. He represented Block Island in the Rhode Island General Assembly and was intimately associated with Roger Williams, John Clark, and other distinguished persons of his day.

In early days, when the Indians outnumbered the settlers twenty to one, Terry learned the Indian tongue and bravely managed the relationship with the Manissean tribe, even assimilating into their culture. His tactics were considered by some to be heavy handed but unquestionably provided security and safety to the pioneers. There were famous stories of his intervention when traders supplied the Indians with large quantities of rum and were ready for mischief. While the other islanders gathered in the Sands's stone garrison for safety, Terry confronted them and turned away their wrath.

The most famous story was of Terry's leading the sixteen men and a boy to face a challenge from the Manissean Indians. From the small Fort Island in the waters just south of the Great Pond and not far from Terry's home, he returned the Indians' threats with a challenge to fight. As a man by the name of Joseph Kent nervously beat his drum, the Manisseans gathered to meet the challenge. However, the sound of the drum so terrified the Indians that they refused to fight. It was then that many of the Indians chose to leave the island, and relations began to improve.

When Alexander and Rebekah reached Corn Neck Road, Alexander playfully spurred his stallion to a fast gallop, causing Rebekah to competitively spur her mare, Swan, to join the race. They rode through the glorious sun and breeze until Alexander reared Nimbau to a sudden stop. He stood up in his saddle to survey the eastern horizon over the blue ocean. A speck of sail from a ship had caught his attention.

"Alexander, please," Rebekah called to him. "I don't want to lose a minute of this glorious day together on our Eden. Please ride with me."

Alexander turned his attention to Rebekah. After stealing a quick look back at the ship, he called, "Oh, I'm sorry, my dear. The last I saw, you were determined to humble me in a horse race. I was only allowing you a head start as an advantage." He spurred Nimbau on to catch up with her, and together they put their horses to a leisurely walk along Corn Neck Road. The road ran north from the Pier Harbor along the island neck and on to the northernmost tip of the island. At the end of the trail lay Sandy Point. Just off the point was a hummock leading out to a small island. The island was accessible only by foot at low tide.

The island crag was a small spot with rocks, brush of beach rose and blueberry, a patch of bluestem, and bushy rockrose grasses. Each year, under the constant push and pull of the rip-tide, the small island grew even smaller. Many of the islanders believed that all it would take was one great storm to make the spot a mere memory.

Along the Corn Neck, at the narrowest part of the island, where the elevation was only a few feet above sea level, they could see across three bodies of water. Alexander again stopped and stood in his stirrups to survey the ocean to the east and then over to the Great Pond and onto the waters of Long Island that lay to the west.

As they passed the pond, he spotted Richard and Edward Jess, along with their bondservants, clamming in the mud in the shallow waters of the pond. He waved, and they stopped to wave back.

Alexander looked at the thick bushes of beach plum mixed with various tall beach grasses. Beyond lay beach grass and bluestem-covered sand dunes. Between the dunes, he could see some of the beach. The dunes and the half-moon stretch of beach had always been his favorite place to play. The long green reeds waved to him, as if the dunes themselves remembered their good times together.

Farther along the trail, Rebekah suddenly kicked her heels and bolted down a small path that led east to the cliffs of Clay Head. The two rode through a small grouping of sycamore maple trees. Alexander spotted the holes in the trees where he had explored island nesting birds. They continued to gallop through a meadow of black-eyed Susan, Queen Anne's lace, daisy, and butter-and-eggs.

The lovers stopped for a moment to take in the view across the milkweed swamp to the Atlantic Ocean and south to the pier at Harbor Bay. Clay Head swamp was Alexander's "secret" fishing place. It was one of the few places he could catch brown bullheads and golden shiners on the island.

Alexander and Rebekah's ears perked up at the call of the yellow warbler. They looked at each other and smiled. Rebekah mimicked the call, saying, "Sweet, sweet, sweet—I'm so sweet."

"Yes," Alexander replied, "the bird sings the truth. However, the lady is not so sweet when competing in a horse race!" With that, he yelled "Yah!" and Nimbau was off.

They raced along the edge of the tallest section of Clay Head, with the rocky beach below and the ocean to their right. The pounding of the horses' hooves shook the homes of the bank swallows as the two rode past. The vibrations sent the birds streaming out of their nests that were cut into the face of the bluffs. It looked as if a string of muskets were being fired in a row just below the riders.

They turned in sync back east, past Little Chagum Pond, perilously close to the bluff's edge. Several great herons flapped their wings and flew off with the sudden disruption to their solitude.

Turning back on to the Corn Neck Road, they continued to race north. Rebekah and Alexander arrived at the northernmost stretch of beach that curved to a sandy point and led out to their little island sanctuary. The tide was now at its lowest, so there would be no problem coaxing their horses across the exposed rocky path to their private plot.

The little cove on the ocean side of the trail was known as Cow Cove. It was there that Thomas Terry and the other fifteen men, including five indentured Scotsmen, arrived on a large barque with their cows and livestock. At that spot, there was only some one hundred feet separating the ocean from Chagum Pond. The pond was the largest freshwater pond on the island and had been named after the Indian, Samuel Chagum, who ran away from his master by stealing a canoe but was then caught on the mainland and returned to the island.

Alexander took the opportunity to fill their flasks with drinking water from the pond, and he and Rebekah cooled their hands and faces with its clean, clear refreshment.

The two riders continued along the rocky beach and out across the narrow hummock to the small island. Soon, they had their horses' saddles off, their blankets spread, and a picnic laid out. Both settled in and lay with their backs against their saddles. They began one of their long conversations, which could often last hours—provided they did not touch upon certain subjects.

Under the shade, Rebekah breathed a content sigh as if the day could not be made any more perfect than this. "Alexander," she whispered, "do you think we might take this spot for our home one day?"

Alexander took her hand. "This is indeed perfect, but I will bring you out on another day and another season, and let you decide then."

She made a playful pout. "Alexander David Hawkins, let me have my fantasy for today! We shall build a beautiful home, like my father's house, and have ten children. With a few slaves, it would be a simple but bountiful life."

He did not want to spoil the moment, but he could not help himself. "I shall let you have your fantasy—for today. Yet as I recall, we used to make our way out here with the other children in the summer evenings. We would look for the ghostly lights from the *Palatine* wreck of '49. Finally, one evening, when they did appear, you were the one who disappeared, only to be found later hiding under your bed. It was years before you would venture out here again."

Rebekah did not like to speak of the *Palatine* lights or of the other ships wrecked on the hummock. The *Palatine* was known to be a ghost ship, still seen on occasion by islanders and sailors, burning over the waters of Block Island Sound where several ships were sunk. The idea of a ghost ship scared Rebekah. Alexander always felt as if there was a strange silence and change of subject from the islanders any time the *Palatine* ship was brought up.

Alexander changed the subject. "More important, I will not suggest that to put your father's house on this land would mean that half of it would be in the ocean. Nor would I suggest that the world is changing around us, and we might not have the luxuries we have today. But let us pretend where we lay is our bedroom, and this is the glorious view to which we would awaken every day."

She chose to ignore Alexander's pragmatism and only listened to the part she wanted to hear. "Yes, it is brilliant! We could have a large fireplace over there, and big, bright windows all around. At some point, I'm sure I'll have Mother's china and silver, and our Negroes shall bring us some fine Indian tea and biscuits in the morning."

Alexander's love for Rebekah had grown beyond what he ever could have imagined. However, more recently he was beginning to realize that he was feeling unsettled about Rebekah's reliance on slaves and her acceptance of slavery itself.

Chapter Thirty

When Alexander awoke the following day, the sun was streaming through the window. His head pounded, and he barely felt the strength to move. He looked over at Martin and found him sitting up, awake and deliriously smiling.

Holly, the woman who had spoken to Alexander the day before, entered the room looking drawn and somber. "Captain Hawkins," she said in a weary voice, "it is good to see you are awake again. I've brought you some water."

Alexander realized only then how dry his mouth was. His tongue was swollen and seemed to fill his mouth. "Yes," he answered eagerly. "Water…please." He struggled to sit up to take a drink but fell back on the bed. He was weak, true, but something else was wrong. Something stopped him from sitting up properly.

Holly propped up his head and slowly poured water into his mouth. He eagerly drank the whole cup. When he'd finished, he looked over at Martin. "Miss? How is Martin doing?"

She answered hesitantly, "Martin's surgery was…very difficult for him…and quite traumatic for the family that assisted.

He seems alert, but his mind is not right. He does not seem to know where he is."

The woman gingerly lifted up the corner of Alexander's blanket and continued, "Your arm wound, Captain, is relatively clean, so the surgeon decided against surgery. He will return in a few days to assess your condition."

Alexander's heart began to race, and he felt faint again. "My…arm? What of my arm?" The blankets were tucked around him, with his arms underneath, and he hadn't had the strength to lift them. He thought, though, that he could feel the fingers on both hands move as he tried to test them.

The woman did not answer his question; she simply said, "You should rest now, Captain. You have had a very difficult time and will need to regain your strength."

Alexander had lost all recollection of the recent traumatic events and struggled to recall what had occurred that left him in this condition. He wasn't sure that he wanted to hear the truth, yet he felt compelled to ask. Clearing his throat, his voice cracked as he called to Martin, "Sailor, can you report to me what transpired that has left us in such a state?"

The young sailor slowly rocked his head, rolled his eyes, and started to whistle.

Alexander repeated his question, but the young man only shook his head back and forth. The captain didn't have the strength to push farther, so he lay still.

Then, quite suddenly, Martin began to talk in a singsong way. "We won! We won! We had da buggers on da run! But we dint see da damn Rose's infernal gun! She's black at the bottom, never ta see da rays of anudder sun!"

Alexander's heart pounded, and every wound began to ache. A huge knot formed in his throat. Tears streamed down his face as the events of the fateful evening came flooding back. Certainly there had been a mission, but he couldn't remember what the mission was about. He choked out the next inevitable question. "What of all the men and the mission?"

Martin didn't answer straightaway. He only rocked back and forth until he formed the words. "All dead or in chain! All dead or in chain! They'll never see free mates again! Nothin' delivered before dey was slain."

Finally, Nathan's name crept into Alexander's mind, and he forced himself to ask the question, "What of our quartermaster, Nathan?"

This time, the young sailor quickly returned, "Off he swum! Off he swum! Savin' da cap'n, but leavin' me scared and dumb! So raise da sail an' home we come!"

Alexander lay back and shook his head in despair. He supposed that Martin's words might simply be the rantings of a madman—but what if there was truth in his words? Had it all been a devastating failure? He didn't have the strength to consider it.

The shame he felt at that moment was unbearable. To be a naval captain, alive, and to have lost every ship and—by the looks of Martin—every man under his command, was unthinkable. His thoughts then turned to the islanders who were lost. Their poor families could now only guess at what terrible disaster had consumed their husbands, fathers, and sons.

Alexander shuddered at the thought of confronting his neighbors' despair. He thought of Molly Mum and the promise he had made to protect her son, and he was crushed by the hopelessness he felt at that moment. All he wanted now was a weapon and the strength to take his own life. The darkness penetrated his being down into his bones. *What is there to live for?* he asked himself in agony.

And then a vision of Rebekah came into his mind, he felt faint and then drifted off back to the memories of the last day they had spent together.

Chapter Thirty-One

Alexander's thoughts returned to that last July day he was together with Rebekah. The two lay across the blanket on the small island at the end of the hummock, the northernmost tip of the island. He leaned over and kissed her; she looked in his eyes and kissed him back.

"My dear 'Rebekah-at-the-well', how undeserving of your love am I. I love the thought of living in your fantasy and even more so in your reality. Whatever our state, I shall always be yours."

Rebekah again lifted his chin and kissed him, running her fingers through his hair. "Our world is so perfect. I pray it may never end. Let us hold each other and close our eyes to see us, when married, enjoying our splendor."

"My splendor is simply to be with you through it all," he said. "I know my time at sea and the inevitable war may prolong the day of our dreams, but even when separated, I will hold you like this in my heart."

She immediately pulled away and stared out to sea. "Alexander, I have shared my feelings with you on this before, and you fail to comprehend, so I will speak more plainly. I cannot bear the thought of being alone, month after month, while you are away at sea. Why can't you be content with that which your farm and this island hold for you? And why do you choose the sea over the one whose heart claims your allegiance?"

Alexander was stunned. He had shared his thoughts and aspirations with Rebekah since he was a boy. His heart's desire was to captain ships and perhaps to play a part in the creation of a Continental Navy. Now, he was awaiting the arrival of the large merchantman ship where he would serve as a senior officer. Alexander could not miss this opportunity. It had always been evident that a navy career did not please her, but he had thought she had accepted his desires. It was part of the world to which, he assumed, she was willing to render herself. These were his plans for his whole life. Now the time was at hand. She evidently could not hold back her true feelings any longer.

After a long silence, he said, "My Rebekah, it will be a matter of days, maybe hours, when the ship will anchor to take us aboard. I know your heart now speaks to try to hold time still, but a man must labor in his own passion, and to share that with his perfect helpmate is his ultimate glory. My desires have been set from the beginning. My father has recognized that I must test myself with the sea and has given his blessing. Yet he still harbors hope that I will one day return to our island farm life."

She turned away coldly and remained silent.

"Rebekah, I would not be the man you love if I did not go."

She stood, her back still turned toward him, and began weeping into her hands. "I don't understand any of it! How can you leave me and our perfect world?"

He stood up behind her and wrapped his arms around her. "Our love should stand forever, but this world is changing. I do this thing to make sure we can control our destiny in a world free of a tyranny that would take away that which is rightfully ours."

She struggled to free herself from him and cried out words that had been begging to be released for a long time. "I don't care about any of that! I just want our perfect life to go on uninterrupted. On this island, we can be as independent and as free as we want to be. There is no reason to ever leave." He finally released her, and she turned to face him. "If you leave me now, I'm afraid my love will dissipate with every league of the sea you put between us."

He grabbed her again and pulled her to him. As she wept, he held onto her as if he might physically stop their hopes and dreams from sifting away. Her voice had something in it that said she would not relent. She was giving him no other choice but to give in. Though he wanted to say whatever she wanted to hear to make everything right, he could not. The relationship he wanted could never be built upon the demands of one and sacrificing the dreams of the other. It came to his mind that they stood at the pivotal point of whatever life they might have together.

Just like the sea was eroding the little island oasis they stood upon, a powerful force was grating away at the foundation of their relationship.

Rebekah sobbed and shook her head. Alexander stared to the east through teary eyes, past the wisps of her dark hair whipping in the breeze. From a cloud of dust, a rider came charging up the point and caught Alexander's attention. Right away, he could tell it was Nathan, and he groaned to himself.

Rebekah did not care for his relationship with the black slave, and like most other island slave owners, she did not understand the relative freedom the Hawkins family afforded their slaves. She believed her own family cared a great deal for their slaves, but they certainly would not treat them as brother and sister, nor son and daughter. Her resentment of Nathan had grown over the years. The more like family the Hawkinses treated their slaves, the more the other islanders were made to feel that they were doing something wrong. She didn't like the way it made her feel, and she could see what kind of trouble it caused her family and the other owners. Rebekah suspected that Alexander's choosing the sea had something to do with Nathan, and now, Nathan's presence upset her even more.

Nathan pulled his steed to a dramatic stop at the other side of the hummock, sending sand and rock flying into the air. He stood tall in his stirrups and excitedly shouted across to Alexander, "She's here! She's here! The *Sea Mistress* is 'breast to the wind! Alexander, you must hurry. She won't stay at anchor for long."

Upon hearing the name of the ship, Rebekah pulled away and threw herself on the ground. Alexander gestured to Nathan, indicating that his friend should be quiet and wait. Alexander then knelt down and pleaded with Rebekah to understand. He begged for her to come with him so he could take her home, but she refused.

She cried out, "Go! Go be with your Negro and your mistress, the sea, but I shan't wait for your return!"

The hatred in her voice for those things he loved sent a chill down his spine. He'd never heard this venom from the woman he loved. Certainly, he had known for some time that his love of the sea and his friendship with Nathan were things Rebekah struggled to accept. He could not fault her for not wanting him to leave her for months at a time, nor could he fault her for holding the same attitudes toward slaves that most others held. His understanding of her feelings, however, made her words no less hurtful.

They were words born of love and desperation. This was her last chance to dissuade Alexander from his plans. *She must certainly know that no matter what she does or says, I will not be moved from this course.* Still, her pain appeared so great that she would not simply see him off and wish him a fond farewell. Perhaps, at that moment, she only wanted him to feel some of the heartbreaking pain she now felt.

"You will be constantly in my mind and my heart," he told her, his voice cracking with emotion. "I'll love you forever, and my greatest hope will be to return to find your waiting arms stretched out from the shores of our Block Island."

Nothing more could be said or done. She refused to speak or to listen, so he departed, feeling a hurt that conjured up an old but familiar feeling. As Nimbau gingerly stepped across the path from the little island oasis, Alexander had a vision: A woman—he assumed she was Rebekah—was in the ocean, slowly sinking. She waved to him before disappearing under turbulent sea. There was no anger in her face, only the look of a loving farewell. This was exactly the look he had hoped for as a fond parting. It comforted him, in spite of its being a confirmation that they might never be together again.

Alexander rode across the rocky hummock as the tide was just beginning to cover the path to the small island. When he met Nathan, he pulled his hat over his eyes and kept his head down. "Nathan, ride ahead and fetch Rebekah's brother, Benjamin, to bring her home," he instructed. "I'll follow shortly. I have something to do."

"Alexander," Nathan said, "Rebekah might not be the one for you. She's got some different notions. If it is meant to be, she'll be waiting for you. You best hurry on."

"I'll be along shortly," he responded, even as he stared back at his Rebekah, still lying face down on the grassy patch.

Nathan rode off, and a few moments of worry convinced Alexander that there really was nothing else he could do. He dejectedly turned to follow Nathan to the harbor. He wondered how long this pain would last, though even then, he was certain of its permanence.

As he rode south along the Corn Neck Road, he stopped at Minister's Lot on the east side of the neck. Riding east through a pasture of long grasses and milkweed, he reached the plot's highest point. From there, he looked over the short bluff to see the *Island Mistress* anchored off the island.

The early settlers dedicated this parcel as land consecrated for God's use. It was an offering to give back to God a portion of what God had provided to them. Though no pastor or parson had yet fully accepted a call to tend the Block Island "flock," the islanders left the plot untouched until that time would come.

He dismounted Nimbau and, on this consecrated ground, he asked God for wisdom—wisdom to know whether the path he was now choosing was the right one. Then he asked for the strength and courage to face the results of his choice. Alexander offered up his love for Rebekah as a sacrifice to God's divine will, hoping that the sweet incense of his sacrifice would circle back to embrace him again one day.

Chapter Thirty-Two

It was now several days after Alexander had first been brought to the Bush house in Coe's Cóbh. He awoke—at least he believed he was awake—with a head that was cloudy from the pain pulsing through his whole body. He shook his head and strained to focus. There was a woman standing over him who seemed to be speaking to him. Yes, her voice was sweet and familiar, and she was repeating something. Caty Littlefield. She was saying "Caty Littlefield." *Why does she say that?* He shook his head, acknowledging he didn't understand.

The woman spoke louder and more insistently, "Alexander. Captain Alexander Hawkins. It is Caty Littlefield Greene here. Can you hear me? Divine providence has brought me to your side. Do you understand me?"

Alexander's mind began to break through the cloud. Yes. He understood. Could it be true? Caty Littlefield? She looked familiar but was not the image of the little girl that was burned into his memory—the glossy black hair, brilliant violet eyes, clear-cut features, and transparent complexion. Yet the lovely girl now was a beautiful grown woman. He tried to speak, but his throat felt coarse and dry. As Alexander began to get his bearings he looked over to see that Martin was gone. "Where's...seaman...Martin?" he croaked.

Caty replied, "Alexander, I know nothing of a Seaman Martin. I only just arrived."

Alexander strained to make sense of his surroundings. The sudden appearance of an old friend only added to the nightmarish quality of his reality. "How did ... you come to be here? Is this really Caty...or an angel?"

Caty smiled. "An angel? My loving husband may refer to me as such, but angelic has rarely been used to describe this island lady."

"But how is it...? What are...you doing here?"

Caty put one hand on his shoulder and stroked his forehead with the other. "Captain Hawkins, you must rest. I was on my way back to Manhattan Island to be with Nathanael. He returned me to Coventry weeks ago. The general was insistent that I not come back to Manhattan, but I cannot bear to be apart from him. I am traveling by carriage, accompanied by a driver. The trip through Connecticut has been tedious, requiring two long days." She shook her head in disappointment. "Now my driver refuses to go on. While stopping at a nearby lodge, I heard of a navy captain who was badly wounded. I came to provide assistance and realized my worst fears." Caty choked up, "I found my dear friend so badly wounded." She began to cry.

Alexander gathered himself, trying to be strong. "I do not know what will become of me, but you must return to your lovely home on the banks of the Pawtuxet. I fear things are not well for our troops. Manhattan is not the place for the general's wife."

"Alexander, I must be with Nathanael. I can't go back to Rhode Island. I won't!"

Alexander's pain and disappointment spilled out into anger, "Go! I am dying, as is this revolution. Leave your husband to fight. We no longer play a child's game, Catherine. Spare yourself and your son. You have no choice. Go! If you want to aid your husband, go back to Coventry and pray for him." He turned his face away from her to end their conversation.

Caty stepped back from the force of his words, trembling, with a look of shock on her face. "Alexander Hawkins, I refuse to believe any of that to be true, as I am certain you do not believe it either!" She clutched at her chest and then dabbed her forehead with a handkerchief. "I will return to Coventry, and I will pray for General Greene, and I will pray for you. And you, sir, will *not* give up." She looked away for a moment as something out the window caught her attention. "The doctor has just arrived. I am certain he will mend you back to health," she informed him. When he did not respond, she said resignedly, "I will follow your orders and return to my home, Captain. I will also speak with the physician to implore him to do all he can for you. You will *not* leave us." Then her voice softened as she said, "We shall see each other again, my good friend. I will send word to your family on Block Island so they may make arrangements to bring you home."

She kissed him on his temple. When he still did not respond, she quietly left the room.

Chapter Thirty-Three

The woman named Holly entered. Alexander asked again, "Where has Seaman Martin been taken?"

She shook her head and said only, "The doctor will be right in to speak with you," before quickly exiting.

Alexander didn't bring it up again, for in his heart, he knew Martin's fate. Still in great pain and with a cloudy mind, he prayed that the doctor either would bring him great relief or would deal a final blow to end his misery.

The doctor entered the room with a somber look. He pulled a stool up close to the bed, and Alexander thought that with the doctor's long gray hair and spectacles, he looked much like the patriot Benjamin Franklin. This further confused Alexander—he knew that Caty's family was close to the great American.

Alexander had met Mr. Franklin on one occasion when he had come out to Block Island to visit the Ray and Littlefield families. Franklin was an intimate friend with Caty's aunt Catherine, and he had a particular fancy for the island's cheese and dairy delights. He was a man who left a lasting impression for his warmth and charm, as well as for his brilliant mind.

When the doctor leaned over to speak softly to his patient, Alexander said, "Doctor Franklin?"

The doctor chuckled. "No, I'm sorry, Captain. I'm not your friend Benjamin, although this is not the first time someone has suggested I look something like the Philadelphian. I can only hope, for your sake, that I'm as successful and as effective in my treatment of you as with everything that man puts his mind to."

Anxious to confirm what he had gleaned from Martin's ramblings, Alexander asked, "Do you know what has become of my men and my ships?"

The doctor shook his head and offered, "Captain, the Bush family has sought information and, unfortunately, has found very little. Word was that there was a battle in the East River in the late evening, several nights ago. Some have described what they heard, but there seems to be no eyewitnesses. Unfortunately, the British still occupy Long Island, and it sounds as though they are about to drive Washington off New York Island. The people in Westchester are scattering. We here in Greenwich are preparing to do the same, and a whole contingent of our militia has suddenly disappeared, feared to have abandoned their post."

Alexander could not speak; the darkness sank even deeper into his soul.

The doctor drew back the blankets and lifted what was left of Alexander's arm. For the first time, Alexander saw the damage. Adrenaline rushed through him, and his breathing came quick as the air seemed to recede from the room. He nearly passed out from the shock. Struggling to control his panicked breathing, he felt sweat beading on his brow and heard his heart beating in his ears. As the doctor removed the bandage from the end of Alexander's right forearm, he grimaced in pain.

"I'm sorry, Captain," the doctor said. "I thought you already knew. Take heart; you are doing well, and I do not see much indication of infection." The surgeon pulled the lamp over to take a closer look at the wound, sniffing. "No, there is no odor of gangrene," he confirmed, "although I do see some discoloration around the wound. Captain, I'm feeling quite confident you will survive your wounds, but I must remove that which is below the top of your elbow. This should not hinder you any more than your current wounds, but it will likely assure that your life will be saved."

Alexander looked away. "Then I will take my chances as I am, Doctor. Leave me be. If it is God's will that I survive, then I will survive. If not, I pray that God just take me home."

The doctor stood up and with the authority of a strict schoolmaster dressing down his young student, he boomed, "I'll hear none of that! Navy captain or not, the good Lord has given me certain talents and has arranged for me to be here to heal, if it is his will. You may think you are the sorriest salt on the face of this earth, but without even knowing you, I can assure you that you have much to live for."

Alexander groaned and kept looking away, not able to think of what there could possibly be to live for.

"You, sir, may not be able to see beyond the pain and darkness that hangs over you at this very moment," the doctor continued, "but this Revolution will need every man. Even if we are so fortunate as to prevail and gain our precious freedom, that will only be the point at which the real work will begin. This country will need good men, right arms or not."

Alexander did not have the strength to argue with the doctor, so he simply nodded in agreement.

"Very well," the doctor said. "Let us get started." He grabbed a brown jug and a wooden tankard from the nightstand and began to pour. "This will be difficult at first, but I need you to drink as much as possible of this medicinal brew." He raised Alexander's head and brought the tankard to his lips. That was the last thing Alexander remembered for several more days.

~~~
~~~

Word of Alexander Hawkins's stay in Coe's Cóbh made its way to Philadelphia, and during Esek Hopkins's return to Providence, the commodore stopped to talk with him. When the navy leader asked for an account, Alexander maintained the story that he had originally devised. British sympathizers had stolen the *Adrian*. He and his crew chased them down in the schooner and caught up with the ship in the East River. During the course of the battle that ensued, which included the British battery at the pinfolds, both ships were sunk and all the men were lost.

Though Hopkins tried to console him, it was impossible. The only hope for any kind of a life for Alexander was to go back to the place he loved most—back to the lush green jewel set in the crown of a deep blue sea, back to the soil that touched his senses and aroused his spirit like no other. He also clung to the hope that he would soon hear that the effort of his heroic men had sparked Washington and his troops on to victory.

~~~

Alexander recognized immediately the three male Hawkins slaves—Stepney, Cujo, and Bolico—when they arrived at the Bush home in Coe's Cóbh to retrieve him. When he saw the looks of fear and sadness on their faces, he could not utter a word. He was weak and his mind was blurred. The silent trip back by wagon and then ferried to Block Island by coastal packet was excruciating. He held on to the small hope that his reaching the island would make things all better, but the pain, the failure of his mission, and the darkness were all still too real. When he saw the condition of his island farm home and his father's own delirium, his darkness became complete.
~~~

Chapter Thirty-Four

November 1776

Stepney sat in the kitchen, leaning over the table, exhausted. The fire in the big open hearth burned brightly and cast large dancing shadows across the room. Molly wept softly as she added another black pot to the others hanging over the cooking fire. Stepney was cold and wet, but he simply did not have the strength to move closer to the fire to warm himself. He tried to offer consolation. "Molly, everyt'in's goin' to be all right. You can cry but not for too long. Master Hawkins is at peace, an' we have our Alexander. We's goin' to be all right. You'll see."

Molly only cried more loudly and spoke through her tears, "All right? Stepney, what does you see dat I don't? We just buried Master Joseph, an' Alizander is like a livin' dead man. We don't know what's become of our Nat'an. De only words Alizander says is dat we slaves is free to go. We ain't no family no more. What is we goin' to do? Where is we goin' to go?"

Stepney had the same questions and concerns. How could he convince her otherwise? He wanted to cry himself, but he was just too tired. He tried to muster the energy to be strong for her and prayed silently, *Good Lord, help us.*

The trip to and from Coe's Cóbh to retrieve Alexander had been extremely difficult. The three male Hawkins slaves were horrified to find Alexander shattered and despondent. Stepney had also expected to find some word on Nathan, but Alexander would not talk with them. On their return, there was hardly a word spoken among the four men.

Now, Stepney actually felt some relief. To him, Master Hawkins's death seemed something of a blessing. He just couldn't stand to watch his master decline any more. The condition of Joseph's health and mind had been getting steadily worse, and when they arrived back on Block Island, just the sight of Alexander's broken body ended his father's will to live. He locked himself in his study and refused to eat. Within a week, Joseph was dead, and Stepney was graveside, burying Joseph next to the grave of his wife, Elizabeth.

The graves sat high up on the southeast corner of the farm, near the highest point but below the crest of the island hollow, not far from their neighbor and at one time the island's only doctor, John Rodman. From the gravesite, Stepney could see the once-manicured and sizable salt box Hawkin's farmhouse, with the sound of the majestic surf crashing on the beach, rumbling from the other side of the crest.

All the islanders came to Joseph's graveside ceremony. Alexander could not attend under his own strength and was carried there in a large wooden chair. Stepney looked around at the mourners and realized that Joseph's death marked the end of a way of life on the island. Joseph Hawkins's estate was perhaps the last of the once prominent island homesteads.

The overwhelming sadness of his master's death took Stepney back to the day of Elizabeth's burial over twenty-five years earlier. He'd thought that was the saddest day he'd ever seen, but now, this seemed worse. For many at the service, their grief went well beyond the loss of Joseph Hawkins and a way of life. Only weeks earlier, two local sailing vessels mysteriously disappeared, and it was reported that a number of islanders were part of the crew. Many families were shattered and grieving, perhaps even more so because they were unable to learn anything about the disappearance of the islanders. Many of the surviving families had now given up hope of ever seeing them again. As they all gathered at the first funeral service held after the disappearance, the reality of their losses hit home, and their grief spilled out. Alexander, despondent and weak, sat in a chair, showing no emotion.

As a late autumn rain turned to near freezing, the cold, dark day heightened Stepney's sour state of mind. He kept looking to Alexander to rise up, to provide strength and encouragement to the other islanders in this time of trouble, but the young man never made a move or tried to speak. Others looking to him for a word—any word—that might provide some ray of hope to break through their darkness; answers that might make sense of the series of tragedies the community had weathered. But there was nothing. Alexander sat in silence, with crushed body and spirit—and it spoke volumes about how their world was unraveling.

In the kitchen, Stepney now struggled to take off his wet coat. Molly grabbed a blanket warmed by the fire and draped it over her husband's shoulders.

Stepney let out a loud sigh. "Molly, dat feels fine. Oh, good Lord, dat's what we needs is warm island sunshine, an' we all be feelin' better. You'll see, Molly, our Alexander will be feelin' better soon."

The heavy black woman turned angry and threw a spoon she was using to the floor. "Dat ain't Alizander. I don't know who dat is, but dat ain't our Alizander. He can't even tell us where our Nat'an is at. If Alizander is alive, lookin' like dat, den I fear our boy must be dead."

"Molly," Stepney said, trying to reassure, "calm yourself. Just give him some time."

Molly only became angrier. "Time? Give him time? Our Nathan could be out dere somewhere, hurt or dyin', an' we may never see him again. Alizander knows what's happened to our boy. Does I have to shake it out of him?"

Stepney struggled for something to say to give her peace about Nathan. The fact was that he had already come to grips with Alexander's shattered state and silence as clear indication that Nathan was gone. He knew it from the moment he first saw Alexander in Coe's Cóbh. On the long trek back to Block Island, he silently wrestled with his Almighty, begging for his son's life. By the time he arrived on Block Island, he prepared himself to accept whatever God had planned for his son. He didn't know when, but he was assured he would know what happened to Nathan one day.

Stepney was not prepared, however, to steal a mother's hope that her son might still be alive. Yet he could think of nothing to say to comfort her when in his heart he knew Nathan was gone. He stood up from the table and went over to Molly, putting his hands on her shoulders. "Molly, we knows dat God gave us two special gifts—first Alexander an' den Nat'an. We knows he has somet'in' special to do wid dem. Nat'an done promise Master Joseph he would protect Alexander, an' we have him back. I's sure Nat'an done somet'in' to save his life."

Molly shook as she cried. "Alizander promised me dat he would protect Nat'an. What about his promise? I want my boy back. I want both back." She paused, and shaking her head, then added, "What's de use in it all? Dis family has all come undone. It's all come undone, an' dis island got not'in' more for us."

Stepney felt the same desperate resignation, but he chose to cast it aside. "Alexander just made us freepersons, but we is stayin'. I talked wid Cujo an' Cuff. We's all stayin' an' goin' to manage de farm. Not'in' else is goin' to change. Molly Mum, dis war is just startin'. Dis is only de beginnin'. We is all goin' to face a lot more, so we gots to decide to face whatever it is. Alexander is back an' we pray he gets better, but one good t'ing—we know's he's done fightin', an' we'll have him here. As for Nat'an, we know de good Lord gots a hold of his life. We don't know what's happened to him, so why t'ink it's somet'in' bad until we know? We got a roof an' food, an' we'll be all right. We'll find our boy."

Cujo entered the kitchen and silently sat down at the table, holding an envelope in his hand.

"What ya got dere, Cujo?" Stepney asked.

"Captain Spats delivered dis," Cujo answered. "It's for Alexander from a Captain Geste. I tried to give it to Alexander, but he took one look at who it was from, an' his eyes got angry. He just t'rew it to de floor. What do we do wid it?"

Molly got excited and grabbed the envelope. "Dis might have word of Nat'an. We gots to open it."

"Hold on, Molly," Stepney was quick to say. "You don't know what's in dere. We can't go openin' de master's mail."

Molly ripped open the envelope. "Do you forget dat we's freepersons? If we're goin' to manage dis farm 'til Alexander is better, den we got to do what we got to do." She handed the letter back to Cujo and demanded, "Now you read dis out loud."

Cujo took the letter out and pulled the candle closer. He looked up to Stepney to confirm it was all right to read it. When Stepney reluctantly nodded, he began:

Dear Captain Hawkins,

It is with deep sorrow and great disappointment that I write this letter. I know it was my pleading that set you on this disastrous mission, suffering a total loss. It causes me profound regret and brokenhearted sorrow.

I only know what I have heard from Cmdr. Hopkins, and it was clear you have maintained the secrecy of your mission. This war, for the time being, will tax every moment of my life. Washington is on the run, and our young revolution is close to collapse.

Following our defeat on Long Island, we were forced to abandon lower New York Island. The militia was able to briefly keep the British at bay at Harlem Heights, but

Washington was again forced to retreat off New York Island to White Plains. Once more, reports told of a ragtag, beleaguered army beaten badly at White Plains, only to narrowly escape over to New Jersey. I don't know what keeps these men fighting when facing so awesome a foe, but I continue to pray for a miracle.

My solemn oath to you is that, God willing and in his time, I will uncover the truth to what happened to you and your men.

I must now set sail on a mission to collect desperately needed gunpowder for Washington. His stores are alarmingly low.

I humbly ask for your forgiveness for the part I have played in your demise. I now ask your permission to one day come to Block Island to meet with you personally and to beg your forgiveness.

Most sincerely,
Captain Nicholas Geste

The three sat silently for a few moments before Stepney said, "Well, it don't looks like dis revolution will go on too much longer."

Molly gave him an angry look and then grabbed the letter out of Cujo's hand. "I'm goin' to get some answers from Alizander," she said as she headed for his room.

Stepney looked at Cujo and shrugged. "Maybe Alexander needs to get shook up to snap him back from where he's at. An' maybe Molly's de one to do it."

A moment later, they heard Molly cry out from Alexander's room, "Oh, God! No, Alizander!"

Stepney and Cujo immediately ran to Alexander's room to find Molly kneeling in the doorway, crying as she softly prayed. Stepney hesitated for a moment, afraid of what he would find inside the room. As he peered around the door, he saw Alexander sitting in his chair. His face was contorted, and tears were streaming over his cheeks.

At first Stepney thought it was only the frightening look on Alexander's face that had upset Molly, but then he looked down into Alexander's lap. Stepney felt his heart jump into his throat. There, in Alexander's hand, was his flintlock, cocked and ready to fire.

Stepney couldn't think of any words to speak, but from somewhere he heard himself command, "Alexander, no! Dere is still so much I have for you!" The old man startled himself. He didn't even know what it meant, nor did it sound like something he would say. The uniqueness of the commanding voice seemed to break though to Alexander for a moment. He looked up to Stepney and quietly muttered, "It's just too dark. It's all too dark."

Chapter Thirty-Five

Earlier that day, Alexander had sat in his room, struggling to cope with the pain from his wounds, a pain that also sharpened the memories of his failure. Rum was the only thing to numb the pain, and perhaps even more welcome was the fact the rum also numbed the mind. Molly knew it was medicinal and saw that it was available whenever Alexander called for it.

In his stupor, he struggled to put the pieces back together, but it was all too incomprehensible, and he gave up the struggle. Making sense of it all was just too hard, and everything was so dark. The strain of trying to see through the darkness was exhausting.

When he'd arrived back on Block Island, he'd found his father's decline was just as upsetting. Joseph appeared to have physically manifested every bit of the disrepair and decline of his farm. To Alexander, it seemed as though years had passed since he had last been home, rather than weeks. He wanted to escape, to retreat to the dark place of which he was becoming more and more accepting.

The captain struggled to recall the images of his father's funeral from the day before. *Was it really just yesterday?* He'd sat graveside, unable to move or feel any emotions, just the constant pain. He could sense the emotions from the islanders cascading forward, as if a dam had broken. It all came rushing toward him, yet he felt nothing but the pain.

He retreated emotionally and ran from the torrent chasing him down. He found a dark cave in his mind where he was safe from the pain—his own, as well as the pain he had brought to so many others. He had failed his country, his family, and his fellow islanders. It was all too much to bear.

With his father's death, what was left of Joseph Hawkins's holdings became Alexander's. But the world, as he knew it, was crashing down, and he did not want any of what was left. The only thing he could think of was to let it all crumble and to completely fall apart.

Though it was always his plan to do so, now giving the family bondservants their freedom would only be the final piece to dismantling the Hawkins legacy. When they returned to the house after the funeral, Alexander spoke the only words he'd said since his return. As the slaves stood around him, he struggled to say, in a raspy, gravelly voice, "Each of you is free now. You must leave this place and make a life for yourselves."

Molly Mum began to cry, and Stepney said, "Alexander, dat is generous of you, but we can't leave you like dis. Real freedom gives us de choice to stay."

Alexander stared at the floor. "You all should leave. This life is over here. I want you to go."

"But Alexander," Stepney argued softly, "you know we can't leave wit'out manumission papers. We ain't really freepersons wit'out dem. Where we goin' to get dem?"

"Sands," Alexander said. "Have Sands draw them up." Alexander was done. He retreated and said no more.

It had always been Alexander's expectation that freeing the slaves upon his father's death would be a reward for their service; a celebration. But now, in Alexander's mind, it was only a means to the end of it all.

The slaves somberly returned Alexander to his room and left him, sitting up, staring at the floor. The curtains behind him flapped in the wind, and the soft breeze made Alexander think of the sea. *No!* He had to close his mind. There was too much pain in memories of being out to sea. He let the darkness take over.

Later, Alexander thought he noticed someone come back into the room. *Cujo?* He felt something put into his hand. *A letter?* The slave said something about reading it. He said a name, a name that made Alexander's heart pound in anger. Suddenly, his injuries began to hurt, and the pain made his mind alert. Alexander focused his eyes on the letter, and the name jumped off the envelope: *Captain Nicholas Geste.* Alexander threw the letter to the floor in a mixture of anger and horror. "No! No! Never!" he cried. He continued to stare at the envelope as if it were a dangerous animal about to pounce on him. Cujo quickly picked up the letter and left the room, but the name continued to pulsate in Alexander's confused mind. He tried to drive it away, but the name remained. He needed to make it go, but it would not go away. *I must kill Geste! It was Geste who shattered my world. Geste must pay.*

Still in an emotional stupor, Alexander willed his body to get up to fetch his flintlock. *I will put an end to Geste, and that will put all back to order.* After retrieving his pistol from the drawing room, he turned to make his way back to his bedroom. He paused, exhausted from the effort, and heard the slaves talking in the kitchen. He strained to listen and heard Cujo reading "... disastrous mission, suffering a total loss." The words made Alexander's darkness turn to red, and his driving heartbeat drowned out the rest of the words.

Alexander looked at the pistol, then made his way back to his room. He had failed completely, and he decided to put an end to his own miserable failure. He collapsed into his chair. Priming the pistol was almost more than he could handle.

After cocking the flintlock, he dropped the piece into his lap to gather his strength. The world around him grew darker. He prepared to raise the pistol to his temple and pull the trigger, yet one thought circled in Alexander's mind: *Such a complete and horrible waste! All of the ships and all those men sacrificed for nothing.* The most crippling pain stabbed as Nathan came to mind, and he let out a desperate groan. Alexander was always certain his life held significant meaning and purpose until that terrible evening in the East River at Hell Gate—when his faith in God's divine will for his life was completely and utterly destroyed.

Now, he was growing more certain that this God was mocking his life and that his childlike faith had deceived him. It was not only the terrible sacrifice on that fateful day but all the other things he'd sacrificed throughout his life. He had believed a lie about the primacy and virtue of the freedom struggle. He had sacrificed time with comrades, neighbors, friends, family—even love.

Love? He tried to focus on Rebekah, but the memory hurt him as much as the loss of Nathan and the pain from his miserable failure at Hell Gate.

With the little strength he could muster, Alexander raised the pistol. Suddenly, there were muffled voices at his door. Cutting through the darkness and the din of his angry heartbeat, he clearly heard the words, "Alexander, no! There is still so much I have for you!"

Chapter Thirty-Six

June 1786

While the two black servants busied themselves with loading supplies into the stout sloop, Captain Alexander Hawkins approached a large, weathered-looking man in a dingy uniform. The officer handed Alexander a letter.

Most times, Alexander didn't care, but news was so rare to come by on the island that he could not resist asking a few questions. "Excuse me, Constable. Do you have any news of General Washington, the newest delegates to Congress, or the plans for a constitutional convention in Philadelphia?"

The constable seemed more than happy to tell all he knew, but Alexander didn't have the energy to listen to his tedious report. As the man talked on, Alexander simply walked away. He wandered back to his sloop to stare across the harbor at Point Judith and out to Block Island Sound.

Alexander rarely received or entertained social correspondence, but he glanced down at the letter and realized he held in his hand a letter from Caty Littlefield Greene. Just holding the letter with her name on it caused warmth to flow through his body and cheery memories of his childhood to surface. He grinned and nodded his head. He decided he would wait to read it until he returned home; then he could carefully meander through it in the solitude of his own room, slowly enjoying every morsel of it and allowing her clever wit and childlike spirit to revive him.

But he couldn't wait. Right there on the wharf, Alexander tore it open with his teeth and let the envelope fly away. He snapped the letter open with his one hand and read...

Dearest Alexander,

Please forgive my negligence in not writing for so long a time. Since our financial troubles necessitated our move from Newport to Savannah, we have endured many trials, with which I shall not burden you. Now, it is with great joy and happiness that I can share how well we all are in our new rice plantation home, Mulberry Grove. I am well, Nathanael is well, and all five children are well. Our future looks bright and financially prosperous.

I do hope you will visit to see for yourself, but let me try to describe the beauty of our expansive plantation.

Driving several miles up the Augusta Road, you enter through a majestic gate and turn down a lane surrounded by a vast forest of spreading live-oak laden with moss. Its dense network forms a shadowy arch above the carriage trail. Wild vines, shrubs, and masses of yellow jasmine make the woods almost impenetrable on either side of the lane. As you approach the river, the forest ends, and you look out upon a great marshy wilderness, checkered with dikes and levees of the rice fields.

A hundred yards from the water's edge on the western bank of the Savannah River sits the estate's large main house. It stands in the midst of a grove of mulberry trees, the vestige of bygone days of a silkworm farm. The two-story brick residence has large chimneys on either end. In the living room, wide glass panels flank the central double doors, offering a fine view of the river, with its bluff covered by enormous trees and, in the distance, the midstream islands and South Carolina shore.

Behind the house are several outbuildings, including the kitchen, smokehouse, coach house and stables, poultry barn, and pigeon house. I have enjoyed restoring the large garden that contains a great variety of shrubs and flowers.

While I had hesitated throwing myself into the demands of learning and operating such a large venture, I have become determined to make Mulberry Grove a success. We have now planted over two hundred acres of rice and corn. The garden is delightful. The fruit trees and flowering shrubs form a pleasing variety. We have green peas and as fine a lettuce as can be seen. The mockingbirds surround us morning and evening. The weather is mild, and the vegetable kingdom is progressing to perfection. We have orchards of apples, pears, peaches, apricots, nectarines, plums, figs, pomegranates, and oranges. And we have strawberries that measure three inches around.

With all the demands of the plantation, my life is one of arduous domesticity but still rewarding. Most dreaded of all duties is dealing with the health problems and daily ministrations of our many troublesome slaves…

Alexander stopped reading and dropped his hand. He had hoped to be encouraged and uplifted by the letter, but now the darkness began to enter in. He was pleased that General Greene and Caty were well and prospering, but there was something that struck him as very wrong. The Georgia state legislature had awarded a vast Tory estate, a rice plantation known as Mulberry Grove, in appreciation of General Greene's service in the South. Alexander had no problem with accepting the reality of "to the victor belong the spoils," but one of the revolution's great Northern heroes had accepted ownership of a plantation operated by a large number of slaves? *Was this the reason we drove out the great oppressor, only to take over their horrid business?* he thought. *We are now a nation of free men, yet with people enslaved among us? What has really changed?*

He thought of an argument he'd had with Caty before the war on the subject of slavery.

~~~

Caty precociously said to Alexander, "Please give me one good reason why slavery should be abolished."

Alexander replied, "Perhaps the greatest argument against slavery is that I would not be a slave myself. Freedom is the most natural impulse to man."

"Nor would I," said Caty, smiling. "But would not your reason operate as strongly with respect to riding your horse—that you would not be willing to be ridden yourself?"

"That is ridiculous. There is a great difference between the two," responded Alexander. "The Negro man has a soul as much as any of us; a horse has not."

"Will you undertake to prove," asked Caty, "that a horse or any other animal has not a soul?"

"Most certainly," answered Alexander.

"Then I would thank you, sir, for your proof."

Alexander hesitated and bit his lip.

Caty offered a smug smile, presuming Alexander to be caught in her intellectual trap.

He calmly answered, "The biblical record is quite clear that man was created in God's image and his soul is eternal. Animals, however, were made for man's use in this realm."

Caty shook her head and laughed. "I fear, Alexander Hawkins, you rely on that one book too much. I dare you to look in the eyes of your favorite steed or the family dog and tell me it has no soul."

"Fair point, my lady. There is certainly a spark of life in our animals—a mind, feelings, devotion, affection, and personality—but I dare say no eternal soul. However, I will certainly
~~~

endeavor to think twice about its feelings the next time I prepare to climb atop my horse."

The two shared a laugh that broke the tension of so volatile a subject.

Alexander added, "And as for that *one* book, I rely on it so because it has proven to be so reliable."

Their conversation moved on to family and politics. Alexander, though, was disturbed once again by another patriot who was so devoted to the pursuit of American independence and yet remained so callous and accepting of the institution of slavery.

~~~

Alexander dropped his arm and stared blankly out to the water. The letter from Caty slipped from his hand and fluttered away in the wind. He walked away, unaware that it was gone.

The constable called out to him as he walked away, "Captain Hawkins! Captain Hawkins! Did you hear the news of General Nathanael Greene?"

Alexander stopped to hear the report but did not turn around.

"Our great and good son of Rhode Island passed away from sunstroke only days ago."
~~~

Chapter Thirty-Seven

Alexander tried to muster the energy to care at all about his former passions, but those same passions and desires had been stripped away ten years earlier. Trying to care again only brought back pain and anguish.

His head began to throb, as it often did, and his mind clouded over. The dark claws of depression dug into his back, its paralyzing poison seeping into his veins.

His servant Cujo was suddenly behind him, pulling him back out of the cloud and into the present. "Cap'n, Bolico and I is finished storing de provisions, and de sloop is ready to sail."

Struggling not to appear totally lost to this world, Alexander replied, "Very well, Cujo. Let us put out. Our Block Island awaits."

The small sloop, heavily laden with supplies, was paddled away from the dock and the rigging pulled taut. The tide was high, the wind was good, and the sun hung low in the sky. After the sloop sailed from Narragansett Bay and out into open water, they took a southwesterly heading. The setting sun painted a brilliant picture of deep blue water set ablaze by strokes of orange and red, bursting through soft purple clouds in a pink sky.

A cool, damp wind brushed their skin, even as the sun's waning rays were still upon them. The three men lifted their faces to the warmth. All was quiet, except for the lapping water and the gentle luffing of the sails. For the captain, these were the coos of a sweet lullaby.

He did not feel good about much of anything anymore—and hadn't for years. His physical being, countenance, and demeanor had all turned sour. He could not shake this feeling, and he asked himself, *Is this it? Is this what it is all about? Is this what the struggle was for—to merely own this moment?*

Suddenly, he realized just how good he *did* feel in this rare moment—but just as quickly, the darkness descended again, as he realized that this moment had always existed at one time or another. *You can't own it.* The struggle for freedom didn't matter. The result of the war was only that there were fewer family and friends with whom to share such a moment. His expression turned even more dour, and Cujo and Bolico looked at each other and shook their heads.

Bolico spoke up to encourage him. "Cap'n, you wants us to sail round her to take in her glory?"

The black men did not care much for the open sea, but they knew there was something about the views of Block Island from the water that picked up their captain's spirit. He would occasionally choose to circle the island when departing or arriving.

"No," Alexander responded evenly. "It will be pitch black by the time we reach her."

"Wid de sky so clear," Bolico said, "I doubts it will get dat dark. But wid de sea and de weather, you never seems to be wrong, Alexander."

As he had anticipated, they had to search to find their landing in the darkness that fell upon them. He was home, and the work of transferring their supplies to the cart and battening down the boat before heading to the farm helped to sober him. He was home, back on Block Island soil.

~~~

The following day began with a typically cool and damp morning. Fog hugged the ground, blanketing the lower portions of the island but allowing the higher elevations to be exposed, as if they were small islands unto themselves, softly breaking through the dewy clouds. The mist rolled down to the open window of the Hawkins house and into Alexander's bedroom.

His window was rarely closed—he welcomed the elements rather than the feeling of entrapment in a closed room. The family had grown used to this. His Molly Mum had told him that he had spent many a sleepless night as a child, with anguished cries and wailing, after his mother had died. Once the family realized that the open door or window was all that was needed to calm his fears, they were all allowed a good night's rest.

Damp mornings were troublesome for Alexander. His battle wounds ached so much that he had difficulty raising himself out of bed. The stump of his right arm was always the worst. He had long since ceased feeling his arm as if it were still there, with the pain pulsing as if his forearm and elbow were being crushed under the weight of a heavy wagon. Now, it felt like the stump that it was but as if it had been beaten much of the night with a hammer.

He willed himself to roll out of bed, while fighting off the relentless question: *For what purpose?* But he was a New Englander, an islander, a seaman, a farmer. Even if that question came into his mind, his body—at least what was left of it—would will itself to do what was required. Ultimately, he didn't have a choice, even though that question and others like it would continue to float in and out of his thoughts.
~~~

What could occupy his mind to fight off the darkness that could grip him at any moment? His once-brilliant mind had deteriorated to the point of existing on whatever he could cope with, only for the day in front of him. A few drinks of "medicinal" rum helped limit his focus. When there was nothing else to focus on, there was always the "rock".

This particular day's work would consist of moving one of the great rock piles from the cleared fields to build a stone boundary to mark the southwest boundary of the Hawkins property. Fields were created near Dr. Rodman's property as part of the island's beautiful hollow—property previously part of the Hawkins's large farm—now owned by Lawrence Tuckman.

The island's hollow was a ravine that dropped down to within several feet of sea level, then rose up again briefly before dropping off as a steep cliff face. The immense bluffs of eroded clay, mixed with gravel, rock, and huge boulders, extended out into the sea to form the dangerous reefs off the island's coast. The top of the ridge offered a dramatic sight, overlooking the horizon. The expansive view included the entire island, with its lush green vegetation, golden fields, and pockets of silvery freshwater pools. The white, shimmering beaches framed the island's distinct shape. Along the edge of the beaches lay a ring of light blue-green shallows that slowly darkened into the endless deep blue of the ocean. Far beyond, to the north and west, lay the shadowy landmasses of the mainland and Long Island. The massive blue canopy above stretched in all directions, like a shimmering soap bubble covering this heavenly realm.

Alexander struggled to put on his clothes. With one hand, he slapped a cold-water wash onto his face before dragging himself into the kitchen. Molly Mum made a slab of corn bread—still hot—and thick black coffee. After applying a liberal portion of their famous rich butter on the cornbread, he ate half the bread, washing it down with several cups of hot coffee. The coffee gave him a rush, numbing his pain. As he was wrestling with his sheepskin coat and putting on his three-corner cap, there came a knock on the front door. Molly Mum and the others were gone to get an early start to their chores, so he was left alone to face this unwanted visitor.

He paused for a moment and considered just waiting for the visitor to simply turn and go away. But whoever was at the door was persistent. Once he concluded the visitor would not disappear, he went to the door.

Without opening it, he asked, "Who's there, and what is your purpose?"

"Alexander," the visitor replied, "it's Benjamin Beach. I bring greetings from my family and a matter to discuss. Perhaps we could warm ourselves with some coffee or perhaps a morning pint?"

Alexander froze. He cared very deeply for Benjamin as a longtime friend, but the Beach family was another source of pain for him. Without a hint of familiarity, Alexander replied, "I'm sorry, but I have a long day ahead of me. We will have to talk another time."

"Alexander," Benjamin said impatiently, "what have I done to you that you won't even open the door to greet me, face to face? If you don't have the time, then I'll be brief, but please open the door."

Alexander was embarrassed. Realizing how rudely he was behaving, he sheepishly opened the door. "I'm sorry, Benjamin; please come in. How can I be of service?"

Benjamin resumed his cheery demeanor and went right to the point. "Actually, I'm going house to house to give notice of a town meeting that's been called for six o'clock tomorrow evening. The issue at hand concerns our island slaves. Considering your disposition with slavery and emancipation, we felt your presence would be paramount."

Alexander's mental focus was limited. He was trying to concentrate, but he only caught a few words here and there. He heard enough, though, to get the gist of what Benjamin was saying. It was something about freeing the slaves. He felt a sense of relief that the subject seemed unlikely to turn to Benjamin's sister.

On the matter of slavery, he couldn't help but feel something inside of him snap to attention. Human freedom was still a passion that shot beyond his mental state, arresting his depression and getting his mind engaged more clearly again.

"Benjamin, you know that on such a subject I would be happy to oblige, but why is this a matter on which the town council will decide? Emancipation is something each family can set straight on their own paper." He sensed something was not right, and his mind started to drift. His emotional impulse to withdraw kicked in again. "I'm sorry," he mumbled, "but I don't believe I can attend."

"Alexander," Benjamin persisted, "this is a topic with which you are well acquainted. You yourself have freed your own slaves, and your experience can bring leadership to this issue. I won't take no for an answer. I will come by myself to pick you up shortly before the hour." He slipped out the door before Alexander could quarrel, adding, "It will do a world of good just to get out. And afterwards, we can share a pint and talk of the old days. Good day, my captain!"

With that, the door clanked shut, leaving Alexander silent and still. The words "my captain" made his face flush with embarrassment. The islanders, mostly out of respect, referred to him in that way. But he felt he was undeserving. His duty and valor had been too short lived. He didn't feel he had earned his share of these United States' freedom.

In spite of giving up his right arm for the cause, he had tried to persuade the islanders to refer to him differently. Still, it was a source of pride for many of the islanders and one that they were not willing to relinquish.

Chapter Thirty-Eight

An hour later, Alexander arrived at the field on the southern end of the hollow. One of the few remaining forests occupied the ridge bordering the hollow. Looking up at the trees, he thought back to years earlier when the island fathers had fashioned the original town ordinance prohibiting any more trees from being felled without the town's approval. His memory was foggy now, and he struggled to recall why that concern had seemed so important to him then.

The three black men had been working at an even pace since the early morning. The fields were now cleared and the ground ready for planting. However, it was well past the time for planting. Several huge rock piles had been built up to be used primarily for the stone walls that would set the boundaries for the lots being split off from their once-large farm.

Stepney, Cujo, and Bolico left what they were doing and approached Alexander as he rode up on a large white mare named Endicott. The men all smiled at the sight of their captain coming out on his own effort to monitor their work. Alexander suddenly felt a rare sense of optimism and vitality. He fearfully wondered how long it would last.

Stepney spoke first. "Greetin's, Cap'n! We bin movin' right long an' makin' good progress. What says you?"

"I say, well done," Alexander said as he climbed down from his mare. "Your progress is steady, and by the looks of these walls, they will stand for the ages. I thought I might try a little physical exertion and see if I could lay a few stones myself."

His servants tried to politely suggest it wasn't necessary, but Alexander could tell they were excited to have their former master working alongside them.

He remembered a time, before the war, when he tirelessly led the way and worked harder than any of the slaves, servants, or paid employees. No one could keep up with him, but he would notice all worked that much more vigorously in trying. Alexander recalled his natural inclination to lead.

He thought back to when he was a young man. Alexander particularly enjoyed challenging himself and those with him to see who could pull the most rock and build the longest stretch of wall in one day. At the end of the day, he would pace off each section—he never lost the challenge. His reward would be to prop himself up against the base of a large shade tree and share a pail of cool water with his comrades and competitors. The group would then look back at their creation and poke fun at the quality of each other's work.

He always amazed the others with how he could creatively describe the unique features of each section of wall. Whether it was its particular physical beauty or its functionality or the many symbolic meanings of walls, it entertained the men. The value Alexander placed on the wall made the men believe their work was much more meaningful than piling up rocks.

The stone itself was rich with colorful minerals and elements that sparkled in the sun. The shadows, too, changed as the sun moved, creating dark and light features. As they sat in the shade, each man would take turns recognizing the shapes as pictures of different things. On occasion, the creative thoughts would even stimulate the slaves' minds to images of their past lives and bring some to tears.

One time, Alexander had himself become emotional as he described the wall. "And look, there," he said, "that large rock with the white vein running down the middle—it looks much like the bow of a great ship plowing through the water. And next to it, yes, surely that is a woman sitting, holding a baby in her lap..." His voice slowed, as he seemed to recognize the image. The slaves looked on as he fell quiet. Tears welled up in his eyes as he softly said, "My mother."

The group looked at each other. Alexander somberly stared at the image he saw. Cujo quickly broke the silence. "But look over dere. De rocks dere must be de head of a elephant. De narrow white rocks is de tusks, an' dat long twisted rock is de trunk."

Alexander broke away from his thoughts to see what Cujo was describing. Stepney spoke up and asked, "You talkin' 'bout dem rocks right dere?"

Cujo nodded, and Stepney said, "Now I knows you ain't from Africa, 'cause dem rocks don't look like no elephant I ever done seen!"

Cujo smiled, and the men broke into laughter. Alexander looked back to find the image of mother and son, but the shadows had already changed. He went back several times in the coming weeks to see if he could find the shadow picture again, but the image was forever gone.

Now, several decades later, Alexander joined the servants once again to work on the wall. He grabbed a rock from the large pile with his one arm. He felt a vitality he had not felt in a very long time and remembered the rush that physical exertion brought—it felt good. Even as he struggled with the stone, he told himself that only with persistence could he learn to manage carrying bigger and heavier rocks again. He determined within himself to continue this mental and physical exercise.

However, after a few rocks, he leaned into the pile to extract a stone over his head. Leaning too far, he fell into the pile.

It left him stretched out and in such an awkward position that he could not right himself. His hand still held the rock that he had grabbed to keep the rock from coming down on him. His elbow and knees pushed against the rocks, but they shifted, and he couldn't get a hold with his feet. He lay against the pile, squirming and being reminded of just how much he missed his right arm. Alexander thought to call out for help, but he couldn't bring himself to do it.

The former slaves were busy at the wall and had their backs to the struggle going on behind them. Just as Alexander pushed the rock above him aside, the bright noon daylight turned to darkness. He found himself back on the rocky bluffs of the northern shore of Long Island, ten years earlier, in the fall of 1776. His right arm was now returned to him, and he flexed his hand and forearm to make certain it was all in working order. Crouched a short distance behind him, he could see the anxious face of Nathan.

"Nathan!" he called back. "Keep your head down! I'll not lose you!"

Above him was the British battery that threatened passage of the shipping through Long Island Sound, the East River, through Hell Gate, up the Harlem River, and onto New York Island. Musket fire and grapeshot rained down upon him and the others trapped on the rocks. Captain Alexander Hawkins once again relived the nightmarish events that had forever changed the course of his life.

~~~

Stepney was enjoying making fun of his two coworkers. "How is it dat dis ol' man does as much work as de two of you's? Still, as slow as you is, you makin' a mess of dis wall. How's it, all dese years an' you still don't know how to put rocks toget'er?"

"Stepney," Cujo answered back, "de day you can work faster dan de two of us is de day we is dead."
~~~

"Well, den," Stepney said with a grin, turning back to get more rock from the pile, "when was it you two died?"

Stepney headed back toward the pile but stopped cold. He was stunned to see Alexander down, partially buried by rock, flailing as if in some great struggle. The old man reached out and grabbed hold of each man beside him. "Sweet Savior in heaven," he uttered in an even but disbelieving tone.

All three men raced over to clear the rock away and then dragged their captain to an even patch of grass.

They had seen this on a few occasions, but this latest time was just as upsetting as the first. Alexander continued to jerk his arms and legs, screaming out unintelligible orders, repeating Nathan's name, and then, oddly, referencing his mother.

"Nathan, don't go!" he would shout. "Forgive me!" And then calling out to his mother, he would repeat over and over, "Mum, your boy is well! Your boy is well!"

The black men held him to the ground to stop his movements, and Stepney spoke softly to calm him. Alexander's face was a distorted blur with his eyes rolled back into his head. Slowly, he began to calm down, and his face came into focus.

Although his head cleared, his disorientation continued. The violence dissipated, but his speech remained strangely in the past. References to times and events that were no longer a part of the current-day Hawkins farm were particularly upsetting to his servants.

"Don't you mind, boys," Stepney instructed. "Just go along wid what he is sayin'. Just act like we all livin' back in de days wid Master Joseph."

The three men brought Alexander back to the main house, where Molly Mum dressed his wounds and gave him rum to settle his still-agitated state. Alexander calmed down, but he continued to quietly drink pint after pint until he passed out completely.

Stepney had the other two men carry Alexander to his bed. When Cujo and Bolico left the room, both Stepney and Molly fell to their knees. They cried and prayed. They cried for the terrible deterioration of the family, and they prayed for its resurrection. At one time it had all held so much promise.

Stepney had seen the worst of times on the farm, but they had survived and always moved on. Now, with Alexander's darkness, they couldn't seem to move on. Every time they sensed things might improve, the darkness would take over. Stepney silently prayed, *What could you possibly be doin'? Lord, can you make anyt'in' good out of all dis?*

Chapter Thirty-Nine

The two friends toiled in the morning sun; both had stripped off their shirts. The Indian's slender, copper-toned physique contrasted with the deep black, muscular torso of the African.

Quepag was growing tired of the work. He really did not like to work this hard; it seemed pointless to him. There was always tomorrow. But he liked to be with the African, and really, Hannibal did most of the work. After the black man pulled the rock and stone from the ground, if it was not too big, Quepag would carry it over to the pile. Most of the time, Quepag would just stand there and quietly watch Hannibal as he worked.

They often worked side by side, silently, for hours. The men could communicate with each other without even speaking a word. While Quepag had taken on the role of teaching Hannibal the island ways, he realized that the black man would teach him many new things. There were qualities in Hannibal that Quepag liked. Most of all, he was quiet, and the two never felt it necessary to waste many words. When they did have conversations, it was when they both felt like talking.

Also, there was a strength and an authority in the man that Quepag respected more than any other man on the island. It reminded him of his grandfather. Even many of the whites had respect in their eyes when they looked at Hannibal. It was clear to the Indian that if Hannibal were not a slave, he would be a leader and a chief.

The Indian squatted and sat back on his haunches, wondering about the slave. *Why didn't Hannibal just leave? Why was he working so hard and so long to earn his freedom? He was so powerful, why didn't he just take a boat and leave?* Quepag didn't think there was anybody on the island who could stop Hannibal.

Coincidentally, Hannibal suddenly spoke up. "Quepag, why don't you leave dis island? Dere are so few of your people left. Why do you stay?"

"Why do you always work so hard?" Quepag returned. "And why don't *you* leave this island?"

Hannibal shrugged but did not respond. "Quepag," he called back, "tell me again about your father's father and how the white men came to the island."

Quepag didn't like to answer questions, but if he was in the right mood, he liked to tell stories. This way, he could just squat and talk about the past while Hannibal did the work.

He thought for a moment, and then began. "For many seasons—by the white man's measure, hundreds of years—my people lived alone in this place. The Mohegans would come and try to take our riches of clams and corn, but we always drove them away. Then one time, after we drove the Mohegans off the great bluffs for our final victory, my people saw the first of the great *mishittouwand*—canoe ships—with white clouds hanging over them. The canoe was caught by the wind, and it floated past the island. Our people knew it was the spirits of the Mohegans we had thrown off the great bluffs, escaping from the island and returning to their hunting grounds.

"Many seasons later, another great mishittouwand canoe floated up to the island, but this one stopped in the water for a time before being carried away by the wind."

Hannibal continued his work as he listened but now stopped to say, "But Quepag, you know it was white men coming to take your land."

"Yes, the white men came," he answered, "and we let them come to the island—to see what form the Mohegan spirits had taken. When we saw their desire to take our things, we knew for sure they were the Mohegan spirits. Our braves agreed that they would attack and destroy the next great mishittouwand canoe and kill the Mattanit spirits to finish our battle with the Mohegans, once and for all."

Hannibal asked, "How did your people know dat de white men were Mohegan spirits?"

Quepag thoughtfully answered, "My people feared in their hearts that the way we had tortured the Mohegans—letting them hang from the bluffs, starving—might cause great revenge to come against us. When the trader named Oldham came, Sachem Audsah took his ship and killed Oldham and all his people on board. We hoped it would be the final end to the vengeance, but it was not. Many white men returned, led by the captain, Endicott, wearing shining tortoise shells and carrying fire sticks. They killed as many of our people as they wanted and burned our villages and cornfields. We could not stop them. Many of our people believed we brought this on ourselves.

"Then, the first whites came to settle the island. They came over with their cattle to make their home on the island. Our tribe did not stop them. They hoped they could live with them. But again, the whites started to take whatever they wanted. Our braves grew angry and went to attack their camp. Just when we were ready to attack, the sachem chief stopped our braves, and our people never tried to fight the whites again. He did not want to see the same revenge visited upon the people that Endicott brought."

The slave paused from his work. "Why? Why didn't he fight de small group? Why wouldn't your braves fight for your land an' your people?"

"The white settlers had a drum and the beating of the drum reminded us of the many who were killed after Oldham by Captain Endicott. When our sachem came to the white man's camp, he saw a young boy with a fire stick. He was wise enough to know that even a young boy with their weapon was greater than many of our men. Fighting these whites would only lead to more revenge upon his people.

"He saw a vision of the whites as the waves on the beach. They would come, and you could not stop them. It was the Mohegans's lasting revenge for how we had murdered them. Their Mattanit spirit of revenge continues to slowly steal our people each year." After a moment, he added, "The summer is upon us. We are due to lose another of our people sometime soon."

Hannibal leaned over and pulled a large boulder he uncovered out of the soil. He turned and rolled it past Quepag. The slave then dropped down to a sitting position, exhausted. Without looking at the Indian, he said, "I have seen your spirit. I have seen de one I believe is killing your tribe."

"You have seen this spirit Mattanit?" Quepag scoffed. "When, and what did it look like?"

"I think I have not only seen it," Hannibal answered, "but it tried to kill me. It was when I first came to de island, just before Williams found me. It was de spirit who kilt de ot'er African an' tried to kill me. We were on de shore when we saw it swim in from de water. When it climbed up de bluff, we surprised it. It quickly kilt de ot'er. I stab it wid my spear, but dat was not'in' to it."

Quepag was confused, and something in him did not want to believe it was true. "What did it look like? Was it a man? Has it ever appeared to you again?"

"It was large an' strong," Hannibal answered, "but its face was old. It had long black hair, wid lightnin' in it. I have never seen it again."

Quepag shook his head. "No, the spirit who is taking my people is a Mattanit. It is evil and cannot be seen." Still, he was curious and asked, "Why have you never spoken of this?"

The slave shrugged his shoulders. "I don't speak but to you. Dis is somet'in' dat makes you angry. It is not my people, and it has never come to fight me again. Maybe it is not your spirit."

Quepag was puzzled. He thought of his grandfather and his promise to return one day. Was it he who Hannibal had seen? The description did not sound like his grandfather, but perhaps he had taken on another body. It gave him some hope that his grandfather would return as he had promised, even after having been gone for so long.

Quepag felt some indignation that Hannibal would think he might know anything of his people and their enemies. He answered with assurance, "What you saw was not the Mohegan Mattanit spirit. I'm sure it was something else." He changed the subject. "You are tired. Let's both hunt wild turkey. But you will use my bow, and I will use your spear."

Hannibal nodded his head in agreement. "I have made you a gift. I have made another spear for you to hunt wit'."

Quepag was pleased. When the two had begun to hunt together, Hannibal fashioned a spear in a new way, and he showed Quepag its superior design and its advantages over the bow and arrow. Quepag was impressed with the weapon. Hannibal, in turn, began to use and appreciate the Indian's weapon.

Quepag had always coveted the slave's spear but did not want to offend him by making one for himself. He smiled a rare smile and proudly said, "I will make a bow for you, and I will treasure your spear alongside my grandfather's weapons."

As Quepag watched Hannibal get up and collect his tools, he marveled at the bond that had grown between them. He knew the slave did not trust anyone else on the island, and now they were behaving as friends. The slave had even picked up some of the Algonquin tongue. At first, the slave would only ask simple questions concerning the how, what, and when with regard to performing his duties. Slowly, though, his trust in Quepag caused him to open up and ask deeper and more significant questions.

Hannibal continued to struggle, however, with Quepag's relationship to Williams. The black slave understood that the Indian was bound as a servant to Williams in some way, but he couldn't comprehend that there might possibly be something more to their relationship.

Quepag could relate to Hannibal, as both came from people who were hunters and gatherers. Between them, the slave and the servant, they performed all of the household labor for Williams. Quepag, though, was entrusted with most of the responsibility revolving around putting food on Williams's table. The Indian did much of the hunting, fishing, and clamming and tended to a small vegetable garden, along with the kitchen work.

Within the garden, he did the hoeing, picked peas, beans, and turnips, and dug up the potatoes. In some instances, the squaws from the tribe would come in to clean and do women's chores in exchange for Quepag's provision of food.

Hannibal was assigned the most physically demanding tasks, including cutting, threshing, and milling wheat; loading wheat straw into the barn; hilling, hoeing, and gathering hay; digging and carting stones; building walls; and cutting and skidding wood.

It was the same for most other slaves on the island. Their services were important to completing the day-to-day chores of the household—cleaning, making repairs, and putting food on the table. Quepag had accepted this as his life, and over time, he thought Hannibal had come to accept it as his.

As they walked across the field together, Hannibal asked Quepag, "Do you want dis life?"

Quepag looked at the slave as he considered what answer the question was asking for. "It is my life," he responded simply. And, referring to the previous life of which Hannibal had spoken, he asked, "Did the Hutu ever want to do anything but serve the Tutsi?"

The slave paused and shook his head. "No, dat would be a foolish t'ought." He tried again. "But do you want anot'er purpose?"

Quepag pondered the question and then responded, "Sometimes I want to fish or hunt, but I must work the field."

"But why do you not go away from here, like so many of your tribe?"

Quepag mostly assumed that his life was his life, and he accepted it. Now he wondered if he should be offended by the questions Hannibal asked. It made him wonder if he should consider another life. Was he really content with this life? It was not as if he was on a distant land. The island had been the Indians' land before the whites came.

"This is the land of my people," Quepag proudly stated. "The white man came and took over, but our Woonanit spirit is still here. Many from our clan have chosen to leave, but they have taken the Woonanit spirit with them. I have chosen to stay to be closer to the land and the memories that I love. The spirit of my family remains. Even if Williams or the others say I am bound here, I am not. I stay because this is what I want." Quepag nodded his head in emphasis, as his words satisfied some of his own questions. He began to speak again, then hesitated for a moment, as if deciding whether he should say the words in his head. "I have a secret that I have carried alone for many years," he continued. "It is one reason why I have stayed. Only my grandfather knows of this secret—I told him many years ago. He told me to keep the secret hidden until the time when he would return to instruct me. I still wait for his instruction. Now I wonder if I will tell it to you."

The two arrived at the Indian trail and spotted an oxcart heading from the east toward them. Quepag suddenly had misgivings about sharing his secret; he was sorry he had even mentioned it to Hannibal. Hannibal waited, expecting the Indian to continue the conversation, but Quepag turned to walk along the trail. "No, it must stay with me until my grandfather returns."

Chapter Forty

Alexander didn't move. He could hear a muffled voice, but he wasn't sure if it was just in his head. He stared blankly at the floor. Molly Mum had entered Alexander's darkened room that evening to find him hunched over while sitting on a chair in the corner. She announced quietly, "Mr. Beach to see you, Alizander, dear."

Benjamin Beach returned as he had said he would. Alexander was still recovering from the wounds he had received the day before to both his body and mind. His head was pounding, and his body was bruised and sore all over.

Molly Mum tried again. "It's your good frien' Benjamin, sir. You don't wants to make him feel bad, do you?"

Alexander realized it was Molly talking to him, but he didn't want to exert the energy to acknowledge her. He only shifted slightly in his chair to stare at the wall.

The old woman stood up straight and strode into the room. She went right to the window, pushed the curtains aside, and barked, "Now you goin' to listen to me! I ain't goin' to walk away like I always done before. I got to speak my mind. I know you sad, but you still breathin'! You might not never be de same, but t'ings is always changin'. Our Lord always is forgivin', but you just got to forgive yourself. Dis island is God's country, and it's your land, and you are a freeperson. De islanders love dere cap'n an' wants dere cap'n back!"

Alexander shaded his eyes from the rays of the setting sun that streamed through the window. He heard some of what she said but was unmoved by his mum's plea.

The old black woman put her head down and struggled for something to say. She started to sob and forced out the words, "We loves you. We wants our Alizander back. We wants our Alizander back! De ot'ers can never come back, but you is here, and we still can't have you!" Molly fell to her knees on the floor and cried.

Benjamin Beach appeared at the door. "Alexander Hawkins," he said in a stern voice, "you have made your Molly Mum very sad, and I would be offended by your rude behavior if we weren't such good friends." He walked over to Alexander and put his hand on Alexander's shoulder. "We have a matter of freedom to attend to tonight, and unless you plan to fight me, you will dress and come with me at once."

Alexander heard something about freedom, and it stirred him. Still, he thought, he would just wait for Benjamin to leave.

Beach seemed determined. He stood over Alexander, steadfastly refusing to take no for an answer. Molly Mum smiled through her tears and added, "Alizander, you listen to Mr. Beach. He knows what's good for you."

Alexander struggled to comprehend, struggled to care. Benjamin Beach was a friend, and he didn't want to offend him. He decided to get up.

Before he knew it, he was dressed and heading north to the meeting hall in Beach's wagon. Alexander remained silent for the entire ride. The darkness was still there, but the jostling from the wagon helped to make him more alert. Benjamin talked uninterrupted the whole way. It seemed to Alexander as if a bee were buzzing in his ear until they arrived at the meetinghouse, where the center cart path and the main cart path intersected at the center of the island.

Benjamin helped Alexander down from the wagon. They were late and would be the last into the meeting. Alexander was still in a fog and did not fully comprehend where he was going. It wasn't until the two men opened the doors that he realized that almost all of the male freemen residents of the island were at the meeting.

Alexander froze in a panic at the door, but Benjamin pulled him through and sat him down in the back. Benjamin waved to Tuckman, who sat at the center of the table at the front of the room. The Irishman nodded back.

Benjamin whispered to Alexander, "You will note that our ambitious Mr. Tuckman has finally earned the position of first warden, for which he has politicked so long."

Alexander sat there in a haze, wishing he had some rum to deaden the pain. He was able to recognize the town council with Tuckman seated at the center, now as first warden, in the front of the meetinghouse behind a large, rough-hewn table. The officers were whispering among themselves, discussing their agenda before the start of the meeting.

Benjamin continued to speak to Alexander, whispering in his ear. The buzzing was irritating, but he was beginning to pick up some of what his friend was saying. Benjamin was explaining what they were there for, but Alexander, still struggling to focus, just nodded as if he understood.

First Warden Tuckman stood up abruptly to pound his gavel on the desk to start the meeting. Alexander's focus began to clear as the large gathering grew silent. Without addressing the group, he first bowed his head and began to pray; the rest followed suit.

"Our holy, majestic God, we bow before thee, seeking thy wisdom in the matters that lay before this meeting of thy people. May the outcome of our discussion concerning slave freedom be to our mutual satisfaction and to thy glory." He paused, and the entire group waited in anticipation for his concluding "Amen!" but first he interjected a final request. "And, almighty Father, I beseech thee for relief from the painful gout that has proven to be so troublesome to our brother Andrew. Amen!"

The whole group repeated "Amen" in agreement, opened their eyes, and raised their heads for the meeting to begin.

Alexander clearly heard the words "slave freedom" in Tuckman's prayer, and he now strained his focus to follow the proceedings. The darkness seemed to lift, and he could now comprehend Tuckman's familiar voice.

The First Warden spoke up in the coarse tongue that combined many of the accents of the British Isles—Dutch, Scottish, and a hint of his ancestral Irish into a unique New England accent. "We are gathered together, brothers, to address a decision that this entire group reached but one year ago. After personally surveying many of the island families, I have learned that each and every one expressed like concerns. It behooved the town council to call this meeting and see if a collective remedy can be found.

"The problem we addressed one year ago, at its very root, was regarding our bondsmen—and in particular, our male Negroes—and their lack of zeal toward the hard labor required of them. Several owners addressed this with their own Negroes, using every form of promise or threat, yet it was to no avail. It seemed that our own newfound American freedom has given them hope that similar freedoms will be extended to them. In addition, it seems they have educated themselves regarding the emancipation work going on back on the mainland and have determined that some of the same new rights should also be extended to them.

"We continue to struggle to revitalize our economy from the ills that have ravaged us through the war and have continued ever since our freedom fight concluded. Many of these ills linger today."

Sam Williams stood up and interjected, "I still don't understand the need for a town ordinance. We fought a war to control the property that is rightfully ours! If an owner can't get his Negro to work, that is his problem. I, for one, do not want any government to tell me what to do with my slaves!"

"Mr. Williams," Tuckman said, "let us please conduct our meeting in an orderly fashion. The Negroes appear to distrust their own masters' promises and are seeking a public solution to their personal desires for more freedom. And I'm not sure your handling of your bondservants is a good example of responsible property ownership."

Williams shook his head in disgust and sat back down.

Tuckman continued, "At this time last year, we all agreed to a solution, but now many of you owners are making claim that this decision was ill conceived."

The crowd started to get vocal, and with Williams's encouragement, men began speaking over one another as they vented their irritation. The first warden looked to the others in the council as they grew nervous and then tapped the table with his gavel.

The group settled down, and Tuckman continued, "Let me restate the final decision, which was presented, discussed, and agreed to by this entire body." The first warden scanned the group before completing his statement. "It was further agreed that due to the sensitive nature of this subject, it would not be formally ratified and entered into the official town meeting minutes."

Putting on his spectacles, he picked up a single-page letter. "And I read:

> *On this 29th day of July in the Year of Our Lord, 1785, we the people, as inhabitants of the island known as Block Island, the Town of New Shoreham, have agreed and approved the following public decree regarding the manumission of our bondservants:*

Any and all male bondsmen being owned by any and all inhabitants of Block Island shall be allowed, through their labor, to be publicly manumitted for the following service: Any and all male bondsmen who can complete the task of pulling a quantity of rock from Block Island soil sufficient to then construct a wall crossing the island from one end to the other at a distance of no less than three miles shall be manumitted and declared the status of freeman, with all the rights and privileges to that status as prescribed within our current body of laws."

Tuckman put down the document and continued, "Well, now, I am pleased to report, one year later, that the result of our policy has been to spur the productivity of our bondservants to a dramatically new level."

Williams jumped up again, shouting, "Of course they're moving rock and stone! They'll all be off this island by next summer. Meanwhile, there ain't no other work being done!"

Chapter Forty-One

The first warden banged his gavel and gave Williams a stern look. “Samuel Williams, that will be enough! If I may finish, please?” Tuckman paused until Williams sat back down, then continued. “However, for many islanders, this productivity is now causing some alarm.”

A nervous ripple went through the group, with many of the men voicing their agreement once again.

“The Negroes are assisting one another to accelerate their freedom mission. Work has progressed—the fields are being cleared, and walls are being built much faster than we could have ever anticipated. The concerns now being raised are that the bondsmen are ignoring their other work, and at this pace, more of our Negroes will free themselves from our island than we expected. This will soon leave us with a depleted workforce. Many in this room would now pressure us to reverse our decision altogether. Our committee has discussed this alternative and has unanimously concurred that the agreed-upon decision should stand!”

Nathaniel Briggs jumped up. "What do you intend to do once all the slaves are gone? Are you and the committee going to do our chores for us?"

"Neighbor Briggs," Tuckman responded, "I really don't think that will be necessary. The last thing we want to do is risk jeopardizing our bondservants' faith in the public trust. So now we open the floor to recommendations as to how we may amend our decision and make this a policy that may achieve our original goals. We want to give our bondservants the hope for freedom, but our desire would be to control or..." Tuckman paused for dramatic effect, and then continued. "To stonewall their freedom until such a time that is most convenient for us, their holders."

At this point, Alexander was exhausted from the strain of trying to focus. By the time Tuckman made the last statement, Alexander's head and body were pounding. He struggled to understand the meaning of the warden's words. He wanted to stop the proceedings and have it all explained, but he didn't dare.

"We should not try to fool ourselves," Tuckman continued. "Though we live on an island, the pressures from the mainland will inevitably make its way here."

The officers fielded questions and various recommendations from the islanders, and Tuckman let the debates go on. Even in his debilitated state, Alexander could see that Tuckman's mastery of managing these meetings would cause the final recommendations to be those that he had planned to adopt already.

One recommendation, however, was seriously pushed forward and was not Tuckman's. The group was pushing him to extend the length of the stone wall from once across the island to two or even three times across the island.

Tuckman was diplomatic, but he firmly put an end to the discussion. "This has become a very delicate matter. We are not here to anger our coloreds further by withdrawing our promise, nor do we want to achieve our goal by making it so blatantly impossible for them to build the wall. Let's look to clarifying our original intent so our bondservants must earn their freedom on their own merit." The group then agreed to adopt certain clarifications to their original agreement.

The first was a requirement for the wall to be of a standard height and width. After a short debate, Tuckman intervened. "I have uncovered an existing law that has gone largely forgotten," he said. "Back in '21, a law was adopted stating that all stone fences must be a uniform height of four feet. I propose that we refer back to that law and establish that their wall must measure four feet tall by two feet wide." All agreed.

Second, they agreed that a slave's earning freedom would be based solely on his own individual efforts. Therefore, the work had to be completed by the bondsman himself.

Third, while the bondsman could connect to existing stone walls to complete the chain, the property owner and the slave's own holder both had to agree to the need for the walls.

Finally, the time of day when the work could be done had to be approved by the owner and could not interfere with any other priority that the property owner required.

Alexander was in a fog, but he strained to keep up with the proceedings. Finally, though, it became too much. He sat back, exhausted, waiting for the meeting to end so he could return home.

As the meeting was concluding, Tuckman added one more requirement. "I want you all to listen carefully. This provision is key to maintaining our control. Any wall that is completed but collapses, for any reason, must be rebuilt. Under this requirement, we islanders can control whether a bond servant will ever actually gain his freedom."

Alexander looked around the room; the islanders seemed pleased with the results of the meeting. He leaned over to Beach. "I'm sorry, Benjamin, but what has actually happened here? Can you explain?"

"Of course, Alexander," Benjamin whispered. "We believe we have arrived at a solution to providing for slave freedom.

Our public policy will offer the slaves a hope for freedom but will still give their holders some control to delay, or as Tuckman put it, 'stonewall' their freedom until such a time that is most convenient for us."

All Alexander heard was that the islanders were allowing for slave freedom and something about stone walls.

Tuckman rapped his gavel and called for a vote. The measures were passed unanimously. Beach assisted Alexander in raising his hand, but the darkness was closing in on him once again. He looked up and saw Tuckman's face. The interim first warden was beaming, reveling in his success.

As Alexander strained to look more closely, Tuckman's face changed. It suddenly looked more sinister and devilish. Alexander closed his eyes and dropped his head to retreat from the image.

Several other matters still needed to be raised, and Tuckman spoke while the gathering began chatting among themselves as though the proceedings came to a close. He rapped his gavel on the hard table, and the entire group came back to attention.

Addressing the group, the first warden said, "Please, may I indulge your attention with two last matters? I promise to be brief. I see that Thomas Wright is conspicuous by his absence. As many, if not all of you, are aware, an incident occurred several weeks back. For those that might not have heard, Thomas, being frustrated with the progress of the clearing of his field, dealt rather harshly with his slave, Jeb. Thomas's ox had given out. According to those who know him, his beast was poorly cared for, suffering for lack of food and water. Thomas then took the yoke and strapped it to Jeb, whipping him from behind to drag the plow until he collapsed. The Negro is now recovering under my care.

"The entire council would like to put on record our denunciation of such a deplorable action with a public reproach of Thomas Wright. We anticipate removing Jeb if we find his indenture to be of 'no force in law' and will send him to the overseer of the poor in Newport. Certainly, if Thomas, or any other master, engages in such vile behavior as to risk taking away any slave's legal right to life, our judgment and penalty will be swift and harsh!"

One of the islanders spoke out. "We all know that Wright is not of sound mind, but that Negro is lazy and deserved to be whipped. And yet, what Tom done was too much."

The rest of the group all voiced their agreement.

Tuckman had to motion to the gathering to quiet down again, rapping his gavel slightly. The group grew silent as he said, "One final piece of business. I would like to publicly acknowledge the presence of our great island patriot, the Honorable Captain Alexander Hawkins, sitting in the back of the room." The attendees all turned and began to raise their voices in excitement at seeing their local hero out and among them.

Alexander had retreated into his darkness and did not notice he was being singled out. "Alexander," Benjamin said, elbowing him, "they are speaking of you. You need to acknowledge them."

The captain lifted his head. When he saw all the eyes in the room peering at him, he became alert.

Tuckman continued, now addressing Alexander directly. "Our captain, if you would be kind enough to stand and address our group, we would be so honored."

Alexander looked over at Benjamin, who lifted his palms up to encourage him to stand. What choice did he have? He slowly raised himself up as the crowd patiently held their breath to hear anything from the person most of them so admired. His mind was blank; all he could think of was to apologize—to apologize for how he had failed them and for how undeserving he was of their devotion. Rather than their affection, he deserved to pay a terrible price to the families he had torn apart. But all he now could bring himself to say, after a long and awkward pause, was "Thank you." He knew they wanted more, so he continued. "Thank you for your kind support and..." He struggled to think of what else he could thank them for. "And thank you for the good work this august body has undertaken." He stopped and waved his hand to acknowledge he was done.

At first, there was silence, but when Tuckman stood up to applaud, the whole group followed in a raucous ovation, with men whistling and cheering and stomping their feet.

In the midst of the ovation, Benjamin leaned toward Alexander and tried to explain over the din, "Tuckman has what he wanted. Now, for the official town record, he has Captain Alexander Hawkins's support of a town emancipation agreement. This will go a long way toward the Negroes accepting this freedom solution as legitimate and real. There is, most certainly, no other white family in which they put any greater faith than that with the Hawkins name. Good show, Alexander."

Alexander did not understand. It was all too much for him, and the cheering caused him to flush with embarrassment. The captain retreated into the darkness, but in the darkness he, once again, found himself transported back ten years earlier, onto the *Adrian*, addressing his men while anchored off the northern shore of Long Island, just before that fateful battle at Hell Gate.

Chapter Forty-Two

A glorious island day was blossoming from a warm, late June morning. Alexander sat in his wagon parked in the fields along the southern rim of the island under a bright blue sky. He stared out over the field of tall grass, milkweed, asters, daisies, and Queen Anne's lace blowing in swirls by a wind he was sure only his island could generate. Like the long grasses and wildflowers, his hair whipped back and forth. For another rare moment, he felt almost alive.

The captain looked off to the east to see the cattail marsh, with its small fern-covered creek. Beyond stood some of the island's largest shadblow, as big as trees. Off in the distance, he could hear the melancholy call of the white-throated sparrow whistling a refrain that sounded remarkably similar to someone calling out, "Poor Sam Peabody, Peabody."

To the northwest were the graves of the victims of the *Palatine* shipwrecks not far from the Ray family farmhouse. Simon Ray was another one of Alexander's great island settler heroes. He was a selfless man who had devoted his sizable fortune, his talents, and his life to the welfare of Block Island.

He was a man known for great physical endurance, an even temper and mild disposition, sound judgment, kind feelings for all classes, even Indians and slaves, and deep religious convictions that manifested in works of faith and charity.

While others fled to escape from invading pirates and French privateers, Simon Ray firmly and patiently submitted to the worst that might come. Although he had a large fortune, his home was unpretentious and had an air less popular than the more significant stone home of Captain James Sands. He, like Sands, kept a regular meeting in his house on the Lord's Day.

Alexander was particularly impressed with Ray for extending freedom to his Negroes out of the great respect he held for them. The slaves had been raised with him from their infancy, and when they secured their freedom they were allowed take whatever they had been able to produce for themselves by their own labor during their lives.

Simon Ray lived to be 102 years old and was continuously elected as first warden for about half a century. By all accounts, his life was a living example of cheerful submission to the will of God and of loving and faithful Christian virtue.

As Alexander sat in admiration of Simon Ray's example of persistent faithfulness, he felt a stabbing pain of remorse for hiss own failure of faith in his God. Still, he lifted his head up and breathed in deeply. The smells of the grasses and plants, the light scent of salty ocean, and the sweet aroma of honeysuckle vines combined for a satisfying fragrance to clear his mind. The heat from the still-climbing sun was tempered by the rapid, cool breeze, making for a most comfortable sensation. He thought, *Oh, yes! This is a pleasure that allows me to go on.*

Alexander was in awe as he studied the black man off in the distance, moving rock after rock. Hannibal had been at it all through the night, taking advantage of the cool evening. He pulled rock up from the soil, made piles, and then placed the rock into a twisting string of stone that wound its way across the southern width of the island. Shirtless, toiling now in the heat of the rising sun, his pitch-black body glistened. Alexander thought, *This man must be made of iron—as hard and heavy and durable as a cannon casing.*

The slave moved as though there was no end to his energy or strength. The question crept into Alexander's mind, just as it had with many of the islanders: *Why?* What was it that kept the slave pressing on? He was a smart man, and even in the face of the indignation of servitude and slavery, he maintained a regal quality about him. He would rarely say anything, but everyone knew he was extremely intelligent, more so than any of the other Negroes. Many, if not all, of the islanders actually held a sincere respect for him, but they also questioned him and even began to despise him. Did he really think he was something better than a slave? How smart could he really be when he had heard so many say that building the wall—necessary to be granted his manumission—could never be done?

Even if it were possible for one man to build a stone wall four feet high by two feet wide that traversed the island from one side to the other, it couldn't be done, part-time, after all the chores were done. Besides, some of the islanders would never allow it, and even his own master would never release him. All the other slaves were smart enough to eventually grasp it.

Alexander decided to offer the man a ride back to his farm before his master came looking for him, but as he raised his arm to snap the reins, he noticed another wagon approaching. His heart sank. He had hoped to ride quietly with the stoic black man and travel in peace, but now someone was looking for him, invading his solitude. As the wagon came closer, the man at the reins called out, "Captain Hawkins? Captain Alexander Hawkins, may I have a word with you?"

Alexander said nothing but quietly observed the man approaching. He could immediately tell the man was not from the island. As he came closer, Alexander became uneasy. Though he was certain he did not know this man, the way he carried himself—and even his voice—seemed familiar. He was well dressed and clearly a man of means.

Stopping his rig just short of Alexander's wagon, he jumped out, confidently strode up, and shot out his left hand, saying, "Captain Hawkins, it has been a very long time. Nicholas Geste, at your service. It is a great honor to see you once again!"

Alexander was stunned. Suddenly, the infamous Nicholas Geste, the very man whom Alexander had concluded was at the heart of the demise of his life's ambition, was before him. Over the past ten years, Alexander had thought it incredibly galling that Geste continued to send him letters. He never even considered opening the letters before tossing them into the fire.

Now, here was this devil, showing up in person. Alexander was embarrassed. How should he greet the man he had entertained thoughts of killing?

Alexander immediately looked down. His heart began to pound, and his wounds ached. The darkness started to take hold, and his mind began to retreat. Something, though, caused him to respond, and he spoke in a slow and regretful tone. "Captain Geste, I'm afraid I have nothing to say to you. If you have come to this island just to visit with me, I'm afraid you have made the long trip in vain."

Geste seemed taken aback but then confessed, "I was prepared for a sour welcome but was unsure of just how bad it would be. You know, Captain, I have been asking about you over the years, and the reports that came back to me were always of a bitter, isolated man with a crushed spirit. I couldn't comprehend it, but now I see firsthand just what was meant."

Alexander's darkness began to clear, and his mind stopped retreating as his blood began to boil. *How dare he?*

Geste continued, "Throughout the war years and thereafter, I looked for opportunities to come to Block Island to talk with you, but the unceasing demands of the war and the struggles of being a party to building this new country have been extraordinary. The truth is that I have been a coward. I have been too afraid to confront the man for whom I played an instrumental role in devastating his life. With every letter I sent that went unanswered, my trepidation grew. However, I am on a business trip to Newport with my wife, and she encouraged me to finally face this demon. Of all the life-threatening adventures and horrifying battles as a sea captain, this is perhaps my most fearful moment."

Does this man dare to believe that he actually feels some of my pain? Alexander wondered incredulously.

Geste seemed to struggle with what to say next, but he pressed on. "I suppose I should say I'm sorry for being a party to the devastation you have experienced. In fact, I feel compelled to get on my knees to beg your forgiveness, but that would be mainly to relieve my own guilt and anguish. The truth is I am not sorry. You faithfully carried out your duty and served your country with honor and distinction."

Alexander's blood continued to boil, and when he heard the word "distinction," he exploded. "*Distinction*? It was all for nothing! If there was any leader in the course of the revolution who proved to be a bigger failure than I, give me his name!" Though Alexander was shaking and almost to the point of tears, a slow smile spread across Geste's face. Alexander noticed the smile and jumped down from his wagon. Grabbing a fistful of Geste's coat, he pushed him to the ground. "How dare you laugh at me! It was not enough that you were the architect of my demise. Now you come onto my soil and mock me?"

Geste took it. He lay there and laughed. "Sir, I assure you I am not a man to take this kind of treatment without doling out an equal measure, but this is welcome, Captain. And I will call you 'captain' because you are deserving of the title and the accompanying honor."

Alexander turned away and set his face to the sky, screaming "Ahhhhh!" in utter despair and in total rejection of Geste's notion.

Geste continued, "I have spent a good part of the last ten years seeking out those who were in New York at the time of your mission, and I have pieced together a full account to now report back to you."

Alexander wheeled around in shock and asked, "Who? What men of mine survived?"

"None, sir," Geste dejectedly replied. "I'm sorry. I never did find a survivor of any of your crew, but there were others who could account for the result of your mission."

Alexander turned away again in pained disbelief but quietly prepared to listen. "Go on."

Chapter Forty-Three

Captain Nicholas Geste spoke as if he had rehearsed the words over and over as he gave the account. "There were those colonials who lived along the banks of the East River. Many had quickly forgotten the battle because of how early on in the war it occurred and for all that happened afterward, but when pressed, those who remembered all had the same recollection. The cannon fire drew in their attention, and though it was night, there was a bright moon, and they could tell your ship, the *Adrian*, was risking all in the attack on a well-fortified British position. The cannons lit up the sky, and they could make out a valiant assault coming from the river.

"When the night grew quiet, each one who reported his recollection was overjoyed with what appeared to be a patriot victory. But the excitement was dashed very shortly thereafter as, from out of nowhere, the British frigate—the HMS *Rose*—appeared and unleashed its full fury upon the *Adrian*, setting her on fire. She would eventually be consumed in flame and disappear into the river.

"The colonials continued to watch in horror as many of the *Adrian*'s men, struggling in the water, were shot by sailors from the British ship. Only a few appeared to be fished from the river. Other colonials along the shore, farther to the west, recounted that the HMS *Rose* had made quick work of several other vessels returning from the Harlem River into the East River. They searched the shore all night and into the morning, looking for survivors, but only a few dead sailors washed up onto the banks."

Alexander put his head into his hand as the painful memories flashed through his mind.

Geste continued, "It pains me to say, Captain, that none of the vessels in your squadron were ever seen again. Your sloop and two other sloops were sunk, and most of the men were killed. Those who survived were captured and likely became some of the first men to be imprisoned on the British prison ships anchored off the coast of Brooklyn. Perhaps you have heard of the horrors our men experienced in what were certainly the worst prison conditions of the revolution. Thousands of our Americans died and were unceremoniously dumped into the New York Harbor.

"The war somehow continued, though I'm sure the reports you received were filled with dismal news. With the navy in disarray and the war going poorly for the Americans, your fight was forgotten by the few who were aware of it. Captain Alexander Hawkins was given up for lost, along with the *Adrian* and her crew.

"The Brits also heard word that it was Tories who had stolen the *Adrian*. To the British command's embarrassment, the report revealed that when the *Rose* sank the *Adrian*, they mistakenly believed your ship might have actually been acting in support of the British battery. The Brits were told that the *Adrian* was engaging with the Greenwich militia who were trying to overtake the British position on the pinfolds at Hell Gate. In order to maintain good relations with the Americans loyal to the crown, the Brits also chose to keep the incident quiet. On both sides of the freedom struggle, any record of the battle at Hell Gate seemed destined to be lost forever."

As Alexander listened, the disturbing scenes from that evening continued to flash through his mind, and his head began to swim. "I don't want to hear any more," he said softly, "but somehow I must! It has been too long. Good or bad, I will hear it all, but please don't tell me our mission meant just a momentary patriotic lift to a few colonists."

"Captain Hawkins," Geste anxiously continued, "I have sought out any men I could find who survived those early days of the war. Many I found within recent years, right in the Providence area, were part of the original 2nd Rhode Island Regiment under General Washington. On the day of your battle, they had been pushed up to the high ground of New York Island on Harlem Heights. Washington's troops were a defeated group. If not for his constant prodding, pushing, and badgering, his troops surely would have surrendered well before then.

"Every man with whom I spoke who was there shared the same feeling—they were fighting a war all alone against a superior force. I need to remind you that the British force was very likely the best-equipped and best-trained army ever assembled on the face of the earth. The Americans were rightfully afraid. Every time the two forces would clash, the British would charge with their sharp, steely bayonets, making our troops flee in terror.

"That evening, on Harlem Heights, many men—faced with an imminent British attack in front of them, and Washington's officers whipping them to fight from behind—considered desertion. They were ill equipped, with few bayonets, and felt alone—both literally and figuratively—on an island, fighting for a stillborn revolution. As the evening wore on, the men passed words among themselves, and many were preparing to make their move. Just as the moon was at its highest, flashes of light erupted to the east, followed by echoing booms. The men were unaware of any other campaigns being waged with the enemy. Slowly, one by one, the troops stood up to watch the night sky, lit up by the engagement. They could see none of the real fighting, but the men applauded and then cheered, knowing as it continued that it had to mean a proper fight was on.

"Then, like angels appearing in the soft evening light, three vessels flying the rebel flag of a pine tree with the motto 'An Appeal to Heaven' sailed up the Harlem River. At this sight, the men erupted into wild cheers. A detachment was sent down to the river to greet the sailors, and in no time, their cargo was transferred to the shore. Just as mystically as they had appeared, the three angels were gone."

Alexander's legs felt weak, and he stumbled back a few paces to his wagon. He reached up and grabbed the wagon for support. Geste stopped to make sure he was all right, and Alexander nodded for him to continue.

Geste spoke faster, anxious to tell the whole story. "Once back to the camp, the crates of muskets were opened and the kegs of gunpowder and lead balls were distributed. When the crates of bayonets were cracked open, the men greedily gathered them up. This was just the steel courage they needed to withstand the British onslaught. The men dug in and were now ready for the next fight.

"Cannon fire over the East River erupted on and off for several hours, and a large fire lit up the sky for a period but then was extinguished. The troops quietly settled in, and though not much was said about the events that had just transpired, a wave of energy and anticipation passed through the entire camp. The men now knew they were not fighting alone and that they had, at the tips of their muskets, just what they needed to keep the bloody Brits at bay. At four in the morning, the British attacked, anticipating this battle might prove to be an easy and final end to the rebellion. Washington's army fought bravely that day, and for the first time, pushed the Brits back, showing them that a victory over the Americans would not come easily.

"As you know, Washington would suffer more defeats in battle and be forced to retreat many more times. However, this was the patriots' first taste of victory in the Northern Campaign, and it sustained them until their next. I dare say, Captain, though others might say I presume too much, it is my firm conviction that you"—Geste hesitated as his throat began to knot up with emotion—"and the heroics of your men are as much a reason as any other that we stand here as free men today."

He stopped to compose himself for a moment, then continued. "Some of the events that led to the creation of these United States can never be fully explained or understood. Your mission and the effect it had on influencing the course of the revolution could only be defined in the category of a miracle."

As he listened, Alexander's emotions swelled to the point that his body began to grow weak. He stumbled forward, struggling to remain standing. When he heard the word "miracle" from Geste, he dropped to his knees and cried out, "Oh, gracious God!" and fell back into the grass.

Geste stood quietly, watching Alexander's emotions spill forth, uncertain of the impact of sharing the full story with the broken captain. Tears streamed down his own face.

Lying in the green pasture, Alexander wept tears of pain and joy—joy for the rush of freedom he now felt, and pain for the thought of how he had given up on God's goodness and grace. Geste, too, fell to his knees and began to openly cry.

The darkness receded, and Alexander's mind cleared. He sat up and through moist eyes stared into the crisp blue sky. Feeling a great weight had been lifted from his shoulders he could now see more clearly the torturous demons of great emotional burdens both he and Geste had been carrying. The power of truth and knowledge was now ripping these demons from their perches and sucking them into a hole, leading to the pit of hell.

The men stayed where they were, reveling in the bright and brilliant beauty around them—a beauty they were, for the first time in years, able to freely and completely enjoy.

Time seemed to slow. After a few moments Alexander slowly got up, and both men stood there, not even looking at each other. Alexander was embarrassed by his emotional outburst and assumed it was also true of Geste. The emotion felt so good, though, and he stretched out his left hand to feel the tips of the tall grass caress his palm and fingers. With his face flushed from the warmth of the sun, he strode freely through the grass. After a few paces, feeling so complete and so alive, Alexander realized that he was feeling the same sensation in both his left and right hands. His emotions spilled forward—in this newfound knowledge, he sensed he was being made a whole person again.

The sound of a wagon approaching in the distance brought him back to the present. The two men both tried to hurriedly gather together their disheveled appearances and wipe their faces. It was Samuel Williams, coming to get his slave Hannibal. Alexander could hear him yelling and cursing as the black man climbed into the wagon before heading off.

Alexander's thoughts suddenly shifted to the slave. He shook his head with remorse and embarrassment. Had he really ever known anything of the Negro's burden? Now, as Alexander enjoyed the sweet taste of freedom from the burdens he had been carrying, he knew his was nothing to what Hannibal and his brethren carried—to be stolen away, chained, mistreated, and imprisoned on an island, with no hope for the future, no hope to even see his family and people again. No, he most certainly never had known. He watched as the wagon turned around and headed back the way it had come. Williams gave a half-hearted wave but maintained the constant angry scowl on his face.

As the wagon passed to the east along the shore, the rays of the sun bounced off the shimmering ocean to create a blinding light through which the wagon passed. Alexander's eyes followed them, squinting in the bright light. Turning away, something about the scene had registered in his mind. *What did I just see?* He quickly turned back. Again, he was blinded by the great light that now surrounded the wagon that carried Williams and Hannibal. Alexander brought his left hand up to shade his eyes and gasped at what he thought he saw. He blinked again and shook his head to clear his vision. Looking once more, he felt his heart jump as he saw what appeared to be a sinister, shadowy figure hovering over the black man's back.

As Alexander strained to look more closely, the wagon disappeared over the hill. He quickly glanced at Geste to see if he could confirm what he had himself just seen, but Geste was not paying attention. Alexander shook his head in disbelief.

Had the vision been due to bleary eyes from the surge of emotions he had just experienced? He was weary and fatigued. He decided that it was the combination of his weakened state and strange shadows that had conjured up this strange image. Captain Alexander Hawkins was exhausted, but for now—for the first time in what seemed forever—he felt alive and free.